Suddenly Single

Suddenly Single

Shana Johnson Burton

URBAN
CHRISTIAN

URBAN CHRISTIAN is published by

Urban Books
1199 Straight Path
West Babylon, NY 11704

ISBN: 978-0-7394-9145-4

Printed in the United States of America

Dedication

This book is dedicated to my great-aunt, Margaret Daniel, who is the strongest woman I know and to my good friend, Yolandra Dixon. We miss you, girl. Rest in peace.

Acknowledgments

First, I would like to thank God for blessing me with the gift to write and putting me in a position to be able to touch people with my words and for surrounding me with such wonderful people. I am absolutely nothing without Him.

I have to thank my husband, Shelman, for being my biggest supporter and for always encouraging me to follow my dreams. I want to thank my kids, Shannon and Trey, for their patience with me for all those times I locked myself away with my computer when they wanted me to play Scrabble with them. Mommy loves you very much.

To my mother, Myrtice Johnson, this truly would not have been possible without your help and endless supply of printer ink and paper. You are my role model in every way, and I love you so much. To my father, James Johnson, thank you for instilling in me a love for reading and writing. This is, by far, the greatest gift you could have ever given to me.

Thank you to my sister, Myrja Fuller, and her husband, Eric, for your prayers and support. And to my baby brother, James "Jay" Johnson, Jr., I appreciate you and Elisha for always being in my corner.

Thank you to my mother-in-law, Jenny Scott, to my sisters-in-law, LaToya and Rhonda, for your love and support and always making me feel like part of the family.

Thanks also to my girls, Theresa Tarver and Deirdre Neeley. Friendship doesn't even begin to describe the bond I have with you. You are my sisters and two of the best friends that anyone could ever hope to have. Not only have you supported me through this venture, but you two have amassed enough drama to keep me writing for the rest of my life. Theresa, I can't thank you enough for all of the time you put into making sure I made my deadline. You are truly a blessing. To Tanisha, Stephanie, Tralia, and Erika— thank you for letting me borrow pieces of your life to write this book. I can't think of a time when I've needed you and you weren't there.

I would like to thank Anthony and Darolyn Hines from Tony's Photography for always making me look so good in pictures and for always coming through at the last minute. And to my web designer, Shaundra Walker and Trinity Web Designs for launching me into cyber space in style. You are the best.

Thank you to my fabulous editor, Joylynn Jossel. You are a God-send! Your encouragement and kind words always ease the pain of your red pen. And to my agent, Nancey Flowers, who believed in me before I really believed in myself. I don't know if any of this would be happening if it weren't for you.

To my special friends, Demetrius Hollis, Telea Reynolds, Kurtina Cordy, Phillip Lockett, Shameka Hunter, who have served as my unofficial editors and sounding boards. Your unwavering support, friendship, and loyalty have gotten me through more times than I can count. I can't thank you enough for being my friend.

Thank you to everyone at Urban Christian who helped this book see the light of day and all of the UC authors who have offered words of encouragement, wisdom, and prayer; especially Mimi Jefferson.

To fellow authors, Tina McElroy Ansa, Patrick Sanchez, Elaine Overton, and Mary Monroe, your words of wisdom and encouragement have helped me more than you know. I wish all of you success in everything you do. Thank you for sharing your talent with the rest of the world.

I would like to thank my co-workers at Northeast High School and former co-workers at Baldwin High for your continued support as well as all my students. I only hope that I've inspired you as much as you've inspired me.

Thank you to my church family at Beulahland Bible Church and Pastor Maurice Watson for keeping me lifted in my prayer.

Thank you to my GWA cohorts for helping me reach my potential as a writer and to everyone else who contributed to this project. If I didn't get you this time, I promise to thank you in the next book.

And thank you, reader, for spending a few hours out of your life with me. I pray that you label it as time well-spent. Enjoy!

Suddenly Single

Chapter 1

His nervous phone call the night before the wedding should have been a warning. But between the beautician threatening to burn her with the curling iron if she didn't keep her head still, her best friend rattling off the "still-to-do" list, and her mother complaining because her fiancé's family served fried chicken at the rehearsal dinner instead of having it catered, Vashti Hunter just didn't detect the worried quiver in his voice. She assumed that Kedrick's telling her that the last thing that he'd ever want to do is hurt her and his promise to always love her was just his way of reassuring her of his commitment to their pending marriage. Before Vashti could delve any deeper into the meaning behind Kedrick's words, her mother had snatched the telephone out of her hand, informing Kedrick that Vashti had to go, would see him tomorrow, and to be on time for the wedding photos at the church the next day.

The next morning, Vashti thought that it was strange that Kedrick hadn't called to wish her a happy wedding day, and she was a little unnerved when she couldn't reach him at home or on his cell phone. Dismissing the apprehension that churned in her stomach, she simply concluded that, like her, he had a lot of errands to run before the wedding and would call her as soon as things settled down.

By noon, she still hadn't heard from him but remembered that he had relatives flying in from New York that he had to meet at the airport. Vashti was certain that he'd call before the limousine arrived to transport her and her family to the church.

Shortly after two o'clock, Vashti was at the church being primped and primed for wedding pictures, but there was still no sign of Kedrick. She wasn't worried—everyone knew that Kedrick was an advocate of CP time. Perhaps he was still recovering from his bachelor party. Vashti made a mental note to question him about it later.

By 2:45 p.m., everyone rationalized that Kedrick must had gotten the time confused and thought that he had to be at the church by three o'clock, not two, since the wedding wasn't set to start until four. Twenty minutes later, Vashti sneaked away to call the hospital to see if anyone had come in from having an accident. She made a quick plea to the Lord before dialing the phone, praying that nothing bad had happened to Kedrick—wouldn't it be just like the devil to take away her "happily ever after" before it ever got started? None of the patients registered matched his name or description. Then she called his friends to see if they'd seen or heard from him. None of them had.

Doubts were starting to creep in, but she was determined to stay positive. Kedrick loved her and that was all that mattered. He would be there—*he had to be*! Besides, grooms were notorious for having cold feet before the wedding. She eased her mind by recalling her college roommate's wedding. The groom zoomed in at the last minute after getting over his pre-wedding jitters, and then the two were happily married. It was only a quarter until four; if he came within the next fifteen minutes, no one outside of the family would even know that he'd been late.

Around 4:15 p.m., murmurs from restless attendants echoed throughout the sanctuary while the bridesmaids exchanged nervous glances that revealed what everyone was thinking.

By 4:40 p.m., Vashti's mother was hastily drafting a speech to notify the guest that the wedding was being postponed, but Vashti insisted that she wait. Kedrick was going to march through the door at any second.

At 5:00 p.m., the Hunter family began apologizing to their family members and friends as they filed out of the church, reassuring them that all gifts would be returned and thanking them for their support.

At 5:30 p.m., they found Vashti squatting on the floor in her wedding dress inside of Kedrick's now empty apartment, drowning in her tears. Her father picked her up and cradled her in his arms the way he used to do when she was a child. Back then, those strong limbs were a comfort to her; now, she resented them for being necessary.

By 6:03 p.m., Vashti was back at her house—the one that she was supposed to share with Kedrick—crossing the threshold in her father's arms instead of her husband's. Her parents offered to stay with her, but she insisted on being left alone. Walking to her room to crawl into bed and remain there for eternity, Vashti caught a glimpse of her reflection in a mirror.

She turned to look at it, wanting to see the future Mrs. Kedrick Wright one last time. She stood there, staring at this woman standing in the exquisite strapless Vera Wang knock-off gown that she practically had to crack a rib to squeeze into. Her tiara veil sparkled as the evening sunlight shone down on it. The beautiful June afternoon seemed to be making a mockery of the torment she was feeling inside.

She looked down at her $400 Jimmy Choo shoes that gave her 5'4 inch frame a much needed boost and at her great-grandmother's pearl necklace that dangled from her neck. She got one last glance at the flawless nails and the impeccable hairdo, upswept and weaved in for the occasion, her caramel-colored skin that had been buffed and mud-wrapped, and her almond-shaped eyes to which fake eye lashes had been adhered to plump up her own thin lashes. She took one last look at the woman who was supposed to marry the love of her life, the man that she'd spent the last five years loving and for whom she was willing to sacrifice her size three figure for in order to have his babies, and cried. Either the devil had succeeded or God was trying to tell her something.

Chapter 2

"Vashti!" bellowed the voice of Vashti's best friend of 20 years, Monique Channings, from outside of the front door. She knocked but got no response. "Vash, it's me. Open up!" She pounded on the door so hard that the reverberation thundered throughout the house. Not one bound by formalities or protocol, Monique whipped out her key to Vashti's house and let herself in.

Monique wrinkled her nose, seized by the stench of stale onions and tomato sauce when she walked into the living room. Scattered amid Vashti's tapestry sofa and glass coffee table were a wilted bouquet of Gardenias and half-eaten pizzas in ripped boxes on the floor. Vashti's wedding dress was thrown across the recliner, and her veil hung limply on top of the piano in the corner of the room. Empty soda cans, shoes, and shredded pictures of Vashti and Kendrick also cluttered the space.

Monique's manicured, Prada-heeled feet lightly stepped over Vashti's sleeping cat and satin wedding shoes to make her way to the couch, where she found Vashti buried under balled up tissues and a Mexican blanket in the sweltering 98 degree Miami heat.

"Vash, what are you doing?" Monique yanked back the blankets, bracing herself for the worst, and shrieked. "Dang, you could have warned a sista! Has your head even *seen* a comb since the wedding?" she ribbed, hoping to muster a smile out of her friend.

Vashti didn't say anything, staring vacantly into the adjacent wall through swollen, blood-shot eyes. Monique shook her head and fished a comb out of her Coach bag. Her cluster of silver bracelets clanked together as she moved her wrists.

"Do you know what today is? It's Thursday—that makes four days since the last time anyone has heard from you. You won't return my calls; you won't answer the phone. Honestly, I was expecting to find your corpse laying up in here!" She tried to rake Vashti's hair into something that would be acceptable, but she soon gave up.

"Have you heard from him? Did he call?" she prodded. Vashti didn't respond. "You do realize that you can't just sit here and mope for the rest of your life, don't you?"

Monique strode over to a nearby window and pulled back the embroidered drapes that had hung in the windows since Vashti was a child, lifting the dark overcast that overpowered the room. "This gothic look has got to go! Who wouldn't be depressed sitting in this bat cave all day? Let some sunshine in here, clean up, fix your hair, do something!" Vashti continued to lay motionless on the sofa.

"All right, I see that it's time for a reality check. Vashti, Kedrick is gone. I know that you loved him and what he did to you was messed up, but, sweetie, he's gone and he may never come back. It's time that you accepted that. You have a business to run and people who miss you and love you." She tried to rouse Vashti again, but nothing could shake her. "And look at this house! What if your grandmother could see this one-room catastrophe you've created here, not to mention the shop? The *closed* sign has been hanging in the window all week. I'm no business woman, but I know that you can't make a dime just sitting here on your derriere." Vashti continued to look blankly ahead in silence.

"Vashti, I know you hear me—say something!" She snapped her fingers and rode her hand over Vashti's face to get a reaction. "I give up!" resigned Monique. "Look, I promised your mama that I'd come by and check on you to make sure that you're still breathing. I've done my part; the rest is up to you." She hurled a stack of envelopes at Vashti and threw up her hands in capitulation. "And there's your mail. It's obvious that you haven't gone to the box all week either." Monique stepped back over the cat and shoes toward the door.

"We were supposed to go snorkeling today," uttered Vashti, almost inaudibly.

Monique turned around. "What did you say?"

"On our itinerary—snorkeling on Thursday, hiking on Friday, and spending the day at the beach on Saturday. You said that today is Thursday; we were supposed to go snorkeling."

Monique ambled back over to her friend and kneeled down beside her. "I'm sorry that you're not in the Caribbean on your honeymoon right now, but, Vashti, you're only 26-years-old! They'll be more men and, then one day, the right man. And you will have your big wedding and go snorkeling on your honeymoon and have lots of snotty-nosed babies to put off on your mama. You'll see." Monique gave her an encouraging smile and stroked Vashti's head to comfort her.

Unable to suppress her emotions any longer, Vashti began sobbing uncontrollably.

"But I love Kedrick, 'Nique! I'm supposed to have those things with him!" Monique wrapped her arms around her.

"I know, but he wasn't the one. At least now you know that."

Vashti blew her chafed nose into a Kleenex. "It can't be over, not like this, not after everything we've meant to each other." She blotted her eyes with the tissue. "He hasn't even called or tried to see me."

"Maybe it's better this way, you know? Seeing him would only make it hurt worse."

Vashti looked down at her hand. "I went to his place after I left the church. All of his stuff was gone, except this." She extended her ring finger. The silver wedding band that he'd purchased for Vashti was secured around her finger. "I found it lying on the dresser in his bedroom."

"Vash, don't do this to yourself," cautioned Monique.

"He had our names inscribed, see?" She held up the ring. "He wouldn't have done that if he wasn't planning on a future together."

"Sweetie, I don't think that this is a good—"

"I know that he loves me," she told herself. "He's just scared and confused right now, but he'll be back. I know he will, and it'll be like he never left. We'll get married just like we planned, start working on that son he wants so badly, and everything will be fine. He just needs a little more time, that's all."

"Vash, are you sure that you're feeling okay? When was the last time you ate something?" Monique quietly scanned the room for razors and sleeping pills.

"I'll never love another man the way I love him— never!" she vowed.

Monique picked up an empty pill bottle that she spotted underneath the sofa. "You didn't take all of these at one time, did you?"

"I just wish he would call. I know that we can fix everything if he would just call me," continued Vashti.

"But he hasn't—that should tell you something."

Upon that realization, Vashti collapsed into another crying fit. "You know, maybe you should talk to somebody," suggested Monique. "It might do you some good to see to a psychiatrist."

"I don't need a shrink," countered Vashti, wiping her eyes. "I need to talk to Kedrick."

"What about your pastor? Have you talked to him?"

Her face lit up. "You think he's heard from Kedrick?"

"I don't know, and I don't give a flip if he has. You need more help than I can give you. Maybe your pastor can give you a prayer cloth or some Hail Marys or something!" she added emphatically. "Seriously, after my mama's divorce, she talked to her pastor, and he stopped her from setting my dad's car on fire."

"Setting his car on fire?"

"Girl, you know how much she liked *Waiting to Exhale*!"

The thought of being hauled off to jail for arson on top of losing Kedrick brought Vashti to tears again.

She blew her nose and nodded her head. "Maybe I *should* talk to Pastor. It can't hurt, right?"

"You don't know how lucky you are to even have a pastor that you trust enough to confide in. I still haven't gotten used to this Catholic thing that Trent has got me doing."

Trent was Monique's husband of two years. He was a professional football player for Miami and, to the chagrin of most of her family, he was white. His race didn't matter to Monique. In fact, the only color that ever mattered to her was green, and the statuesque, former ghetto princess had perfected the art of acquiring it. By the time she'd hit her twenties, Monique had grown accustomed to having men take care of her and saw no reason to alter her lifestyle.

"Hand me the phone," ordered Vashti. "I'm going to call him."

Monique passed the phone to her. "Tell him that you need to see him *today*," she stressed as Vashti waited for someone to answer.

Vashti "yes-ed" and "no-ed" her way through a series of questions and hung up the phone, appearing to be more at peace than she was prior to calling.

"Well?" egged Monique once Vashti ended the conversation with the church's receptionist.

"Pastor Carey can't see me today. His assistant, Pastor White, is free, though."

"Pastor White—which one is he?"

"You remember him. He came in and spoke to everybody during the rehearsal dinner. He's a good man, very anointed." Monique rolled her eyes and sucked her teeth. "What was that for?"

"You know what they say—all shepherds weren't meant to be followed."

"Meaning . . ."

"Well, my beautician Gina said that she'd heard that he got a girl pregnant back at his old church in Alabama. Supposedly, she was real young, too, around 17 or 18, still in high school. Her parents made her get an abortion and threatened to expose the pastor if he didn't get out of Mobile," reported Monique. "So much for all of that *anointing*!"

"Monique, that is ridiculous!" scoffed Vashti. "Pastor White is married with two kids. His wife is gorgeous. Why would he need to mess around with some kid?"

"Hey, don't shoot the messenger. I'm just telling you what I heard." Monique walked into the kitchen and came back with a large trash sack and began tidying up the room.

"And I'm just telling you that it's not true," contested Vashti. "I know that you thrive on gossip, but slandering an innocent preacher is going too far. Besides, my pastor wouldn't hire someone like that."

"You're way too trusting, V." She shook her head. "Just don't say I didn't warn you."

"Whatever. Anyway, he said that I could come in about an hour. I should probably get ready." Vashti rose from the couch and stretched. "Do you know that I haven't left this spot since Saturday?"

"I hope that you haven't left this *house*, not with your head looking like that!"

Vashti felt her hair. She hadn't washed it since the wedding, and her usually relaxed, neatly-coiffed bob was matted down with crusted gel and hair extensions. The parts that weren't matted down sprang out like wires and were caked with dandruff.

"Look at me," Vashti mouthed sadly, her eyes wandering down to her crumpled and stained pajamas. "No wonder Kedrick doesn't want me."

"Vashti, if you say his name one more time . . ." warned Monique, tossing confettied pictures into the bag. "I just hope that he keeps his triflin' tail wherever it is."

"Don't say that. He's not a bad person, and I know that he is somewhere missing me as much as I'm missing him."

"He's got a funky way of showing it, V. And don't think that I'm going to let you sit here waiting for him to call either. You are moving on with your life starting today!"

Vashti ran her hand over her head. "You're right— I know that. But it's a lot easier said than done. Loving him gave me a reason to wake up every morning."

"I guess loving *you* will have to suffice now. Do you want me to come with you?"

Vashti dropped her mail into the trash sack. "This is something I've got to do on my own."

"Aren't you even going to look at your mail?"

"For what? It's just a bunch of bills and cards congratulating Kedrick and me on our marriage. I can't handle either right now." She looked down at the ring on her finger. Her eyes welled with tears again.

"Come here," beckoned Monique. She let Vashti cry on her shoulder. "V, please go talk to the pastor," she pleaded. "You're a basket case. You need help."

Vashti sniffed. "I'm all right." She covered her face with her hands for a few moments and exhaled. "I'm okay."

"You go on and get dressed. I'll stay here and straighten up a bit."

"You don't have to do that, 'Nique."

"I'm only doing what you'd do for me, and what you may end up *having* to do for me if you don't get your butt to that store soon and sell some flowers!

You know, I would pitch in, but I don't think you could afford me. Besides, Trent and I can't afford to have you standing at our door begging for handouts if you lose all of your customers. We get enough of that from my relatives as it is."

With Monique's help, Vashti was able to make herself look presentable. She tossed out Vashti's ripped jogging suit and dirty sneakers and insisted that she put on a dress, heels, and makeup. Monique was the consummate fashionista, who wore her own coffee-brown skin and jet black hair like a badge of honor and dared anyone to recall a time that she didn't step out of the house looking like she had just walked off of the pages of *Vogue*.

"A break up is no excuse to leave the house looking like a fool," admonished Monique. "And smile; you don't have to *look* like you just got dumped!" she added as she ushered Vashti out of the house and into a situation that was about to make her life a lot more complicated.

Chapter 3

Vashti walked into the church and down the long, dimly-lit corridor that led to the office suites. When she came to Pastor White's office, she saw him bent over his desk studying the Bible and taking notes. He was a slightly older, distinguished man with an aura that suggested he was a man of God.

"Pastor?" she called softly, not wanting to disturb him.

"Sister Hunter, come on in." He removed his reading glasses and stood up from behind the desk to meet Vashti at the door. "How are you, sister?"

She shook her head, feeling a surge of emotions rising in her chest. She muttered, "Not so good, Pastor." The pastor embraced her as she started bawling again.

"I know, sweet sister, let it out." He closed the door. "Come on in, sit down." He led her to a seat across from his desk and sat down next to her. "I heard about the wedding being called off. Tell me what happened." He handed her his handkerchief.

Vashti thanked him and dried her eyes and blew her nose.

"I don't know what happened," she wept. "I thought he loved me."

"I'm sure he does love you, sister. He just wasn't ready to marry you."

"But why? I don't understand what I did wrong."

"This doesn't mean that you did anything wrong, and you can't go around blaming yourself for other people's decisions." He reached out and grabbed her hand. "I can see how much you're hurting. I want to pray for you, sister." Vashti nodded and closed her eyes as Pastor White pleaded with the Lord on her behalf. The heart-felt prayer ended with him asking God to let Vashti's heart be receptive to trusting and finding love again.

"Thank you, that was beautiful, Pastor."

"And so are you, Sister Hunter. Don't ever forget that." He was still holding her hand.

"It's hard, though. When something like this happens, it makes you question everything about yourself—was I pretty enough? Was I too this or too that? Why wasn't I enough for him?"

"You are enough! Any man with eyes can see that. You're just in a lot of pain right now."

She nodded in agreement. "I am, Pastor. The pain cuts like a knife, and it feels like the bleeding is never going to stop. Sometimes, it's so bad that I just want to lay down and die." She looked up at him. "Have you ever felt that way?"

"We all have," he assured her.

"How did you get through it? How did you make the pain go away? I don't think I'm strong enough to take this anymore."

"Sister, there is no magical solution or scripture

that I can give you to make the pain go away instantly, but you can learn to deal with it with the Lord's help. Pray for peace and accept the Lord's will."

"I've done all of that, Pastor, but it still hurts. I close my eyes, and I see him; I still feel him. I don't think I'll ever stop loving him or that this emptiness in my heart will ever be filled again." She snuffled and reached for a tissue on his desk.

Pastor White looked down at his watch. He rose from his chair and stood behind Vashti. "You know, Miss Hunter," he began solemnly, "the pain you're feeling won't leave you overnight, but, in time, you'll get over him and learn to love again." He placed his hands on her shoulders. "But it's times like this that people should rely on family and friends to comfort them and get them through those difficult moments. Never underestimate the value of a true friend. Something as simple as going to lunch together or sharing a joke can do wonders for your spirit." He began gently massaging her shoulders.

"They can't help me. They'll just tell me how it's better that I found out sooner than later or how it's his loss, not mine. None of that's going to do me any good right now."

He nodded. "I see your point. Sometimes those closest to us aren't really equipped to give us the kind of help that we need, that we crave." His caresses were becoming deeper and more intense. "Sometimes we need more than just words to comfort us. Sometimes we need closeness and human contact."

"Yes." Sniveling, she nodded again, concurring with his assessment. She was amazed at how in tuned he seemed to be with her needs. It was as if he was reading the transcripts of her thoughts, and it was a great comfort to know that at least one other person knew how she felt.

His right hand stealthily crept down her chest, nearly touching her breast, but Vashti was too distraught to notice.

"Sometimes we need to be touched, to be held, to feel sexy and wanted," he explained. His soothing baritone voice was hypnotic. "Is that what you need, sister? Do you need to feel wanted?"

"I do, Pastor. Kedrick's rejection has totally wiped out my self-esteem. I feel so . . . ugly and worthless."

"You shouldn't think like that. You're beautiful, Sister Hunter. I don't know what man wouldn't want you. You're one of God's fairest creatures. Your body is perfect, skin all silky smooth. Your lips look so soft, like they were made to be kissed."

"Thank you."

"Your hair is all shiny. You've got it going on all over!" She smiled a little, wallowing in his sea of compliments, growing more relaxed and subdued with every touch and every word that fell from his lips. "See—there's that pretty smile. You just needed to be comforted, sister." He leaned down and whispered in her ear, "And I can comfort you in *every* way." He slithered his fingertips along her jaw line.

Vashti's thoughts were racing, and her heart was pounding in her chest. She wasn't quite sure what to make of the situation or the pastor's words. She shifted nervously in her seat.

"Listen to me going on like this," he chided. "You're probably over there thinking the worst about me. I mean no offense, sister. I just think you're pretty is all. There's nothing wrong with that, is there?"

"No, I guess not," she replied dubiously.

Vashti felt silly for questioning his intentions. Was her self-esteem so low that she couldn't accept a compliment without being suspicious?

"Come here. I think you need a hug, sister." She stood up and complied. The pastor held her for a long time, tightly clasping his body against hers and rubbing her back. He commented on how soft she was and told her how good she smelled. He admitted that he often thought about what it would be like to touch her as his hand then slid down to her behind. Before Vashti could react, his lips were hard-pressed on hers.

"Pastor!" she managed to say, not knowing what else to do. She was still dazed when she realized that he was kissing her again, wedging her between the desk and his body.

"I can make you feel good. I can make you feel like a woman again. Let me comfort you," he baited, kissing her face and holding her firmly.

It wasn't rape, yet she felt powerless to stop him. She knew that it was wrong, but being held and feeling secure felt good. She wanted to tell him to stop and to remind him that he was married and was her associate pastor. Her mind was yelling out to him that they were in a church and shouldn't be doing this, but her body needed it, not so much sex as the need to feel whole again. She needed to feel like she was desirable and that a man could still want her. At that moment, she missed Kedrick's presence more than ever before. She closed her eyes and imagined that it was him cleaving to her, telling her how much he wanted her. That it was his touch, his kiss painting her neck, that it was him intertwining his body with hers with love, not primal lust. She blocked everything else out of her mind. Nothing and no one existed except her and Kedrick. They were back at her house, in love and pledging themselves to one another. For that span of time, nothing else mattered.

As Pastor White was assuring Vashti that no one ever had to know what they were doing, she felt him pulling down her slip and panties. She didn't want to look at him, but she could feel his breath, ardent and warm, against her flesh. She heard the jingling of his belt and zipper coming down. He turned her around, pitting her against the desk. She couldn't remember whether or not he said anything, only that he grabbed her thighs and began fervently thrusting from behind.

When Vashti opened her eyes, it was over. Instead of seeing her beloved Kedrick in her own familiar surroundings, she was back in the pastor's brightly lit office. She looked up to see Pastor White hurriedly tucking his shirt into his pants, resuming his business-like manner.

"Well, sister, like I was saying, you just need to stay strong, pray, and wait for the Lord to work this out. This could turn out to be a blessing in disguise." He went on to quote biblical scriptures as Vashti slipped her panties over her legs.

She was numb, almost dead inside. She nodded and smoothed out her dress, too distracted to search for her slip. Averting eye contact, Vashti grabbed her purse and headed toward the door. Pastor White raced to cut her off and slammed his hand against the door to prevent her from leaving.

"Now, Sister Hunter, you do realize that counseling sessions with the pastor are private and confidential," he said gravely. "Counseling methods vary from person to person. What one person needs can be totally different from what someone else needs. That's why it's so important to keep what goes on in these sessions to ourselves. Do you understand?"

His unmitigated gall was appalling. "Yes, Pastor, I understand perfectly. Good day."

"Should you need more counseling . . ."

"No, Mr. White, I believe that I've had all the *counseling* I can stomach," she spewed and swung the door open. She bolted from his office, running into a young woman as she darted out of the building. She didn't apologize or even look up to see who it was. She jumped into her car and tore out of the church's parking lot. Church had been the one place that she thought that she could always turn to for solace and strength. Now, it, too, had become desecrated. Halfway down the street, she felt nauseated and pulled her car over to the side of the road, violently regurgitating the small amount of food that she'd been able to consume that day and wept as drivers zoomed past her.

When she walked into the house, she found it spotless and smiled to herself, silently thanking God for a friend like Monique. Monique had also left a copy of one of Iyanla Vanzant's self-help books on her coffee table. Her cat, Puddin', greeted Vashti by rubbing its body against her legs and pawing her. Vashti scooped her up, a fluffy, white Persian feline given to her from Kedrick on her 23rd birthday, and walked into her bedroom. She saw a knife lying on her kitchen counter and wondered—only for a moment—if she had the nerve to take the knife and drag it across her wrist. She dismissed the thought as quickly as she'd conjured it up and treaded into her bedroom, locking the door behind her. Puddin' disappeared underneath Vashti's bed as if she, too, was utterly disgusted with her.

She stripped away her vomit-singed clothes and looked at herself in the full-length mirror, barely recognizing the woman who stared back at her. Her recent behavior was as unpredictable to her as it was to everyone else. It was not like her to neglect her family, friends, and her business or to allow her problems to consume her. And having sex with her married pastor, humped over a desk in his office, was a transgression that no one could have paid her to believe that she was capable of committing.

She had always been taught that suicide was a sin; yet she'd found herself contemplating it more than once. She was glad that her parents were living miles away in Georgia and that her grandmother was peacefully sleeping in her grave. She didn't want them to see the kind of person she was becoming.

Vashti realized that she had two choices: she could continue on the self-destructive path that she was paving—acting out and hurting herself and those she cared about—or she could start over. She could accept that her life was on a different course than the one that she had mapped out and see it as a chance for a new beginning.

She decided to choose the latter. She wanted to be able to accept and love the woman on the other side of the mirror, and she couldn't do it if she kept clinging to the fantasy of a reunion with Kedrick or by harboring resentment toward him in her heart. She could no longer be impeded by guilt or desperation. She knew what the first step had to be.

Vashti looked down at the wedding band still locked around her finger. She kissed it and closed her eyes. Taking a deep breath, she slid it off of her finger.

"Good-bye, Kedrick," she whispered and buried it

in her jewelry box to be mailed to his parents later. She knew that she would continue to miss him and might even break down crying a hundred more times before all was said and done. She also realized that a part of her would always love him, but an even bigger part knew that it was time to move on.

She went into her bathroom and turned the hot water faucet on full capacity. Steam began rising out of the shower as she immersed herself in the scalding water. It burned, but its sting felt like redemption to her. She scrubbed off her pastor's sweaty fingerprints and the dried tears that stained her face. She watched the soapy water drain out of the shower, hoping that it had taken all of her sins and pain with it.

She stepped out of the shower feeling revived. After she dressed, she prepared herself to do one of the tasks that she had been dreading all week: she had to excise Kedrick and reminders of him from her home.

It started with small things; the tattered movie stub and the pressed rose—cherished relics from their first date—to the more significant items, like his fraternity paraphernalia and weathered toothbrush. She fought the impulse to replay all of their romantic moments and focused on the task at hand.

She restocked and closed the niche she had created for him in her cramped closet and bagged up the rest of his clothes and possessions that he had already moved into her house. She boxed up the few pictures of him that she hadn't ripped or burned. She looked around the room, beaming with pride. She actually thought that she might be okay after all. That is, until she discovered one of their wedding invitations stashed away in her nightstand.

Seeing the invitation brought back all of the hurt and disappointment. In spite of herself, she saw teardrops sprinkling the invitation that she held in her trembling hands. At that moment, she was again consumed with memories and thoughts of Kedrick. She fell to her knees and was soon on the floor writhing in anguish, asking God why this had to happen to her, and crying so hard that she had to gasp for air. She screamed out Kedrick's name.

The agony of losing him was more excruciating than any physical pain that she had ever experienced. Kedrick was the center of her world, and nothing seemed worthwhile if he wasn't there to experience it with her. For Vashti, death seemed like a gentler sentence than life without him.

It was too soon, she'd concluded. There was no point in trying to forget him or get over the relationship or to do anything if she and Kedrick couldn't be together. The best thing she could do was to get back in bed and grieve as long and as much as she needed to. If the Lord was kind, He would let her sleep and never wake up.

She slinked into her covers but not before digging out the ring and putting it back on her finger and slipping into one of Kedrick's discarded T-shirts. She even hung a few of his clothes back in her closet before drifting off to sleep, clutching his picture.

She woke up around two in the morning, startled from a disturbing dream. In the dream, she and Kedrick were in the middle of the ocean. He was drowning, floundering and holding on to her. She was floating between him and a strip of land. She knew that if she let go of him, she could save herself but that he would end up dying. He was calling her name, begging her to save him, but her friends and family were on the island, telling her to save herself. She woke up before she could make a decision.

She sat up in the bed, her heart thumping wildly in her chest. Kedrick's shirt was still clinging to her body, only now it was damp from perspiration. The wetness was like an omen, a reminder of the choice that she had to make in the dream as well as in real life. She felt her face. Kedrick's picture was stuck to the side of it. She detached the picture and flung the covers back.

She reached under her bed and grabbed her suitcase, which hadn't been unpacked since her aborted honeymoon trip. She tossed out a few items—her wedding trousseau, the unopened bottle of chocolate syrup, the trip itinerary—and replaced them with her old, reliable cotton pajama set and Monique's book. She went online and booked the first flight out of Miami.

Chapter 4

Vashti loved the ocean. Even though going from the beaches of Miami, Florida, to the beaches of Savannah, Georgia, might not seem like a change of scenery to anyone else, it felt like a world of difference to her. The humid Georgia air, the warm beaches of Tybee Island and her mama's shrimp gravy over hot, buttered grits were the panacea that Vashti needed.

To avoid her mother's questions and her father's constant threats to kill Kedrick if he ever showed his face around there again, Vashti spent most of her time during her impromptu visit to Savannah alone on the beach.

She would spend hours in a secluded spot staring out at the ocean, thinking and examining her life. When she wasn't doing that, she was jogging on the beach and splitting her reading time between the self-help book and erotic grocery store novels. She nibbled on Georgia's sweet, juicy peaches and crisp Vidalia onions until she thought she might burst, but the fresh fruit and fresh faces worked wonders for her psyche.

After a week, she felt like she was ready to go back home, but there was one last thing that she needed to do.

Her flight back to Miami was scheduled for ten o'clock a.m. Vashti rose at dawn, slipped into her flip-flops and shorts, and headed to the beach with a tightly-wrapped tissue tucked down in her pocket. When she arrived at the beach, the sun had barely secured its place in the rose-streaked sky. The beach was deserted except for a lone seashell collector several feet away from her.

Vashti kicked off her shoes and waded at the water's edge. Gradually, she walked out into the ocean with the foamy waves lapping around her ankles, then calves, then thighs. The water was cold and the motion of the waves rocked her back and forth. At one point, she lost her balance and slipped. Before she could recover, another wave sent her back under the water.

She remembered the dream she had on the night before she came to Savannah, and it was that dream that had led her to the ocean at that moment. She reached down into her pocket. The tissue was soggy, but it was still there. She unwrapped its contents. Two shimmering wedding rings, one engraved with her name, the other with Kedrick's, lay in her hands. She looked at them both for the last time and threw them as far out into the ocean as she could. She watched as they whirled through the air. Though she had thrown them at the same time, they separated in mid-air, going in opposite directions of each other. Vashti closed her eyes and inhaled the fresh, salt-water air. She finally felt free.

When she returned to Florida and to work the following Monday morning, there was a new spring in her step along with a new hairstyle. Her nape-length bob had been razor-cut and layered on the ends to give it a flipped effect and her dark brown hair dyed a sun-burnt bronze color that complemented her complexion. She felt revived and had even thrown out the rest of Kedrick's belongings. While initially, she had planned to send them, along with the ring, to his parents, she didn't want to risk seeing her almost in-laws and getting sucked back into all of that drama. Plus, there was a certain vindication in watching the sanitation workers load up his possessions on the back of the truck along with all of the other trash.

Vashti was itching to get back to work. It was rare for her to miss even one day of work, let alone two weeks, especially without having anyone there to run the day-to-day operations. Managing her grandmother's floral business made Vashti feel like she was actively contributing to keeping her grandmother's memory and spirit alive. Vashti had spent almost every summer of her childhood in Florida at her grandmother's flower shop and grew to love plants as much as she did. By the time she was ten, Vashti had memorized the floral family better than she had her multiplication tables. At sixteen, her grandmother began training and grooming her to take over the business. Vashti even graduated from college with a degree in horticulture to be better prepared to help her run the shop.

Two months following her graduation, her grandmother was diagnosed with colon cancer. It had already progressed to its third stage and little could be done short of keeping her medicated and as comfortable as possible. Vashti left her family's house in Savannah and moved into her grandmother's Florida home to take care of her and be near her as much as possible. Before she died, her grandmother willed the store to Vashti, who was honored to carry out her grandmother's last wish. Vashti couldn't bear the thought of someone else living in the house, so she continued to reside there despite lucrative offers to sell the property.

Strolling up to the front of the floral shop, Mattie's Garden, Vashti encountered the jilted woman's worst fear: the people that still hadn't heard. When he saw her approaching, Hector, the gray-haired Cuban who rented out the space next to hers, waved wildly and extended his arms out to her.

"So she finally returns!" he announced. "Married life agrees with you, yes?"

"Actually, no. I didn't get married." Having to say the words out loud still hurt.

His smile faded. "Why? What happened?"

"I don't know. He never showed up. I guess he didn't love me as much as I thought he did." Vashti could feel her chest tightening, but she refused to waste another tear on someone who didn't even think enough of their relationship to call and check on her.

"Then he's an idiot!" declared Hector.

Vashti smiled faintly. "Yes, he's an idiot."

"You know my son is single. He needs a good girl like you that he can settle down with. I can make it happen, eh?" Vashti politely declined. Hector's son, Juan, had a propensity for losing both jobs and money.

Vashti looked down and noticed that Hector was carrying a large box. "What do you have in there, Hector? You moving or something?"

He sighed. "Si, the wife wants to move back to California. I have a daughter living out there, and she just had a boy. My wife wants to be closer to her grandbaby."

"But what about your business?" He had run the novelty shop next to Vashti's store for as long as she could remember.

"Well, you know business has slowed down the last couple of years, and I'm getting too old to keep working like this. Plus, the owner wants me to buy the place. I don't want to keep working here bad enough to give up my life's savings."

"Aw, Hector, I'm so sorry to see you go. I'm going to miss you."

"We could still see each other if you were my daughter-in-law," he pitched again, and again, as Vashti continued to turn him down.

As she watched Hector cart away the last box, a thought occurred to her. For awhile now, she had wanted to expand her store but dismissed the idea because she knew that Hector would never leave on his own. And who knew when he was going to die? But his departure made the possibility more feasible.

"Hey, Hector, what do you think about me buying this place?" inquired Vashti.

"Well, it needs work." He wiped his brow. "What do you want to do with it?"

"I've been thinking about starting a new business—wedding planning, to be exact. I've dabbled in it for fun from time to time; might as well do it for profit." Hector agreed. "Besides, I'm not ready to give up on love. Making other people's wedding dreams come true might give me hope that the same thing'll happen for me one day."

For the next several weeks, Vashti researched everything she needed to know about wedding planning. She threw herself into this project because it kept her mind off of Kedrick. As the days passed, thoughts of Kedrick began to occupy less time in her mind. After a while, she hardly thought about him at all, but when she was reminded of him, it always caught her off guard and she had to struggle with herself to keep from sinking into another depression. So far, she was winning.

"So what do you think?" she anxiously asked Monique as she poured over Vashti's business plan during lunch. They had gone to Ago at The Shore Club and sat out on the large, open terrace to take full advantage of the late summer afternoon's sunshine and the restaurant's spectacular view of the beach.

Monique nodded and closed the portfolio. "Looks good," she answered and passed the folder back to Vashti.

Vashti frowned. "You didn't even read it, did you?"

"I skimmed through it," she admitted. Vashti huffed and shot her a threatening look. "Girl, you know that I don't get into all of that technical stuff—that's what lawyers and accountants are for," touted Monique. "I'm only interested in the bottom line: can you do it and will it make any money?" She tapped the handle of her fork against the table to accent each syllable.

"Yes and yes." Vashti flung open the portfolio and flipped through a few pages and dropped it down in front of Monique. "If you had bothered to look at pages five through twelve, you'd know that!"

"Well, our coordinator made a killing off of us! I don't see why you couldn't."

"Most weddings don't cost half a million dollars, Monique."

"They do if they're done right!"

Vashti shook her head. "Anyway, I think I could do it. I've got a couple of weddings under my belt. Plus,

I need the space for my showroom, not to mention the extra money and the much-needed distraction."

"Wouldn't it depress you, though, after everything that happened with Kedrick?"

Vashti looked away from her. "I'm over that," she said with conviction.

"Then why can't you face me when you say it?"

Vashti exhaled and fixed her eyes on Monique's. "I'm over it."

"It hasn't been that long, V," Monique reminded her, biting into her pasta salad. "I remember back in high school when it took you a year to get over that guy you dated for three weeks. With Kedrick, it could take until the second coming."

"It's been almost three months," she interjected. "I can't live my life waiting for him to realize that he still loves me. In fact, I declare that by this time next year, my business will be a huge success and I'll be married to the man of my dreams. You watch."

"Married in a year, huh? Kind of difficult when you're not even dating."

"I just haven't met anyone, that's all," she stammered, cramming a forkful of seafood ravioli in her mouth so she wouldn't have to talk.

"What about Trent's cousin, Ashton?"

"What about him?"

"Why can't you go out with him?"

"Because I'm into the brothers; you know that!"

Monique shook her head and dipped her fork into her salad. "Look, I'm all for you setting goals, no matter how unlikely it is that you'll be rich or married within the next 365 days, but we both know the truth. You still love Kedrick. Resolve that before you do anything."

"Dang, you sound like my parents. Haven't any of

you ever heard of being supportive? When I was depressed about Kedrick, you all were telling me to get over him and go on with my life. Now that I'm doing that, you're saying that I shouldn't because I still love him."

"So you're *admitting* that you're still in love with him?" Monique inferred.

Vashti rolled her eyes. She wiped her mouth and flicked her napkin onto her plate. "Good-bye, Monique." She tucked her portfolio under her arm and prepared to leave.

Monique contorted her face, bewildered. "You're leaving because I asked you if you still loved Kedrick? You're more sensitive about him than I thought."

"No, I'm leaving because I have an appointment at the bank today. I'm speaking with a loan counselor about a second mortgage."

"You know that I would have lent you the money," added Monique.

"I know, but this is something I want to do by myself. I need to stop depending on other people to make me happy or do things for me. It's all a part of the reinvention of Vashti."

"Then you can tell me if the new you gets turned down for loans as fast as the old one."

"Very funny." She stood up to leave. "Aren't you leaving, too?"

Monique reclined in her seat. "I think I'm going to hang out her for a minute. It's not like I have anyone to rush home to."

Vashti waved good-bye and turned to leave but came back.

"You're right," she confessed. "I have been afraid to date again, but I'm working on that, too. I know that it's over. I have to go on with my life, and I will—

not with Ashton—but with somebody. You'll see. I
know that my husband is out there."

"I'll even do you one better. If you manage to get
over Kedrick, meet a man, fall in love—get him to
fall in love with you, too—get engaged, and set a
wedding date for September first of next year, I'll foot
the bill for this soiree."

Vashti crossed her arms in front of her. "You don't
think I can do it, do you?"

"Sure, I do." Monique sipped her drink. "Miracles
happen every day."

"They must do—you landed Trent," she teased.

"And a multi-million dollar home with an Italian
sports car parked in the garage. Not bad for a girl
from the projects."

She laughed. "Then it's on. If I get married in the
next year, you'll pay the tab. And I'm talking horse-
drawn carriages, couture gowns, a lavish reception—the works."

Monique extended her hand. "Let's shake on it."

Vashti sealed the deal. "Now, if you'll excuse me,"
she stated, "I've got a loan and husband to nab."

Chapter 5

Vashti checked her watched as she pulled open the glass doors of South Trust National Bank. It was 3:05 p.m. Being late for her appointment would definitely leave a bad impression with the loan officer. She had concocted a story in her head about being held up by an accident on the highway should the situation warrant's an explanation. It certainly was more plausible than saying she tarried having a "to heck with Kedrick" drink with Monique.

A desk clerk directed her to her counselor's office. She knocked and poked her head through the door. "Hi, I'm your 3:00 appointment, Vashti Hunter."

He jolted out of his seat and rushed over to her. "Come in, Miss Hunter. I've been waiting for you." He extended his hand and warmly accepted hers. He led her into his spacious office and shut the door. She spotted his degrees in finance and business posted in polished brass frames on the wall. "It is *Miss*, isn't it?"

"Yes," she replied, blushing. He caught himself staring at her and abruptly walked back to his desk.

"We've talked on the phone, right?" he asked.

"Yeah, last week." Vashti's heart fluttered in a way that it hadn't in a long time. She was expecting to meet with a frowning, stiff-collard white man, not the tall, buffed chocolate-covered specimen that was standing before her. She knew right then that she was *definitely* ready to start back dating.

"My name is Brentz Washington, but none of that Mr. Washington stuff—call me Brentz. Please have a seat." She eyed the gold cufflinks that shone from the sleeves of his tailored suit as he flipped through a manila folder with her name typed across the label. She also noted that he wasn't wearing a wedding ring.

"I see here that you're interested in a home equity loan to finance your new business venture," he read.

"Yes, I own my house straight out, and I was hoping to take out a second mortgage to pay for everything. Here's my business plan." She handed him the portfolio. He leafed through it, nodding at certain pages, jotting down notes about others.

"I see you've done your homework, Miss Hunter. This is impressive."

"Thank you. This is something that I believe in and want to make happen."

"Do you own the space that your business is in now?"

"No, I'm leasing it, but I hope to be in a position to purchase it when my lease is up next year. The suite next to mine is available and for sale."

He looked up at her. "Why a second mortgage? That can be very risky if your business isn't as successful as you're hoping. You could lose your home."

Vashti shook her head, frightened at the mere thought of losing her grandmother's home. "I can't lose the house; it's been in my family for years. What are my other options?"

"Well, foremost, we offer small business loans. There are a lot of special programs for minority and female-owned businesses. You have several outlets available to you."

"Like what?"

"Here, why don't you look through these." He reached into his desk and handed her some pamphlets. "Read through them tonight and come back tomorrow and let me know what you're interested in. They list the terms and other specifics for the different kinds of loans available to you. Meanwhile, I'll start processing your paperwork and get you preapproved."

"Thanks, I'll start reading through this as soon as I get home." She stuffed the papers into her bucket-styled purse.

"You know some of the jargon is pretty technical, and you may not understand all of it." He raised an eyebrow and flashed his camera-ready smile. "Why don't I discuss it with you tonight over dinner?"

She could hardly contain her excitement but maintained her composure and cast a coy smile at him. "Are you asking me out on date, Mr. Washington?"

"In the banking world, it's called a business dinner."

"You all really do cater to your customer's needs, I see." She crossed and uncrossed her legs to toy with him.

"We do," he agreed. "But I've taken a special interest in your case."

"Why is that?"

He laughed a little. "Because you had me from the first second I saw you—those eyes, those lips. Besides, I never know when I might be in need of a wedding planner myself." He stared at her intently and ran his tongue across his lips. Just watching him made her melt. "I'm sorry. I know that I'm being totally unprofessional."

"No, you're fine," she dispelled, meaning it both literally and figuratively. "I don't mind, honestly." Brentz was perfect—gorgeous, successful, had access to large sums of money. She wasn't going to waste this opportunity by acting offended. "Anyway, I would love to have dinner with you . . . you know, to discuss the, um, loan and everything," she added quickly. "Would you like to meet somewhere?"

"Why don't you come over to my place? I'll cook for you."

He could cook, too! Vashti was ready to dust off her wedding dress and was already visualizing her new Vashti Washington business cards.

"Great, that sounds perfect." He grabbed one of his cards and scribbled something on the back.

"Here's my address and my home number. I'm putting my cell number on here, too." He handed her the paper.

"Brickell Avenue—I know that neighborhood." Who in Miami didn't? The street was lined with pricey condos and beachfront properties.

"Is seven o'clock good for you?"

"It's great for me, but is that going to give you enough time to cook?"

"Sure, I have the meat thawing as we speak. I just have to throw together a couple of sides, maybe chill a bottle of wine, if that's okay."

"Sounds great."

"All right, then. I guess I'll see you in a couple of hours."

Vashti sauntered out of his office, but as soon as she was confined into the safety of her car and out of earshot, she stamped her feet in elation and let out a shriek from the top of her lungs. Remembering that she was still in a public place, she craned her neck to make sure that no one saw her. She couldn't afford to have it get back to Brentz that she was a mental case. After all, she had a wedding to plan.

When Vashti had left Monique on a quest to get a husband and a loan, she had no idea that God had taken her words literally. Maybe she hadn't lost Kedrick; perhaps God had just moved him out of her way to make room for the husband he had for her.

Chapter 6

"Brentz Washington, the sexy loan officer over at the bank? Yes, girl, he is fine. You picked a good one this time!" affirmed Monique, sprawling across the bed as Vashti rummaged through the closet for something to wear. "He handled my sister's loan when she was buying her house."

"Did I mention that he is cooking?" Vashti bragged.

"Girl, if you're lucky, his skills extend far beyond the kitchen."

Vashti shook her head. "You are so nasty," she replied and pressed a yellow tea-length halter dress against her body for Monique's approval. "How about this?"

"Hmmm—it's a little long. Show him some leg." She reached into the closet and handed Vashti a black mini-skirt and a red corset-style top. "Here, put this on."

Vashti slipped the clothes over her head and waist. Monique gave her the once-over.

"Those heels are a little clunky, and they're too low. Do you have anything a little spikier, a little sexier? Aw, heck, take these." Monique kicked off a pair of slinky black Manolo Blahnik stilettos and continued her fashion critique as Vashti wriggled her feet into the shoes. Monique frowned at the blouse.

"What's wrong now?"

"Unlace the first two holes; show him a little cleavage."

"Better?" she asked after tugging on the shirt. Monique clasped accessories around Vashti's neck and wrists.

"You're good now!" commended Monique, standing back to admire her work.

"Can I go?" Vashti asked impatiently.

"Oh, don't act like you ain't grateful!" Monique spat, waving her finger. "This is a big deal for you. It's your first date in five years. I'm trying to help everything go smoothly."

Vashti knew better than to argue with her. "I *am* grateful," she stated. "And I have the best *best* friend in the whole world; now I would like to have the best *boy*friend in the world, too, so I have to leave."

"All right, just don't be too eager. Men can sense when you haven't had any in a while. He might try to take advantage," she warned.

"And I might let him!" exclaimed Vashti.

"What—Little Miss We-Can't-Have-Sex-Unless-We're-Committed is going to give it up on the first date? I don't know if I'm impressed or *de*pressed."

Vashti's mind flashed back to the tryst in the Pastor's office. There was no point in acting like she was still the girl who held on to those beliefs. Even if she tried to deny it, God knew the truth.

"Well, I'm not saying all that, but I'm tired of being this passive, on the sidelines Vashti. I'm going for what I want from now on—no more of this waiting for a man to decide when and what happens. I did that with Kedrick but never again. From now on, I'm controlling my destiny in my business *and* personal life," she declared. "I have a wedding deadline to meet. Either Brentz can roll with me or get rolled over." With that, she pranced out of the door.

Driving down Brentz's exclusive neighborhood with its rows of high-rise, stately condominiums was a little daunting for Vashti. The moxie that she'd displayed minutes earlier with Monique had become a distant memory. She was just a simple girl from Savannah, and she prayed that would be enough for him. She found his address and walked up the brick steps leading to the front door. She knocked and waited with baited breath for him to answer.

He came to the door smiling and as handsome as Vashti remembered. His suit had been traded in for a pair of tapered jeans and a blue collared shirt. Suddenly, she felt over-dressed, but Brentz complimented her on how wonderful she looked and greeted her with a kiss on the cheek as he invited her in.

"Oh, this is nice, Brentz," complimented Vashti, looking around at the immaculately furnished home. She could hear jazz playing in the background and a woman with a deep alto voice wailing over the instruments. "I love Jacob Lawrence," she gushed, admiring one of the paintings on Brentz's wall. "Wow, you have Romare Bearden, too!"

"That's nothing compared to the news I have for you." He paused. "The bank approved your loan!"

Vashti gasped and she flung her hand over her chest. "Are you serious?"

"Yes, and not the second mortgage either; they're giving you a small-business loan. That way, if worse comes to worst, you won't lose your house."

She clapped her hands together. "Brentz, I can't believe it! Thank you so much!"

"Whoa, don't thank me yet; there are still a lot of details to be worked out and forms to be signed."

"But other than that, it's a done deal?" she asked hopefully.

He grinned. "It's a done deal!"

She squealed and impulsively threw her arms around his neck. "Thank you, Brentz! You have no idea what this means to me."

"It wasn't me, really. It was your good credit and the success that your store has had over the years that did it. Plus, you put together an incredible business plan."

She released him from her embrace. "Still, I don't think that this would be happening so fast if it weren't for you."

His expression changed. "There's a downside to all of this, though," he acknowledged.

"What? They're not giving me the full amount, are they?"

"Oh, no, your loan amount was approved."

"Then what's the problem?"

"The problem is that I asked you here to discuss loan options. Now that that's no longer an issue, I'm sure you want to go home," he teased.

She smiled and playfully poked him in the chest. "Why would you think something as silly as that?"

"Isn't that what you women do once you get what you want?"

"Who says that I've gotten what I want?" Armed with her exhilaration and regained sense of confidence, Vashti took the initiative and kissed him. Once their lips met, there was no denying the chemistry between the two of them.

"I like a woman who knows what she wants and isn't afraid to get it," said Brentz, rubbing her back and looking down at her salaciously.

"Well, that's not exactly what I wanted," she replied bashfully, putting a little space between them. "I just wanted to thank you for getting my loan approved."

He pulled her to him again. "I know a couple of ways you can thank me."

"I just did," she answered stiffly, backing away.

He grinned, taking the hint. "Where are my manners? You must be hungry. Let me pour you a drink before we eat." He led her out of the foyer and to the sofa in his living room. Two chilled flutes and a bottle of Acacia Pinot Noir were waiting for them on an ottoman.

When Vashti sat down, something poked her in the rear, and she immediately jumped up to see what it was. It was a toy car. "Aren't you a little old for these?" she kidded.

"The one that I play with is parked out in the garage," he retorted as he took it from her and laid it on the coffee table. He poured a glass for her and one for himself. "Taste your wine; tell me what you think."

"This is good," she affirmed, sipping carefully so she wouldn't spill it on his white chenille sofa. For all she knew, it could be occupying a space in her living room one day.

"You know what else was good? Those sweet kisses of yours. How about another one?" She smiled and complied, only now the kisses were more passionate and intense.

Vashti put a halt to it before she ended up naked and on her back. "I think that this wine is getting to me. Maybe we should . . ."

"Should what?" he asked softly, tracing her lips with his fingertips.

". . . should eat dinner!" She moved his hand and stood up. Brentz looked a tad disappointed, but he laughed it off.

"Okay, you got me that time, Miss Hunter."

"I'm sorry, I wasn't trying to lead you on," she explained.

"It's too soon, I know. Heck, it's just the first date! We haven't even had dinner yet. You stay right here; I'll fix your plate." She was glad that he had lightened the mood. As he returned with her food, Vashti began to think that he was someone she could actually fall for. Who was she kidding? She *was* falling.

"So do you believe in love?" Brentz asked over the tarragon poached chicken breast he had prepared. Vashti nodded her head and swallowed.

"Sure, I mean, I had a bad break up a few months ago, but I'm not letting that turn me into some bitter, old spinster. I want to fall in love again, get married, the whole nine."

"I think that falling in love is an incredible gift. I know that a lot of men shy away from commitment and relationships, but I don't. I love being in love and having someone to share my life with. I'm just waiting for the right woman."

Vashti sipped her wine, fully convinced that she would make her wedding deadline after all. After dinner and two hours of conversation, they shared another lingering kiss as he walked her to her car. It was well pass midnight by then.

"I had a wonderful time, Brentz; I really did," said Vashti, trying to remember a time when someone had made her smile as much as Brentz had.

"Me, too. This is the best date I've had in a long time." It had also been a while since she'd been able to make a man blush, but Brentz hadn't stopped blushing since she arrived.

"I'm glad. I hope that we can see each other again."

He brushed his lips against her cheek. "I'm counting on seeing *a lot* more of each other."

Vashti was encouraged by his enthusiasm. She told him good night again and ducked into the car. He tapped on the window.

"Yes?" she asked after rolling it down.

"Nothing," he answered coyly. "I just wanted to hear your voice again, maybe get another kiss while I was at it."

"Don't you think you've had enough kissing for tonight?" she taunted.

"I get the feeling that I could never get enough of you." She smiled and ruled that his words were enticing enough to earn him another kiss.

"Now, I really do have to go, Brentz."

"I know. Will you be thinking about me tonight?" She broke into a smile, unable to refute that she would be. "Give me a call to let me know that you got home safely, all right?" She nodded and pulled out.

After arriving home, Vashti floated into her house, replaying her date with Brentz in her head. She even indulged in another hour long conversation with him when she called to let him know that she was home. She went to bed smiling that night, deciding that Vashti Washington had a nice ring to it, and, for the first time in three months, feeling like she could be happy again.

Chapter 7

"Lewis, hi!" greeted Vashti when she saw the wood-dusted figure lumbering through the door, ducking underneath the frame. Lewis Brown was a church friend of hers who Vashti commissioned for the construction of her new office and, in turn, he hired her to direct the upcoming nuptials for his daughter, Sabrina. "How does it look over there?"

"It needs a lot of work, but it's nothing that me and my boys can't handle," Lewis replied.

"That's great. I want to get started right away."

"I haven't seen you in church lately," he noted, wiping sweat from his brow with the back of his hand. "I guess you've become a member of the good ol' SAHB."

She wrinkled her nose. "What's that?"

"Stay At Home Baptist," he replied. She chuckled. "So who presided—Bishop Pillow?"

"Yeah. You should have been there this weekend. Deacon Sheets spoke a powerful word. And you know that we united box spring members are always willing to rollover for the Lord."

Lewis shook his head and cracked, "I don't think that's what the good book had in mind about the Lord being a comforter."

"I know. I've been sort of laying low since the wedding fiasco," she confessed, pruning a hanging basket that dangled near the entryway. "A bunch of people from the church have been calling and asking me to come back, but I don't want to face anyone with a million questions." She neglected to tell him that the thought of coming face-to-face with Pastor White was just as terrifying.

"Well, you're missing all the gossip." He plunked down in one of the whicker chairs adorning the reception area. "The church just hired a new assistant pastor. Word is that Pastor White got caught with some young girl in his office."

"Oh," replied Vashti, trying to appear disinterested.

"Sho 'nuff! Pastor fired him right on the spot. This was right 'round the time of your wedding, about a week or so afterward."

"He could have been counseling her or witnessing to her, Lewis."

"*Mrs.* White found the woman's slip behind the trashcan. Now what kind of witnessing is that?"

Vashti swallowed hard, digesting the information, recalling that she never recovered the slip that she was wearing that day. "Do they know who the girl was?"

"Naw, she took off so fast that all anybody saw was a blur running out of the church. That's what's on everybody's tongue now—that and Deacon Stubbs getting caught stealing $500 from the missionary offering. You and Kedrick—that's old news. You can come on back now."

Vashti tossed the wilted leaves into her trashcan, praying that Lewis wouldn't be able to sense how nervous she was. "I'll think about it."

"Well, tell me, are you getting back out there dating again? A nice, pretty girl like you shouldn't be cooped up in the house or hiding out behind these flowers."

"I'm getting out a little. I met this guy at the bank yesterday. I think I might like him." She smiled to herself as she slid off her soiled gardening gloves.

"That's what you need; a good, stable fellow like that. That Kedrick was always rippin' and runnin'. You're better off without him, trust me."

"I don't know, Lewis. I really loved him."

"I'm sure you did, but that doesn't mean that y'all were meant to be." He ascended from the chair and looked at her curiously. "You've got an old soul, Vashti. What you need is a man with some age on him, some life experience."

"Who, like you?" she joked.

"Girl, you ain't ready for ol' Lewis here!" he boasted, pulling up his pants at the waist. "I'm 46 years old, and I got 40-year-old women who *still* ain't ready!" They both laughed. "Well, Miss Hunter, I guess I'll check you out later."

"You're leaving?"

"I just came by to sit with you and to give you this." He reached into his pocket and handed her a slip of paper. "Sabrina told me to give this to you. She said something about wanting the cloud bouquet for her and the dyed flowers for the bridesmaids."

"Yeah, yeah, I know what this is about," she said, scanning the request.

"That's a relief because I didn't have a clue!" Vashti walked him to the door. "And good luck with your banker fellow and if he doesn't see how special you are, he's the biggest fool in the world!" He winked at her and walked out.

Vashti watched him walk down the street. Lewis was charming and sweet. Even with his "salt and pepper" (as her grandmother would say) sprinkled throughout his hair, he was still attractive. His deep-set, bedroom eyes and sly smile let Vashti know that he must have been a real player in his day.

Vashti was startled by the sudden ringing of her phone but smiled when she saw the bank's name and number register on the caller ID.

"You can't stay away from me, can you?" she kidded.

"Actually, I've done very well," Brentz countered. "I've fought the urge to call you all day and had been successful. Then I saw your file laying here on my desk and had to give in."

Vashti was elated. He seemed to be as smitten with her as she was with him. "Well, why don't you put us both out of our misery and meet me for lunch today?"

"As much as I would love to, thinking about you all morning has gotten me behind in my work. I'm going to have to work through lunch today. Work is really the reason why I'm calling. We need to set a time for you to come finalize everything with your loan."

"I can do that on one condition," she cited. "You have to have dinner with me tonight. I was thinking that maybe we can try that new Thai restaurant that everyone has been raving about." Brentz didn't say anything. "Hello?"

"I'm here...um, listen, about dinner tonight—
let's just stay in. I'm not ready to share you with the
rest of the world yet. Why don't you come back over
to my place? I can throw a couple of steaks on the
grill, and we can listen to a little music—how does
that sound?"

Her heart leapt. "I can't wait. So I'll meet you
around seven?"

"Better make it a little later than that. I'll probably
end up having to take some work home, and I want
to be finished with it by the time you come over. I
want you to have my undivided attention." The more
he talked, the more Vashti could not believe how
lucky she was to have found him.

"All right, I'll see you tonight." She hung the
phone.

"*I'll see you tonight,*" mimicked a voice behind her.
It was Monique.

"What—are you slumming today?"

"It feels like it. You know I try to come to the unat-
tractive parts of town as little as possible." She flung
her armload of shopping bags into the chair. "So that
was Brentz, I presume?"

"Yes," Vashti answered dreamily. "It was Brentz."

"And I'm assuming by that dopey look on your face
that the date went well."

"Monique, it was perfect. *He* was perfect!"

Monique exhaled loudly and shook her head. "You
gave him some, didn't you?"

"No!" she balked. "But we connected just the
same."

"That's a lot easier to do when a man is *connecting*
with some finances as well."

"Speaking of which, he got my loan approved. Isn't
that great?"

"Yes, now you can finally move out of this place," replied Monique, grimacing as she looked around the store.

"I don't want to move, Monique, just expand. Lewis has already agreed to do it and everything."

"Lewis . . ." Monique tapped her finger on her cheek. "You know if he wasn't so old, he might be dateable," she remarked.

"*Lewis*? Please—he's like my father. He has *kids* our age for heaven's sake!"

"Yes, but rumor has it that his pockets run pretty deep. In the end, that's usually what counts."

"And you wonder why they call you a gold-digger. Now, is there a reason for this visit?"

"Yes, they're in the bags." Vashti grabbed one of the sacks and opened it. She pulled out a stunning, champagne-colored décolletage gown. "Consider this to be an early birthday gift—or a belated one."

"Monique, this is beautiful! Are you giving this to me?"

"Sure," she replied and shrugged.

"Why?"

"Well, I bought it to go to this political fundraiser that Trent and I got an invitation to. It was really an honor to be asked to attend—one of those black-tie, thousand-a-plate deals. But he called from Houston last night. He's not going to be able to go." Even though Monique didn't admit it, Vashti could tell that she was disappointed.

"I'm sorry, Monique."

"This is like the third time he's cancelled on me this month, you know." She stared at the ground. Instinctively, she plastered a smile across her face and let out a forced laugh. "Who wants to spend the night with a bunch of boring old politicos anyway? I would much rather lie around the pool at my beautiful mansion with a glass of champagne any day. I thought that you might want the dress since I won't be wearing it. Now that you're seeing Brentz, the two of you will probably be attending events like that all of the time."

Vashti sensed that Monique was more upset than she was letting on. " 'Nique, are you okay?"

"Sure! Girl, you must didn't see what was in the other bags—two new Chanel suits. See, that's one advantage to having a husband who's never home— you can do all of the shopping you want and not have to answer to anybody!" Monique scooped up her bags, donned her over-sized Christian Dior sunglasses, and sashayed out of the store. She didn't want anyone, not even her best friend, to see her crying.

Chapter 8

"Mmm, that was delicious!" raved Vashti as she swallowed the last of the decadent hazelnut chocolate cheesecake that Brentz was feeding her. He put down the saucer and fork and stretched her legs across his thighs to rub her feet.

The past two weeks of their whirlwind romance included nights of sampling imported wine in front of his fireplace, having private dinners on his balcony, and renting romantic movies that they usually ended up kissing through. Time that in her previous relationships was marked by her obsessing over whether or not the man loved her or was being faithful was now spent thanking Brentz for one of his surprise gifts or listening to him request "their" song over the radio. If this wasn't bliss, it was a fine imitation.

"You know, I could sit here and stare at you all night," he crooned, gazing into her eyes.

"And I could let you." As with almost every other statement, this, too, ended with a kiss.

"Have we become *that* couple?" he asked, twirling a lock of her hair around his finger.

"Which couple is that?"

"The couple that makes everybody sick because they are so disgustingly happy."

"According to Monique, we crossed that threshold after our first date!"

"I can't help it. I've never been so content with any one person. I can't imagine my life without you in it. Just last night last, I was thinking, 'what was I doing before I met her?' "

"I feel the same way," she shared. "It's like we've always been together, you know? Like the people we dated and the things we did before we met don't even matter."

"Life is funny like that sometimes. It's amazing how one person can be the answer to every question you ever had or every prayer you ever lifted. That's what you are to me."

"I never thought it could be like this. You're like a dream come true for me." She rested her hand on his shoulder.

Brentz sat upright and cleared his throat. "Vashti, I want to tell you something, but I don't want you to be afraid by what I have to say."

"What is it?" she asked, concerned.

He looked down at his hands as he spoke. "I know that we haven't been seeing each long, and I have never done this before, at least not this early in the relationship . . ."

"Done what, baby? Now you *are* scaring me."

"No, it's nothing like that," he reassured her, grabbing her hands. "It's just that . . . I think I'm falling in love with you, Vashti."

She sighed and lovingly touched his face. "You thought telling me that would scare me?"

He kissed her hand. "I didn't want you to think that I was crazy or something for feeling that way. It's only been a few weeks."

She sealed his mouth with her finger. "I think I love you, too."

Their lips joined in an amorous kiss. Brentz laid her down on the sofa and began caressing her. Their attraction to each other was as much physical as it was emotional. She knew that he wanted to make love to her, but something inside of her wouldn't let him despite how strong her feelings were for him. She sprung up quickly, gently pushing him away.

"Brentz, I can't, not yet."

He smoothed her hair and kissed her on the cheek. He was a little flustered but had gotten used to her thwarting his attempts at intimacy. "It's okay; we'll wait as long as you want to." His willingness to be patient and wait for her made her fall even deeper for him.

"You're so good to me," she declared and sighed.

"I love you; I don't mind waiting." She nestled her body in his arms, and she rested her head against his chest, listening to his heartbeat. He ran his fingers through her hair.

"Vashti?" he said after a long silence.

"Huh?"

"Were you serious about what you said earlier?"

"About loving you?"

"Yeah."

"Of course I was serious. I wouldn't have said something like that if I didn't mean it." She sat up and looked at him. "Unless you're trying to tell me that you didn't mean it."

"No, no, I meant every word of it! I love you. You never have to question that."

"Then what is it?"

He paused before answering her question. "Vashti, you're the woman I've been waiting for my whole life." He swallowed. "I'm going to marry you one day."

She seized his face and pressed her lips against his. Brentz was her destiny, the one that she had been waiting for to make her feel whole again. He was the one to fill that empty place in her heart that remained vacant since Kedrick's departure.

They dozed off in each other's arms in front of the crackling fireplace. Vashti was awakened by Brentz affectionately nudging her.

"It's after one o'clock." He yawned. "You can stay, but I didn't want you to sleep too long if you had to go."

She stood up and stretched. "No, I have to go. I'm expecting a big shipment first thing in the morning." Brentz grabbed her hand and playfully jerked her back into his arms.

"You're not going anywhere until I get my good night kiss." She smiled and acquiesced. "I can't wait until you're my wife," he whispered. "Then you can stay all night every night, going to sleep and waking up right here in my arms."

Vashti took a deep breath and said aloud what she was thinking. "Why should you have to wait?"

Brentz blinked, thinking that he had misunderstood her. "What did you say?"

"Baby, this is fate, right? We both know how this is going to end. I'm not afraid to say it anymore."

"Are you talking about marriage?"

She nodded. "You said yourself that that's where we're headed."

"Yes, down the road, not right now. Marriage is a very big deal. I don't know if we're even ready to have this conversation."

"I am," she affirmed. "What about you?"

He laughed nervously and rubbed the back of his head. "Oh, man, this is crazy!"

"Is it really? I mean, when it's right, you know it."

He looked up at her. "I knew that you were the one for me the second I laid eyes on you. I never believed in love at first sight until then."

"I know that it takes some people years to figure out that they want to be together, but we're not like those people. We already know what we want."

Brentz fidgeted about uneasily and cleared his throat. "Okay, then." He rose from the sofa and got down on one knee.

"Brentz, what are doing?"

"I'm not really sure, actually; I've never done this before." He took her by the hand. "You said that you love me, right?"

"Yeah."

"And you want to be with me?"

"Uh-huh."

"And all of that ex-boyfriend stuff that you told me about is history?"

"Yes, Brentz; I don't even think about him anymore." That wasn't completely true, but she did know that Kedrick was a part of her past; her future belonged to Brentz.

"I want you to know that I have to watch the game on Sundays, and sometimes I snore. And I'm not that good at fixing things around the house, but I promise to be the best man that I can for you."

"Baby, that's all great, but why are you telling me this?"

"Because I want you to know what you're getting into."

"What I'm getting into?" she repeated.

"Yes . . . I'm asking you to be my wife; I'm asking you to marry me, Vashti. I know that it's too soon to press you for a date right now. I just want to know if you'll have me as your husband."

"Ohh, baby!" she cried. She was trembling, overcome with emotion. This perfect man was giving her the most unromantic and awkward proposal she'd ever heard, but that is what made it so wonderful to her. She didn't even have to think about her reply. "Yes, I'll marry you!"

Brentz's face melted into a large smile, and he hugged her. "I know that we can't set a date yet, but knowing that you want to marry me is enough."

She disengaged herself from him. "That's not true."

"Oh," he said sadly. "I guess you need to think about it some more, huh?" He lowered his head in penitence. "I'm sorry, Vashti, that was so stupid of me. When you said that you loved me and that we were meant to be together, I got carried away and—"

"No, I meant that I *am* ready to set a date," she clarified.

"Are you serious?" She nodded, and he kissed her again. "Do you want to wait a year or two? I know that some women like long engagements."

"No, that's too long," she refuted.

"You must want to be a spring bride?" .

She smiled and shook her head. "Spring is six months away!"

"What date did you have in mind?"

"I was thinking Christmas."

"Are you sure? Christmas'll be here before you know it," he reminded her.

"I know, but like we said, why wait?" She climbed into his lap and wrapped her arms around his neck. "Besides, wouldn't it be great to wake up Christmas morning as husband and wife?"

"And unwrap my gorgeous wife under the tree," he added.

"Yeah, we can put up a little tree and sit by the fire. After that, we can bring in New Year's together. What better way to start off the year than as your wife?"

"Are you sure? Christmas is, what, eight weeks away?"

"Yes, I'm sure, but we'll wait if you think that we're moving too fast."

"Girl, I would marry you tonight if I could!" he replied with a wide grin.

"All right, Christmas it is then! Christmas Eve night I will become your wife." He stitched his fingers into hers.

"And who knows—maybe this time next year, they'll be another reason to celebrate." He rubbed her stomach.

Her eyes sparkled. "Are you talking about a baby?"

"Yeah, don't you want kids?"

"Of course—I love kids," she gushed.

"Me, too. I want a whole house full of them." They both looked at each other and laughed.

"Is this really happening?" she asked him. "Am I really this happy?"

He kissed her hand. "It's happening, baby."

"Two months ago, I wasn't even dating. Now, we're *engaged*! I still can't believe it."

"I guess I'm going to have to get you that ring then, so you can have proof."

"I have all of the proof I need right here." She touched her heart.

"Who would have guessed when we got up this morning that we'd be engaged now?"

"Not me, but that's the way love works, I guess." She stood up and looked around the room and back at Brentz. "Wow, I've got my new business, my soon-to-be new husband. We're thinking about having a baby. My life is so perfect right now!"

"I'm going to spend every day keeping it that way. I love you so much, Vashti Hunter." He stood behind her, circling his arms around her waist. She closed her eyes and let his love surround her but, for a split second after she opened them, it wasn't Brentz's face that she saw. It was Kedrick's.

Chapter 9

"Hello," croaked Monique's sleepy voice on the other end of the phone. She glanced over at her clock, which read 3:23 p.m.

"We're getting married!" blurted out Vashti, still on a high from her night with Brentz.

"What!"

"Brentz asked me to marry him, and I accepted. Talk about romantic!" She slung her purse into a corner and curled into her recliner. "You better start warming up that checkbook."

"Are you sure that he didn't just yell it out in the middle of sex? I had a guy propose to me like that once. He didn't even realize that he'd said it."

"We were not in bed, Monique. We're waiting. We were talking about how much we loved each other and then he asked me to be wife."

"How much you love each other? V, you met him, like, two weeks ago."

"It's been six weeks but when it's right, it's right.

He's my destiny." Monique was quiet. "I know that you're in shock—I mean, who wouldn't be? I still have trouble believing it myself. Anyway, the wedding is in about eight weeks."

"Eight weeks! I know you're on a deadline, but don't you think that's rushing it?"

"I know that it may seem like it, but we want to be married before Christmas. Besides, my parents had only been together a couple of months before they got married."

"Yeah, and they've been fighting ever since!" Monique interjected. "And what about Kedrick?"

Vashti squirmed in her seat. "What about him?"

"Do you expect me to believe that you're over him?"

"What you believe doesn't matter," she answered, perturbed. "He's out of my life now. I belong with Brentz."

"Then won't you *still* belong with him six months or a year from now?"

"Yes, but we don't want to wait. I really expected you to be more supportive, Monique."

"How can I be supportive when I think you're making a mistake? You're on the rebound, Vash, not to mention that you know absolutely nothing about this man."

"Monique, I *love* Brentz!" she reaffirmed. "That's all I need to know."

"Then why haven't you slept with him?"

"I told you. We're waiting!"

"Are you sure it isn't because of Kedrick? Maybe a part of you feels like it would be unfaithful to him."

"How can I be unfaithful to someone who's not even here?"

Monique paused. "What if Kedrick were suddenly back in the picture?"

"But he's not! Kedrick made his choice, and it obviously wasn't me. I've moved passed him. That part of my life is over."

Monique hesitated before speaking again. "I wasn't going to tell you this, but I've talked to him."

Vashti's heart stopped. "You what? When?" She was shaking all over. At that moment, nothing was more important than hearing what Kedrick had to say.

"He called me a few weeks ago. He wanted to know how you were and if he still had a chance with you."

"And you didn't tell me? How could you keep something like that from me? You're supposed to be my friend!" she ranted.

"I didn't want to upset you. You finally seemed so happy."

"I need to know everything he said. Is he coming back? Does he want to get back together? How did he sound? Does he miss me?" she rambled, her thoughts speeding faster than she could articulate them.

"Why do you care? You're engaged to Brentz now."

"Monique, just answer the questions. Does he want me back?"

"I don't know."

"What do you mean you don't know? How could you be so stupid? Didn't you ask him?" Vashti took a moment to breathe and regain her composure. "You know what—never mind. Did he give you a number where he can be reached? I'll call him myself."

"No, I don't have his number and, no, I don't know

whether or not he wants to get back with you."
Monique closed her eyes and braced for Vashti's reaction. "I lied; I didn't talk to him. I only wanted to
prove that you still have feelings for him, and it's obvious that you do."

Vashti felt as if she had the wind knocked out of
her, and her blood ran cold. Her eyes squinted into a
livid stare. "So, you made the whole thing up?" she
asked, dumbfounded. "Why would you do that to me?
How could you be that cruel?"

"It was the only way to make you see the truth. I
know that you don't want to hear this, but Brentz is
the rebound guy. You're still in love with Kedrick.
And if Brentz can't see that, then he's as screwed up
as you are!"

Vashti didn't know if she was angry because
Monique had lied to her or because she had hoped
that Kedrick calling was true. Either way, the emotional damage was done, and her best friend was to
blame for that. Rather than admit the truth, Vashti
jumped on the defensive.

"I can't believe that I didn't see this before," she
snarled. "You're jealous!"

"Jealous?"

"Yes, jealous!" charged Vashti. "I have a man who
loves me and wants to spend every second that he
can with me. But where is Trent? Is he with you
tonight?" Monique's silence answered her question.
"No, you're over there in your two million dollar
home, under your 800-thread count Egyptian sheets,
on your imported sleigh bed, alone. You're miserable, so you want me to be miserable, too."

Monique shook her head. "Vashti, you're wrong.

I'm worried about you, and I'm just trying to look out for you."

"I didn't ask you to look out for me. Furthermore, I don't *need* you looking out for me. I have Brentz for that now. If you can't support my decision to marry him . . ."

"Then what?" prompted Monique.

"Then I can't have you in my life. We don't need this kind of negativity in our marriage."

"Let me get this straight, Vashti—you are willing to sacrifice a twenty-year friendship for a guy that you have known for twenty minutes?"

"I'm willing to sacrifice a non-supportive person in my life for the man that I love and plan to marry, yes," she answered boldly.

Monique stood her ground. "Then do what you have to do," she stated callously. Vashti hadn't expected Monique to respond that way. She was sure that once their friendship was on the line that Monique would back her decision. But now that Vashti had put the ultimatum out there, she felt like she had to follow through with it.

"Monique, you know I never thought I'd say this, but you really have turned out to be the witch that everyone says you are!" Vashti chucked the phone across the room. The happiest day of her life was turning into one of the saddest.

She loved Monique like a sister. Even though growing up they only saw each other during the summer when Vashti came to visit her grandmother, they never lost contact. They wrote each other every week, emailed, and drove up their parents' phone bills calling each other. Vashti couldn't imagine this friendship that had been such an important part of her life being over, but she knew that it was what she had to do. If there was ever a time in Vashti's life that she needed support, it was now, and Monique had made it painfully obvious that she wasn't going to give it to her.

Chapter 10

"What do you think about this one? It's kind of fun and flirty at the same time," said Vashti, holding up a wedding catalog. She flipped through the book as her beautician, Shawnna, combed out her hair.

Shawnna frowned. "I don't like it. The sleeves are too puffy. Why don't you ask Monique? She's the expert on clothes. Isn't she your matron of honor anyway?"

"Monique and I don't really talk anymore," Vashti replied in a huff.

Shawnna's jaw dropped. "You two were like sisters! What happened?"

"People grow apart. Our lives are taking off in different directions now."

As Vashti was saying that, Monique waltzed in complaining about how all the rain had destroyed the curls that Gina had sewn in the day before. She stopped short when she noticed Vashti. The two hadn't spoken since their phone call three weeks prior.

Monique rolled her eyes and sat down in Gina's chair adjacent to Vashti. Both stylists looked on as they shot heated glances in the other's direction.

"So, what, y'all aren't speaking to each other?" Gina directed to the two of them.

"Oh, hey, I didn't see you there," lied Monique to Vashti.

"Yeah, right," jeered Vashti and continued weighing her dress options.

"Instead of buying a new dress, you could just use the same one you had for your other wedding," Monique remarked. "It seems appropriate considering that you're in love with the same guy."

"Why don't you let me use yours instead?" she hurled. "I'm sure that Trent wouldn't miss it. He barely even knows *you're* there, much less your wedding dress."

"At least he showed up for the wedding!" Monique snapped back. "Can't say that about ol' Kedrick, can we?" That last slight riled her, but Shawnna shoved her back down in the seat.

"Hey, now, play nice!" warned Shawnna. "We can't have you scaring the customers."

"She's mad because she knows I'm right," disclosed Monique.

"Go to you know where, Monique," muttered Vashti, surfing through her catalog again. "Just because you've screwed up your marriage doesn't mean I'm going to do the same to mine."

"Are you really dumb enough to think that this so-called marriage of yours is going to work? Who are you trying to fool, Vashti—me or yourself?"

"Girl, hush!" ordered Gina. "You're out the 'hood now, remember?"

"So, what's your mama got to say about this wedding?" asked Shawnna to break the tension. "I bet she's more excited than you are."

Vashti cleared her throat. "We haven't really talked about it," she replied softly. "I haven't exactly told my family yet."

"What?!" exclaimed both Shawnna and Gina.

"It's not like I'm ashamed or anything—"

"Humph!" sneered Monique.

Vashti ignored her and went on. "Well, you know how she is! She'll overreact and put me through about a year's worth of lectures. I'm not trying to hear that right now, not while I'm this happy. And don't you go blabbing to her either," she directed at Monique. "I don't need you telling her my business."

"You don't have to worry about me telling her a thing," retorted Monique, standing up to go to the sink. "And good luck on your little wedding. A word of advice: try to keep the names straight when you're saying your vows."

Vashti wanted to cry. She hated being this way with Monique, and she hated keeping her pending marriage a secret. She felt in her heart that Brentz was the one for her, but she was still fighting off thoughts of Kedrick everyday. In spite of the close connection that she shared with Brentz, she had a nagging feeling that something about their relationship wasn't quite right.

Vashti was still glum when she dragged herself to Brentz's later on that night. She had gathered the courage to tell her parents about her engagement only to have them denounce her decision as being immature and impetuous. Like Monique, they accused her of using Brentz to substitute for Kedrick and refused to have any part in the wedding.

"Baby, just give them a little time; they'll come around," consoled Brentz.

"I know, but Thanksgiving is next week, and I was hoping that you could go down to Savannah with me to meet my parents. Now, it looks like that's not going to happen."

"Be patient, sweetness. It'll all work out. In the meantime, I have something that I think might cheer you up!" He reached down in his pocket and pulled out a small velvet box.

"Is this what I think it is?" she asked with a smile spreading across her face.

"Open it." She lifted the lid. Inside sat an exquisite princess cut diamond ring set in platinum. The sight of it took her breath away. "Do you like it?"

"Brentz, this is beautiful!"

"I picked it up today. I can't wait to see it on you." She extended her left hand, and he slid the ring on her finger. "It's a perfect fit, just like us." Seeing the ring and how much Brentz loved her allayed Vashti's doubts about their marriage. She was ready to prove to herself and everyone else that Brentz was the man she wanted.

"You are the best thing that's happened to me in a long time, Brentz. I never want to lose what we have."

"I'm not going anywhere, baby, 'til death do us part."

"Yes, but up until now, I've withheld a part of myself from you. I don't want to do that anymore. I want you to have all of me."

His interest and his libido piqued. "Do you mean . . ."

She snuggled up next to him. "I mean that I want to be with you in every way—mind, heart, and body."

"I thought that you wanted to wait until our wedding night?"

"Well, we're getting married in a few weeks anyway. We're in love, and we're both consenting adults. Let's make it official."

"Are you sure about this? I meant it when I said that I was willing to wait for you."

"I know you did—the fact that you are willing to wait makes me love you even more. But I don't want to wait anymore. I want you to know that I'm yours, now and forever."

Brentz told Vashti that he loved her and began kissing her hungrily. She forced out the voices in her head that were telling her that she was making a mistake. She closed her eyes and prepared to completely give herself to Brentz. She was at peace with her decision until she was distracted by a strange noise.

Vashti cautiously lifted an eyelid and tried to peer over Brentz's shoulder. She thought that she heard whispering and giggling, but she knew that they were alone in the house. She concluded that Brentz must have left a television on in another part of the house.

She grabbed the back of his head and drew him into another kiss. She bent her thigh over his leg. He slid his hand up her thigh and began nibbling on her neck. She kicked her shoes off and lay down on the couch, pulling him down with her. She could feel him penetrating through his pants.

He slid her right strap down low enough to expose her breasts and his tongue danced across her shoulders. She pulled down the other strap and lowered the dress down to her waist. His hand rode over her satin bra on its way to unsnapping it.

"They doin' it!" exclaimed a child-like voice. Both Vashti and Brentz immediately jumped up and turned in the direction of the sound.

In the doorway separating the living room from the hall stood two boys in their pajamas. One was a tall, leaner and younger version of Brentz and the other was a small, chubby-cheeked boy covering his eyes with his hands. When the older boy spotted Vashti's dangling bra, he squint his eyes shut, too.

Vashti ducked down and quickly slipped the straps back over her shoulders.

"You didn't tell me you had company! Who are they?" she asked in a loud whisper.

"Those are my kids, baby—Brentz, Jr. and Chance," he answered calmly.

Her eyes widened. "Your kids?!"

"Yeah, baby, I told you about 'em, remember?" He turned to address the boys. "B.J., I thought daddy told you two to stay back there in your room tonight."

"I know, but Chance said that he was hungry," expounded the boy in a cracking voice that was in the inchoate stages of puberty.

"All right, there's some fruit in the fridge. You can eat that and go on back to bed," he ordered. The boys shuffled out of the living room and into the kitchen.

"You never said that you had kids, Brentz!" she reproached, still seething from the revelation.

"Don't you remember the other night?"

"No, what you said was that you *wanted* a house full of kids, not that you already had a house full!" She stood up and pushed her foot into her shoe.

"So you're just going to leave like that?" he fired back.

"You didn't tell me about the kids," she reiterated. "They almost walked in on us. What kind of way is that for them to find out about me or me find out about them?" She snatched up her purse, bound for the door.

"Hold up—so we can't be together because I have kids? What kind of mess is that?"

She turned around. "It's not only that," she admitted and paused. "Everybody keeps saying that we're rushing things, that we need to get to know each other first. Maybe they're right." Her eyes shifted to her flawless ring, and she thought of the commitment and responsibility that came along with it. "I think we need to slow things down."

"But why? Yes, I have kids, and I should have made that clear to you from the beginning," he acknowledged. "But what we have is special, V, once in a lifetime. Don't walk away from that."

The part of her that was telling her to go was equally balanced by the part of her that wanted to stay. His eyes were pleading with her to fight for their future together. If he really was her true love, she supposed that she at least owed him the opportunity to explain himself.

"Who is their mother? Where is she?"

"Well, Terry, Brentz's mom—"

"There are two!" She rolled her eyes and sank into the couch.

"As I was saying, Terry was my high school sweetheart. She had him when we were sixteen, and Chance and Grace's mom—"

"Who's Grace?" she broke in.

"She's Chance's sister. Don't worry, she's not mine. Grace was born long before I met her mother." Vashti closed her eyes. Visions of child support payments and baby-mama-drama danced in her head.

"Anyway," he went on, "I met Chance's mother,

Keista, around the way. We dated for a few months, nothing serious, but then she turned up pregnant. So here we are."

"Where are the mothers? Do the kids live with you or are they just visiting?"

"Um, a little bit of both, actually. B.J.'s mom is in the military. She was deployed about a month ago, so she had to sign custody of him over to me before she left. She comes home in about eight months, though. Then he'll go back to live with her."

"What about the other kids?"

"That's a little more complicated," he hedged. "You see, their mom is sort of messed up right now. Chance's teacher found marks on him from where she had been hitting him. When children's services came out to her house to investigate, they found drugs. They would have put both kids in foster care if I hadn't stepped up to claim them, and I couldn't take Chance and leave Grace. Her father is dead, so there was no one else to take her in."

"And they've been here the whole time?" He nodded. "I guess that explains why we never go out." He told her that the kids were usually in bed by the time she would come over.

"This doesn't have to change anything between us," he insisted. "This is destiny. Look at how we have connected in such a short time. I know you still feel it."

"Brentz, I don't know . . ." He grabbed her hand.

"Come on, let me introduce them to you. Before you know it, you'll love them as much as I do." He led a reluctant Vashti into the kitchen, where the two boys were devouring peanut butter and jelly sandwiches.

"Hey, fellas, I've got someone that I want you to

meet." He positioned Vashti in front of him. "This is Vashti Hunter. She is a very special lady, and I wanted her to meet the other special people in my life."

"Hi," she replied and waved shyly.

"Hey," mumbled Brentz, Jr., looking down, still a little embarrassed about seeing her topless.

"Are you my daddy's girlfriend?" added Chance.

"Yes," she confirmed. "I'm his girlfriend."

"Actually, she's a little more than that," Brentz clarified. "We want to get married."

"Oh," muttered B.J., sounding disappointed. "What about mama? Does she know you're getting married?"

"Son, there's no need to worry about all of that right now. I'll sit down and have a long talk with your mother as soon as I get a chance. In the meantime, is there anything you want to say to or ask Vashti?"

Brentz, Jr. shook his head then thought of a question. "Do you have any kids?"

"No, but I love kids. I've always wanted to be a part of a big family," Vashti answered.

"Are you mean?" he inquired.

"No, I don't think so."

"She's the sweetest person in the world," finished Brentz and kissed her on the cheek.

"What are we supposed to call you?"

"Vashti is fine with me."

"Chance, do you have anything to ask Miss Vashti?" asked Brentz.

He licked peanut butter off of his hands. "Can you make peanut butter and jelly sandwiches? I like peanut butter and jelly."

"Yes," she said, smiling. "I make an excellent peanut butter and jelly sandwich!" With that, the

Washington men seemed content. Vashti, on the other hand, questioned if she was really ready to add "step-mother" to her repertoire and wondered what other skeletons did her fiancé have lurking in his closet.

Chapter 11

"Say it ain't so!" exclaimed Lewis when he looked down at the glittery diamond on Vashti's finger.

"Yes, it's so, but I told you that I was getting married. Don't tell me that you forgot," she reproached as she bagged up customer's poinsettias. She waved as the woman walked out of the store.

"Naw, I didn't forget; I had hoped that you'd changed your mind, though."

"No, I haven't changed my mind. The wedding's four weeks from today on Christmas Eve."

"It's getting close, huh?"

"Yep, but don't worry—I haven't let it distract me from Sabrina's wedding. We're not having anything nearly as **elaborate** as all that, just something small and intimate. We're only inviting about fifty people. Plus, it's on a Friday night. Those kinds of weddings don't usually have all of that fanfare. We just want to say our vows and be pronounced man and wife."

"Are you going on a honeymoon?"

"We don't know yet. It all depends on what Brentz can work out with his kids."

Lewis's face twisted into a frown. "I don't remember you saying nothing about no kids."

"Yes, he has two boys, but it's really not a problem. They're both very well-behaved children." She decided not to mention Grace seeing the troubled look on Lewis's face.

"Vashti, I don't know about all this. Taking on somebody else's children is a big responsibility. Even though my baby girl, Kirsten, is a teenager, I would still be weary about bringing another woman into her life."

"I know that, but we're in love. We'll work it out."

"That's even more reason for you to come on back to church," reasoned Lewis. "You're going to need all the prayer you can get."

"I'm coming back, Lewis, but now is not the right time. And I would appreciate it if you asked the deaconesses to stop calling to check on me and pressuring me to come back." The truth was that she was still ashamed of her dalliance with the pastor and wasn't ready to face the condemnatory eyes of the congregation for her spotty church attendance.

Lewis shook his head. "Girl, you know that Mattie Hunter would be turning over in her grave to hear you talking like this. If there's one thing your grandmother believed in, it was going to church."

"I'm trying to sort some things out with my life, Lewis, but I'll be back. I promise."

"And what about that busybody friend of yours? Y'all talking yet?"

Vashti shook her head. This was the longest that

she and Monique had ever gone without speaking, and it made her sad to think that they wouldn't be friends anymore.

"Well, you got some things to work on, Miss Lady. You ain't right with your friends; you ain't right with the Lord. What's going on here?"

"It'll all be fine. Once Brentz and I are married, everything will fall into place."

Lewis gave her a distrustful look and went back to the other side of the store. Vashti looked down at her ring, trying to convince herself that she really was doing the right thing.

The next day, she and Brentz were scheduled to finalize their gift registry. Vashti couldn't think of anything that would raise her spirits more than the prospect of receiving presents. An added bonus was that the children would be spending the day at home with the sitter. It wasn't that Vashti didn't like them, but neither Vashti or the kids were particularly at ease around the other. She welcomed the opportunity to spend time with Brentz away from their prying eyes and happily leaped up the steps leading to Brentz's front door.

Brentz took longer than usual to answer the door. "Come on in," he said. He looked frazzled and was ordering the children to sit down and be quiet. Grace screamed as the other boys chased her around the room.

"Sounds like your sitter's got her hands full with the kids today," Vashti said to Brentz. "You ready?"

"She had to cancel, and someone from the bank called a few minutes ago. They need me to go in."

"Okay, well, I guess I can do it alone. Just call me, and we can link up later on today." She kissed him and was about to turn to leave when he seized her arm.

"Vashti, wait! I hate to ask you this, but I need you to stay here with the kids. It'll only be for a little while, just until I can fix this problem at work."

Vashti wanted to ask if he'd lost his mind, but they would be her stepchildren in a few weeks. She needed to get used to babysitting them.

"Sure, I'll watch them," she answered dryly.

"Thank you so much, baby!" He gave her a quick kiss and bolted toward the door. He put his hand on the doorknob then turned around to face her.

"What's wrong?"

He exhaled. "There's one other thing that I need to tell you about." She could tell by his tone that it was serious. "Braxton's here."

"Who?"

"Braxton—she says he's mine, but I don't know. We're getting a paternity test," he explained quickly.

"Who is *she*?"

"Ashley Walker—she's a teller at the bank. She was seeing me and some guy named Fred at the same time, so he could just as easily be his baby."

Vashti was flabbergasted. Brentz darted into one of the bedrooms and came back out holding the infant. He plunked the child into Vashti's arms.

"He's a really good baby; all he does is sleep. You won't even know he's here."

Forty-five minutes later, Vashti was balancing the screaming baby in her arms and chasing Chance around the house. She heard something in another room crash as it hit the floor, followed by a "sorry" from Grace.

Vashti was at her wit's end when she heard a key

turning the lock on the front door. She let out a sigh of relief. As much as she wanted to be Brentz's wife, there was no way that she was ready to be his children's mother, and she had decided to tell him as soon as he walked in.

When the door opened, however, it wasn't her baby-making fiancé on the other side but a woman in a spiky blonde and red wig wearing hot pants.

"Who is you?" spat the woman. "Where is Brentz?"

"He had to go to work. Who are you?" Vashti replied, still in shock.

"I'm Keista. Oh, you the babysitter or something?"

"No, I'm Vashti."

"Vas what?" She smacked her lips. "I came to see my son." At this point, that could be for any given child. "What the . . ." she muttered as Chance zipped across the room naked and covered in suds. "Boy, where are your clothes?"

"I'm taking a bath!" he announced, jumping up and down on the couch.

"Chance, don't do that! Please stop jumping," pleaded Vashti to no avail. His mother whacked him across the back of his legs.

"Boy, get your butt down from there! Ain't nobody playing with you." She snatched him by the arm and dragged him down. He scurried out of the room. She turned and faced Vashti again. "Like I said, who is you?"

"I'm Brentz's fiancée."

"His who?" She spotted the ring on Vashti's finger and rolled her eyes. "You 'bout the third one he's had this year! I don't know when you tricks gon' figure out that Brentz likes falling in love, but he don't stay there. He told me that same trash four years ago, and we ain't married yet."

"He said that you two weren't even serious," Vashti pointed out.

"I don't care what he told you." She held up a ring cut and shaped identical to Vashti's. "Heck, I knew about Tanisha, but he ain't said nothing about you. It don't phase me none, though. Share and share alike, ain't that what they say?"

Vashti leaned in for a closer look at the ring. "Did Brentz give you this?"

"It wasn't the tooth fairy!" she spewed. "You stupid if you really think he's gonna marry you. You've got to go through me first and ain't none of you skeezers did it yet."

This was definitely more drama than Vashti had agreed to. "Didn't he tell you that he was seeing someone?" asked Vashti.

"What I care about him *seeing* you? Brentz can't get enough of this."

Despite having written Brentz off moments earlier, Vashti's pride would not allow her to concede to a woman that she considered beneath her. "Things have changed. Brentz and I are together now. We'll be married in a few weeks and you need to accept that," she explained.

"I ain't got to accept nothing!" Vashti shook her head and rocked the baby. "I don't know what you shaking your head for! What—you think you better than me?"

"I didn't say that, but I do think you should leave."

"I got a right to be here," she boasted. "I have visitation on weekends."

"Then leave and come back when Brentz gets here," replied Vashti and laid the baby down in the playpen.

"I ain't going nowhere." Keista parked her hands on her hips, challenging Vashti.

"Then I'm calling the police."

"Tramp, I wish you would try to call the folks on me!" She shoved Vashti in the chest.

"You're crazy." Vashti turned away to retrieve the phone. Then Keista toppled her from behind and wrestled her to the ground, reaching for the phone. During the scuffle, Vashti bruised her arm, scraping it against the edge of the wooden coffee table. She shrieked and groped the air for something to hit Keista with.

"Shut up!" Keista wrapped her hands around Vashti's neck, strangling her.

Vashti was on her back, gasping for air and digging her fingernails into Keista's wrists when she heard Brentz's voice telling Keista to stop. He pried her hands away from Vashti's neck and hauled Keista off of her.

Vashti sat up, inhaling deep breaths of air. Brentz rushed back to her side while Keista stood fuming in the foyer.

"Are you all right, baby?" She nodded. "What's going on here? I was on my way back when I got a call from B.J. saying that you and Keista were arguing."

"She—she tried to kill me!" Vashti stated breathlessly. "Call the police, Brentz. I want her locked up."

He stroked her back. "I'm here; you're okay now. We don't need to involve the police."

"She tried to kill me!" Vashti repeated shrilly.

"I can't lock her up, V. She's Chance's mother."

"I don't care who she is! I'm your fiancée. She attacked me, and I want her thrown in jail." Brentz made no moves toward the phone. "Brentz, I know that you are not going to let her get away with this."

"Vash, you're blowing it out of proportion. It was

just a little scuffle. I'm here now and everything's all right."

"So, what you're telling me is that you don't intend to do anything about this, that my feelings really don't matter?"

"I'm saying that she doesn't need to go jail over this. You're overreacting."

She narrowed her eyes. "Maybe I'm not making myself clear to you, Brentz. She assaulted me and I want her arrested. Either you are going to support me or you're not."

Brentz glanced back at Keista and then to Vashti. "She's my son's mother," he answered softly. "I can't call the police on her, not about this."

"That's fine." Vashti nodded, swallowing her anger and disappointment in Brentz. "That's fine." She stood up, nursing her bleeding arm, and hobbled toward the door.

"Baby, wait!" Brentz raced to catch her. "You're not leaving, are you?"

She looked into his eyes and shrugged her shoulders. "There's nothing for me here."

"Baby, I love you. We can work this out!"

"No, we can't. I have limits, Brentz, and you've gone way passed them."

He stepped back. "What do you mean?"

"What I mean is that I can't deal with my issues and your drama, too. First, there were the kids you didn't tell me about, your stable of baby-mamas, girl-friends and fiancées; now, the deranged ex that you refuse to have arrested. She could have killed me, and you don't even love me enough to make sure she pays for it! I need a man who can put me first, and you can't do that." She slid the ring from her finger and placed it in his hands. "It's over."

Brentz followed her out to her car. "Baby, I can fix this! Just tell me what you want me to do," he pleaded.

Vashti stopped to look at him. "Tell me, Brentz—is this the same speech you gave to Ashley and Keista and Tanisha? It's obvious that we all get the same ring, the same lies, and the same promises." She marched to her car and swung open the door.

"Baby, those women don't mean anything to me. You're the one I want."

"But you're *not* the one *I* want!" she stated, strapping on her seatbelt. "You're not the man for me, and there's no point in denying it any longer."

"Vashti, wait—once the DNA test comes back and—"

"Brentz, you know what you are—you're a love addict. You just replace one bad relationship with another one, and here I was trying to do it, too, but not anymore."

He blocked her from closing the door. "It's different this time."

"The only difference is that my name is Vashti and her name is Keista." She shook her head. "I can't believe I lost my best friend over you. This has been a complete waste of my freaking time. Have a nice life!"

As she sped off, she felt light and free. The nagging feeling that had been following her for weeks was finally gone, and she knew in her heart that, this time, she really had done the right thing.

Chapter 12

"What happened to you?" asked Lewis when he came into the store and noticed the bandage on Vashti's arm.

"Oh, this—it's my war injury," she replied sardonically.

"War? Who's been in battle with you? That banker didn't put his hands on you, did he?" Lewis flared up as if he would kill Brentz himself for hurting Vashti.

"No, it was his deranged baby's mama, one of them anyway. We had a little run-in over the weekend."

"What happened?"

"The usual I suppose—fussing, fighting . . . attempted murder."

Lewis was taken aback. "What?"

"Yes, she literally tried to kill me! Plus, I found out the he has yet another child." She shook her head, replaying the ordeal in her mind. "I told him that it wasn't going to work out between us."

"So is the engagement off?"

"Yep, we're through," Vashti said with finality.

"How do you feel about that?"

She shrugged her shoulders. "Angry, sad, love's fool yet again—I cried all weekend. But now mostly I feel relief."

Lewis was surprised. "Relieved? Why?"

"I guess I should have known that we had no business rushing into marriage that way. We barely even knew each other. But when you've been hurt, you get desperate."

"Well, I'm glad that you came to your senses before it was too late. I thought it was a bad idea from the start, but you seemed so determined to go through with it."

"I think that a part of me was just looking to fill the void that Kedrick left," she surmised.

"How's that void now?"

"I know now that only time can fill that void, not another person. I loved Kedrick and it's going to take a while to completely get over that, but I do think that I'm well on my way."

"Don't worry," Lewis assured her, "you'll get there with the Lord's help."

"Anyway, I know that you didn't come to hear me rant about my love life, so what *did* bring you by here today?"

"I wanted to see you," he said with a puckish grin.

"All right, Lewis, seriously—is there a problem with the construction that I should know about?"

"Well, there is a minor problem. We're going to need a little more lumber than we initially projected."

Vashti groaned. "How much more? And by that, I mean in dollars."

"About two hundred."

"Shoot!" She slammed her hand down on the counter.

"But for you, I'd settle for one of your pretty smiles."

"What about the lumber?"

"Don't worry about it; it's on me."

"Lewis, I can't let you do that."

"Yes, you can. You can deduct it from some of those wedding costs." She laughed and agreed to the compromise. "There's that smile that I came here for! I guess I better get out of here before you have me doing the whole thing for free." He winked at her and whistled as he walked out. As he departed, another customer walked in.

"Hi," welcomed Vashti, smiling up at the tall, baby-faced young man entering the store. He was obviously too young for her to lust after, but it couldn't hurt to look and long to be a teenager again. "How can I help you today?"

"Um, I want to get some flowers," he stammered.

"Okay, for a girlfriend?" He blushed and shook his head.

"Naw, naw, they're for my mom's birthday."

"All right, what kind of flowers are you looking for?"

"Roses, I guess. I don't really know too much about flowers."

She touched his arm to loosen him up. "Lucky for you, I know plenty. Come on." She led him into the showroom. He moved cautiously among the begonias and episcias, taking care not to accidentally brush up against them.

"Are you nervous?"

"A little," he confessed. "I don't want to mess up anything."

"Relax . . . it's a flower shop, not a museum." She smiled reassuringly at him. "So, do you have a name?"

"Yes, ma'am, it's Tyrell." Vashti couldn't help being a little insulted by him calling her ma'am. She knew that he was young, but she didn't think that she looked that old.

"What grade are you in, Tyrell?"

"Oh, I'm a senior in high school. I just turned nine-teen. I would be a freshman in college if I hadn't got held back a year in middle school. But I'll be graduating in a few months."

"Congratulations! Are you planning to go to college then?"

"Yes, ma'am." There was that word again! "I got a full basketball scholarship to FAM."

"Good for you." She picked up a potted amaryllis. "These are beautiful. I know that you said roses, but these can last two or three seasons. Do you like them?"

"Yes, ma'am."

"Tyrell, I'm not that much older than you. You don't have to *ma'am* me."

"I'm just trying to respect my elders. My mama always tells me to do that."

"*Elder*! Tyrell, I'm 26-years-old. That hardly qualifies me as a senior citizen. Just call me Vashti."

"I'm sorry," he apologized, blushing. She handed him another flower.

"This is an African violet."

He sniffed it. "It's pretty."

"And if you have your heart set on roses, you might want to try these tea roses. Aren't they lovely?" She held out a bouquet of short-stemmed coral tea roses.

"Yeah," he answered, nodding. "This is what I want. She'll love these."

"Okay, come back up front, and I'll ring you up." She walked ahead of him but could see him checking her out from behind through her peripheral vision. She smiled, thinking *Yeah, I've still got it!*

"All right, you're all set," she said and handed him the vase after he paid for the flowers. His hand brushed against hers during the exchange, sending a tingle through Vashti's body that she hadn't expected.

"Thank you . . . and thank you for helping me out. I guess you can tell I don't usually do this kind of thing."

"Neither do most men, but you did well for a first-timer." He smiled up at her again.

"Well . . . 'bye," he said, seeming like he wanted to say more but didn't know if he should.

"Good-bye, Tyrell, and wish your mother a happy birthday for me."

"I'll do that," he promised. He waved again before leaving. Vashti shook her head at his awkwardness around women and laughed to herself recalling the huge crush she had on her swimming coach and wondered if he saw her in the same bumbling light as she saw Tyrell.

"What are you smiling about? Or should I say *who*?" asked Monique, walking into the store weighed down by a mammoth purse thrown across her shoulders and a massive fedora tilted to the side of her head.

As soon as Vashti had left Brentz's house that Saturday afternoon, she drove straight to Monique's to apologize and ask for her forgiveness. Monique told her that she couldn't accept the apology because there was nothing to be sorry for or to forgive. She only wanted Vashti to promise to take a pregnancy test. Even though Vashti never did have sex with Brentz, Monique said that Vashti probably got pregnant just being in that fertile environment. However, Monique did berate her for giving back the ring.

"It's obvious that I haven't taught you anything!" she'd said. The two laughed and agreed to put the drama with Brentz behind them.

"Oh, hey. I was thinking about Coach Walker from the rec center. You remember him?"

"Do I? He was way too fine to be giving swimming lessons to underprivileged youths. I remember sneaking down to the pool after class just to look at him."

"I remember. He started having closed sessions after that."

Monique adjusted her hat. "What made you think about him?"

"This kid was in here a little while ago. He was kind of cute. I was helping him pick out flowers for his mom's birthday. I caught him checking me out, trying to do it on the sly like we used to do with Coach Walker. If that guy was a little older . . ." Vashti caught Monique eyeing her strangely. "What?"

"Were you tempted to touch?"

"No," denied Vashti. "I'll admit that I may be a little antsy, but I want to be loved, not arrested. Besides, I just got out of a relationship. The last thing I'm looking to do is get into another one, especially with someone who still has a curfew."

"Speaking of which, have you heard from Brentz?"

Vashti brushed her hair out of her face. "He's called a couple times trying to apologize, but it's over. It never should have started."

"Well, I won't say, 'I-told-you-so,' but we both know that I did," gloated Monique.

"You did, and I should have listened. It would have been a lot safer." Vashti looked down at the counter. "Look, that young man forgot his wallet!"

Monique folded her arms across her chest. "Don't act like you weren't hoping for an excuse to see him again."

"I wasn't! He's a *kid*, Monique. If there's a number in here, I'll call and return the wallet, and that will be the end of it."

"By the way, if he's your next prospective husband, please note that the legal age to marry in this country is eighteen."

"I'm well aware of that. Rest assured that when you start doling out checks for my wedding, the groom will be old enough to toast his beautiful bride."

Monique took a seat. "Since you're still determined to go through with this, I suggest you start paying attention to the calendar. You've already used a fourth of your time."

"That still leaves me with nine months. If a woman can bring about another human life in that same amount of time, surely I can snag a husband!"

Chapter 13

"Hey, I thought you might be needing this by now!" said Vashti, brandishing Tyrell's wallet. He stopped in to reclaim it on his way to school the next morning. She couldn't help but take stock of how cute he looked in his baggy jeans and jersey.

"Yeah, thanks." He smiled and tucked it into his back pocket. "I've been looking everywhere for it. My girlfriend thinks I left it at a female's house," he added sourly.

"Oh, you have a girlfriend?" Inexplicably, Vashti was disappointed upon hearing that.

"Yes, ma'am, we've been together since my sophomore year."

"So it's getting pretty serious then?"

He frowned and shrugged. "Not as serious as I'd like it to be."

Vashti recognized that frustrated expression from the countless number of boys who had labeled her a "tease" in high school. "You mean sex, right?"

He turned away bashfully. "I've got to go," he said

through an embarrassed smile. "Thanks for finding my wallet."

"You're welcome, and anytime you want some flowers or just want to talk, stop by." Her conscience reprimanded her for extending the invitation to him, but she couldn't help it. He was so darned cute!

A few days later, he was back. Vashti felt terrible for being excited to see him.

"Did you forget another wallet?" she teased.

"No, but I did forget me and my girlfriend's anniversary. She says that our first date was two years ago today. She's pissed that I didn't remember. I thought maybe some flowers would get me out of the doghouse."

"Well, nothing leaves an impression on a woman like a bouquet of flowers, but that's no excuse to forget your anniversary either," she scolded playfully.

"Between practice and college admissions and school, I can't remember everything. All she has to remember are her choir practices."

"She's not going to go to college?"

"She's a junior, so she has another year. But for me, I'm already a year behind because I flunked the sixth grade. My mom is on me everyday about that college sh—I mean, stuff."

"It's okay," she said, laughing. "You don't have to watch your language around me. You can say whatever you want."

He grinned mischievously. "In that case, is it all right if I tell you that you look kind of nice in those jeans today?" he added, eyeing her figure.

Vashti blushed. She hadn't heard a line that lame since she was Tyrell's age, so why was it having an effect on her now?

"You like that, huh?" he asked a little cocky. They

both looked at each other and smiled before timorously turning away.

As they moved about the store, he took advantage of every opportunity to touch her, and she continued to find excuses to let him. The sexual tension between the two of them was palpable, though Vashti would never admit it.

Monique and Lewis wandered into the store together, laughing. Their countenances changed the moment they saw Vashti with Tyrell.

"What's all this?" asked Monique, sounding more like an interrogating police officer than a friend.

Vashti quickly readjusted her position and backed away from Tyrell. Their presence was like an ice storm in the middle of a sunny afternoon. "Tyrell, why don't you look around and pick out something. I'll be up here if you need any help." He nodded and moved to the back of the store. Lewis immediately grabbed Vashti by the arm and pulled her to the side.

"Girl, what are doing letting that young boy lust after you like that? He looks young enough to be one of Kirsten's friends."

"We were talking, that's all."

"Yes, but he was *talking* with his eyes all over your booty," chimed in Monique.

"He's young and full of hormones. It's no big deal," remarked Vashti, dismissing their concerns.

"It's a *very* big deal," cut in Lewis. "What business does a thirty-year-old woman have messing with a young fellow like that?"

She wiggled out of his grip. "First of all, Lewis, I'm not thirty; I'm twenty-six. Secondly, nobody's *messing around* with anyone. He's here picking out flowers for his girlfriend."

They both looked at her warily, but Vashti was determined not to let them make her feel ashamed or guilty. She went on.

"And unlike the two of you, he's actually a *paying* customer, who needs my help."

"Now, listen," Lewis began gingerly. "You just got out of one bad situation, and nobody wants to see you rushing into another one."

"You'd think that she would've had enough of children," muttered Monique. Vashti stood akimbo and insisted that they were blowing things out of proportion.

"Well, I wasn't trying to get in your business. I came over to tell you that we're done with the lighting over there, and the boys are finishing up your office as we speak. You ought to be able to move into it later on today," informed Lewis.

"He gave me a preview. It looks good," Monique added.

"Thank you both. Now, I really must get back to my customer," she claimed, anxious to get them out of the shop.

"One more thing," interrupted Monique. "Lewis asked if his daughter can have her engagement party at my house and I said yes, so we're going to need to get together and discuss that real soon."

"And we will," Vashti replied, shooing them out. "We'll talk later."

"I didn't give you the date."

"Tell me later!" She pushed them out the door and shut it behind them, hoping that their being there hadn't scared Tyrell away.

"Tyrell, are you still back there?" she called.

"Yeah." He loomed from behind a bushel of plants. "Do you think she'll like these?" he asked, holding up an array of yellow abutilons.

"Sure, she'll love them. You'll be out of the dog-house in no time." He was standing close enough to her for her to inhale his cologne. She was positive that it was something cheap and gaudy that she'd sniffed at the sales counter at Wal-Mart, but at that moment, it was utterly intoxicating.

"Are you okay?" he asked.

"Huh?"

"You had this weird look on your face."

"I'm sorry; I was distracted."

He edged closer to her. "Vashti, can I ask you something?"

"Sure, what's up?"

He sighed and tilted his head a little. "Are women your age attracted to guys my age?"

She cleared her throat and could feel her palms becoming sweaty. The longer he stood there, the more she felt the impulse to rip his clothes off. "How old are you again?" she asked.

"I turned nineteen two weeks ago."

"Some women date younger guys, I guess. I wouldn't, of course," she indicated sternly. "But a lot women find those lean, hard muscles ... boyish charm ... and baby-soft skin sexy."

"But not you?" he asked for clarity.

"No—would you like some water?" she asked, di-verting the conversation. "It's a little stuffy in here. My throat is parched." She toddled over to a water cooler located next to the cash register.

"Why not?" he asked her. "What's wrong with going out with someone my age?"

"Because ... it's wrong and immoral and ... it's wrong," she stuttered, taking a big gulp of water.

"You already said that."

"Yes, because that's how wrong it is!"

He nodded and simpered impishly. "All right, I was just wondering."

"Why would you be wondering a thing like that anyway?"

"If I tell you, you might think I'm gay or something."

"Try me."

He looked around the store before speaking. "I'm a virgin," he admitted. Vashti hadn't expected to hear that. Now she *really* felt guilty for salivating over him. "I think an older woman could teach me how to, you know, be a good lover."

"Um, you do know what a virgin is, right?" she asked. He gave her an exasperated look. "Okay, I was just checking. Well, there's nothing wrong with being a virgin. The world needs more of them."

"Falon certainly thinks so."

"Who?"

"My girlfriend. She wants to wait until she gets married. I didn't want to cheat on her, so I waited, too."

"I take it that you're having second thoughts about that now."

"Yeah, I mean, I'll be in college soon. I don't want to leave, still being a virgin."

"There's nothing wrong with that, Tyrell."

"I know, but I *want* to have sex. She's the one who wants to be a virgin."

"Yes but with sex comes a lot of responsibility— pregnancy, STDs, emotional attachment. I know that you and your girlfriend may be feeling a lot of mixed emotions right now, but you shouldn't give in to that temptation until you're absolutely certain that it's what you both want to do. Maybe you're better off waiting."

He looked down at his plant. "I probably shouldn't be talking to you about this kind of thing, should I?"

"Tyrell, I told you that you can tell me anything. I meant that."

He reached into his pocket then smiled. "Are you ready for me?"

"Tyrell, weren't you listening to me?" she argued, misconstruing his question as a result of her own salacious thoughts. "Just because two people may be attracted to each other doesn't make it right. Sex is a very serious matter. You might not think so now, but you'll thank me for this later—trust me."

He was perplexed by her tirade and held up a twenty-dollar bill. "I meant the flowers. Are you ready for me at the cash register?"

"Oh . . . yeah, sure." With her pride deflated, she silently punched in his order and handed him his change, concluding that this was what six months of celibacy could do to a girl. "I hope that your girlfriend enjoys them."

"Can I come back and see you sometime? You know, to talk about girls and college—things like that?"

"Sure, I said that you could. Think of me as your big sister," replied Vashti although her feelings toward him were anything but familial. Nevertheless, she knew better than to act on her desires for him.

Shortly after his departure, Monique strolled back around to the store. "I waited until I saw your boyfriend leave," she ribbed.

"He's not my boyfriend; he's just a kid."

"He didn't look like any *kid* I know! What are they putting in the milk to have them coming out looking like that?"

"I know, right! Back when we were in school, you

thought you had yourself something if your boyfriend didn't have acne. But now—whew!"

"So are you planning on breaking him off behind the bleachers after school?"

"No, I made it very clear that I don't do the whole Stella thing. Besides, he's a virgin."

Monique frowned. "Do they even make those anymore?"

"Apparently so, but I believe that he's looking to change his status. He asked me if I'm attracted to younger guys."

"Are you?"

"Of course not—that's ridiculous." She thought for a moment. "So what if a harmless fling might do me some good or that I've been on a drought for six months . . ."

Monique propped her arm up on the counter. "So, what are you saying, V?"

"I'm not saying anything," she replied. "You know that I'd never stoop to that."

"Well, how old is he?" asked Monique.

"He said he's nineteen. It doesn't matter, though. I'm trying to find a husband, not a study buddy." A group of chatty women entered the store, and Vashti moved to assist them, but no matter what she did for the rest of the day, she couldn't stop her mind from wandering back to Tyrell.

Chapter 14

Vashti was curious when the name and phone number for a Theresa Jackson registered on her phone at work and was even more surprised to hear Tyrell on the other end of the phone. It had been almost two weeks since she'd last seen him. Between running the store and Christmas shopping, Vashti had ample time and distractions to help her work through her fascination with him. When he asked if he could stop by the store to talk to her, she felt certain that all of her inappropriate thoughts about him had been squelched and saw no harm in talking to him as a friend. She thought that it might even be fun to have someone to mentor.

When he arrived, she was busy pruning rosary vines in the back of the store. She only knew that he was there by the bell signaling his presence.

"Hey, Tyrell! What can I do for you today?" she asked, barely looking away from the plants. Tyrell didn't respond at first. He strode in and looked at her, licking his lips.

"This . . ." Catching her completely off-guard, Tyrell pinned Vashti against the wall, kissing her. After allowing herself to give in to her attraction to him for a few seconds, she broke away from his clutches.

"Tyrell, what are you doing?"

"What do you think?" He tried to kiss her again, but she rebuffed him.

"Tyrell, I don't know what you're thinking, but it's not like that between you and me. Sweetie, you're way too young for me to get involved with."

"I'm over eighteen. Whatever we do is legal, baby."

She pressed her hands against his chest to prevent him from coming any closer. "Legal, yes; moral, no!"

"But I'm ready! I told you that I don't want to go off to college still being a virgin."

"Why not? There's nothing wrong with waiting for the right woman to come along. I think that it's admirable that you held out this long. Lord knows I couldn't, but I've always regretted it."

"But I have found the right woman—*you*!"

"Your first time should be with someone you love—specifically, your wife, or at least your girlfriend."

"Come on, Vashti," he whined, peeling her hands off of his chest and folding them into his. "I can't wait that long. Besides, I want *you.* There's something strong between us. I know you feel it, too. I can tell by the way you look at me."

She dropped his hand. "Yes, I'm a little attracted to you but . . ."

Vashti lost her train of thought and sense of morality as he slid off his shirt, revealing his carved abs and rippled biceps. Even the lion tattoo etched in his muscular chest was enticing. He sure wasn't cut like any teenager she'd ever known; very few grown men had a body like that.

"Umph!" grunted Vashti, ogling his torso. He leaned in for another kiss. This time, she didn't resist. She felt his hands crawl underneath her skirt and yank at her panties. She stopped him.

"Not here," she whispered.

"Don't stop, Vashti. I know you want to as much as I do."

"No, I meant not here in the store. Let's go to my office."

Gripping her from behind, he hoisted her up, and Vashti clamped her legs around him as he carried her to the office. Before they had even reached the door, Vashti's shirt and shoes had been tossed aside. Tyrell set her down on the desk, and she snatched his belt from its loops and unbuttoned his jeans. He pulled his pants down and brusquely proceeded.

"Uh-uh, hold up!"

"What?" he asked impatiently, almost panting.

"Tyrell, I know that you're a virgin and everything, but there are some things that I just can't excuse. This is one of them." He sighed and backed away from her.

"What am I doing wrong? Tell me what I'm supposed to do."

How often had she longed to hear those words uttered by a man, but now was not the right time. She was ready and did not need anything to distract her or remind her of the fact that her having sex with someone who had only been allowed to vote for a year was a testament to her desperation. Vashti had not envisioned herself playing the role of his sex coach, but this way, she could rationalize it as instruction.

She sighed. "First of all, women like it slow. This isn't a race to see who can finish first."

"Okay, I can do it slow." He tried again.

"Wait!" She pushed him off of her. "I'm not a man. I can't just jump in the mood."

He exhaled heavily. "I asked you to tell me what to do."

"You should kiss me, touch me." He leaned down and planted a gentle kiss on her lips.

"Touch you where?"

"Here—feel that?" She was frustrated by his ignorance and the school system's failure to require classes in human anatomy.

"Come on, I'm ready now!" he insisted.

"Do you have a condom?"

"For what? I'm a virgin, so you know I don't have anything."

"You have sperm!"

He huffed and fished a condom out of his pocket. She snatched it out of his hands.

"Hey, what are you doing?"

"I'm examining it . . . okay—latex . . . nonoxynol-9 . . . all right, we're good to go." He tried to pry it out of her hands. "Uh-uh—I'll do it. You might not know what you're doing, and I'm not taking any chances."

"You're acting like my mama."

"Boy, I'm trying to keep from being your *baby's* mama!" He was reticent as she slipped the condom over him.

A few moans and deep breaths later, Tyrell squinted his eyes and opened his mouth, but no sound came out. Then his face contorted and his body stiffened. Then it was over. So much for Vashti's quest to eradicate the two-minute brother.

"How was that?" he asked nervously.

"Great, great." She patted him on the back.

"I guess I'm a man now," he touted.

"It takes a lot more than that to be a man, Tyrell," noted Vashti, searching for her panties.

"At least I'm not a virgin anymore."

"Nope, you're not a virgin."

He zipped up his pants. "Hey, when can we hook up again?"

She jerked her head around and looked at him apprehensively. "Excuse me?"

"Yeah, you know—me and you. I really want to get good at it, and I know you have some more things you can teach me. You can be like my tutor."

"Look, deflowering you was one thing, but we're not going to make this a habit. You might be legal, but I'm way too old for you. This can never happen again!"

Vashti tried her best to ignore the feeling that told her that what she was doing was wrong. She told herself that since she was no longer attending church, God could neither see nor hold her accountable. The devil had a found a crack in her life, and he was slowly but surely creeping through it. Vashti had stopped bothering to try to resist him.

Chapter 15

Her words were still echoing in her head as her back was being pressed up against the wall with her legs folded over Tyrell's strong arms when they were having sex at her house three days after she swore never to sleep with him again.

Tyrell was the ideal student—a quick study, eager to learn, and obedient. She only hoped that he fared as well in the classroom.

Persistent guilt prevented Vashti from revealing her secret affair to anyone, not even Monique. She knew that it was wrong but felt powerless to put an end to it. It didn't take more than a few conversations with Tyrell for Vashti to realize there could never be anything more between them than sex. Everything he talked about somehow always came back to basketball and food, two subjects which he could ramble on about incessantly. She would often have to kiss him just to make him shut up. Once during a moment of passion, she asked him to say her name, then to spell it. The mood was broken when he did so incorrectly.

Within weeks after the affair started, Vashti concluded that she was not one to indulge in casual sex,
no matter how good it was. She needed an emotional
connection—someone she could talk to, someone
she could share her dreams with . . . someone whose
idea of a date was not going to the gas station to pick
up snacks.

She was on the verge of telling Tyrell so when he
called asking her to come over. He had the house to
himself and was aching to see her. It was tempting—
she was in heat and her house was being fumigated.
Against her better judgment, Vashti decided to have
one last rendezvous—just to let him down easily.

She knew that it was a mistake when she looked
around his bedroom. Vashti was used to seeing the
likes of Elizabeth Catlett and Eldzier Cortor nailed to
the wall, not half-naked vixens and posters of the
G-Unit. The bedroom reeked with a fusty combina-
tion of sweat socks and musk. A crumpled denim
comforter was hanging off the otherwise sheet-less
bed. The thought of laying her freshly-bathed and
expensively-moisturized body on his bare urine-in-
fested mattress sickened her. Tyrell caught a glimpse
of the disapproving scowl on her face and quickly
smoothed out the comforter and spread it evenly
over the mattress. He sat down and motioned to her
with his head.

The fact that he was young, broke, couldn't buy
her a drink, and still lived with his mama couldn't
take away from the fact that he was sexy as ever.
Even the peach-fuzz on his face that screamed jail-
bait was an added turn on to her.

She kissed him as she snatched his Danner High
School T-shirt over his head. He lay back on the bed
and closed his eyes as she unzipped his pants and

unearthed the part of him that she was willing to lay in pee for. Within minutes, the heaving, the gyrating, and grinding brought them both to climax, and they fell back on his bed.

Tyrell clicked the stereo on with his remote. The sudden roar of the bass and intelligible, profane lyrics startled her.

"Don't you have anything a little more mellow? Some Jill Scott maybe, or Brian McKnight?"

"Nah, that's ol' school. What you know about this new banger?" He reached underneath his bed and pulled out a school supply box. He popped the lid open and pulled out a dime bag of weed and papers and began to roll a joint. She sat up in the bed in horror.

"Tyrell, what are you doing?"

He licked the blunt to seal it shut and flicked his lighter. "What does it look like?"

"Tyrell, you can't smoke weed! I don't care what your friends say—that stuff is addictive!" He took a long pull from the marijuana.

"So, what, you my conscience now?" He coughed.

"Look, you don't even know how to smoke it!" she chided.

He passed it to her. "You wanna hit this?" He turned his head and coughed again.

Vashti felt that she had reached an all-time low—she was sexing a nineteen year-old man on urine-stained sheets, listening to someone rap about putting her in a body bag while lying naked in his mama's house. The least she could do was get high to escape the reality of what her life had become. She inhaled the joint and released it.

"This isn't laced with anything, is it?" Tyrell shook his head. She took another hit.

"Pass that to the left, Shawty!" he asserted, snatching the joint from her grip. "You're getting too comfortable with that."

Vashti closed her eyes and waited for the buzz. The thought of what her friends would say if they could see her made her giggle. Yes, surely the devil had found a way into Vashti's life.

"Yeah, you messed up all right," drawled Tyrell and passed it back to her. She inhaled and blew out her worries and inhibitions. She even began to think that this thing with Tyrell might work out after all—either that or they were puffing some very strong weed.

"Yeah, I like for my girl to get high with me. Falon ain't havin' it. She can't get down like you can."

"Oh, I'm your girl now?" Vashti asked, smiling up at him with half-closed eyelids.

"Yeah, you my girl." He leaned down to kiss her. Vashti didn't know if it was the drug making her paranoid or what, but she thought that she heard keys dangling and voices in the distance. She ignored it and crept her hand down Tyrell's thigh. She clamped her legs around him. She had just started to get her body in rhythm with his when she heard a voice piercing over the music.

"What the heavens is going on here?! Tyrell, get up from there right now!"

It was the booming voice of an overweight, large purse-wielding woman. She began to beat Tyrell across his bare back with her imitation Louis Vuitton bag. Tyrell jumped up, and Vashti gasped and tried to cover herself when she realized that they'd been discovered. The woman glared at her and placed her hands on her hips. It was then that Vashti noticed a young woman with her. The girl was in shock and tears sprang into her eyes.

"Falon!" stammered Tyrell, trying to shield himself with a pillow he grabbed from the floor. "Don't cry — it's not what it looks like."

"Do you think I'm stupid, Ty," she cried, lunging toward him. His mother held her back.

"I saw her at the grocery store. She came home with me so she could help me bake you some cookies to take with you on the road tomorrow, you triflin' dog, just like your daddy! And who is this hussy you got laying up with you? You don't look like no high school girl."

"She's not! She's a woman! She's a grown woman with her own business and everything," he crowed. Vashti tried to quiet him. Unlike him, she found nothing about the situation to be proud of.

"You ought to be ashamed of yourself!" hissed his mother. "A grown woman messin' around with my boy, and —" She sniffed the air. "Do I smell weed? Have you been giving my son drugs?"

"No, mama," Tyrell answered.

She slung her purse and struck him in the face. "Don't you lie to me, boy! I told you I ain't having that in my house!" Tyrell ducked and slipped into a pair of pants.

"Fine, I'll go stay with Vashti. Come on." Tyrell grabbed her by the arm.

"Wait a minute, Tyrell." She pulled away from him. "You can't stay with me."

"You're my girl, right?"

"I thought *I* was your girl," squeaked Falon, wiping a tear. Tyrell faced her.

"Fal, what we had was cool, but I need a woman —

a real woman. I'll be a college man soon; you'll still be in high school. Vashti and me have a mature relationship," he explained.

"Fool, y'all ain't got no relationship!" ranted his mother. "She just wanted a piece of young meat, ain't that right?" She turned to Vashti, waiting for her to respond.

"Tell her, Vashti. Tell her we're the real thing," demanded Tyrell. Vashti pulled the blanket tighter around her body.

"Maybe we shouldn't see each other for a while, Ty," Vashti suggested quietly.

"Naw, you don't have to be ashamed. Tell them I'm your man!" Vashti looked into the accusing eyes of his mother and the heart-broken eyes of his girl-friend. She knew that she couldn't delude him any longer.

"Tyrell, you're real cool and maybe if you were older or if I were younger, things could be different. But you're about to go to college and—"

"Don't you see—I could go to school here," he interposed. "We could move into your crib together, and we wouldn't have to sneak around anymore. I'm nineteen. I'm a man."

Vashti shook her head. "Tyrell, it just wouldn't work."

"Tyrell, I thought you loved me!" blurted out Falon.

It was then, the moment that Vashti saw tears streaming down Falon's innocent, cherub face, that she realized that she was the cause of it. Sure, Tyrell was fun and games to her, but this was a girl who actually loved him. Suddenly, Vashti felt dirty and ashamed.

She secured the blanket around her body and slid out of bed, scooping her clothes off of the floor.

"Yeah, you *better* leave!" grumbled his mother.

"Ms. Jackson, I'm so sorry for disrespecting your house. I won't see Tyrell again." She slinked out of the room.

"Vashti!" called Tyrell. "Vashti!" Once she was out of their line of vision, she quickly dressed and scurried out of the house.

She fumbled with her keys and dropped them in her haste to get into the car and drive off. Tyrell was calling her name and approached her.

"Vash, what's up? Where you goin'?" he asked.

"Tyrell, you've got a lot of drama going on in there with your mom and your girl. I don't need to be here."

"But you're my girl, right? I mean, I love you, Vashti, and you love me, too. If you didn't, you would've made love to me."

Made love? Vashti had always assumed that their sessions together were nothing more than a good time for the both of them. She never expected him to get emotionally involved.

"Tyrell, you don't mean that. You don't love me; you hardly even know me."

"But we've got a bond. I know you feel it, too."

"You have your whole life ahead of you. You're starting college, and there's a whole world of experiences that are just waiting for you."

"Look, I don't care about the age thing. It doesn't matter to me."

"It matters to me!" she exclaimed. "Tyrell, you're just a kid. You're a kid, and I should have known better."

"A kid, huh?" His expression turned cold. "Was I a kid when I was tapping that the other night? Was I a kid when you were groaning and slobbering all over me ten minutes ago?"

"Yes, Tyrell, you were. I'm the adult. I shouldn't have let things go this far." He looked away from her and snatched his arm back when she tried to touch him. "Look, I know that things look bad now, but you'll be in college in the fall. You'll be partying and meeting new people. You can forget that all of this ever happened. And maybe it's not too late to patch things up with your girlfriend. I know she's upset right now, but she loves you and she still might forgive you. Just tell her . . . tell her it was a mistake, that you're sorry, and that it never should have happened."

Her turned and glared at her with tears in his eyes.

"I loved you, Vashti. It wasn't a mistake to me." He turned and dashed into the house. She called his name, but he didn't come back.

"Get off my property, tramp!" called his mother from the doorway. Vashti jumped into her car and spun off.

Vashti looked through the rearview mirror at her own reflection, wondering what happened to the woman she used to be. She remembered how she condemned Pastor White for the hypocrite he was and realized that she was no different or any better than he. During the drive, Vashti recalled all the times that Lewis had asked her when she was coming back to church. Assessing the mess that her life had become, Vashti now realized that it needed to be sooner rather than later.

Chapter 16

"Girl, where have you been?" asked Monique when the housekeeper led Vashti into the living room, where Monique was taking down Christmas ornaments. "I tried calling you all afternoon. I was going to invite you to go get facials and pedis. It was on me—well, technically, it was on Trent—but you get the idea. I ended up going by myself. Didn't you get my messages?"

"I was busy this afternoon—busy getting busy . . . then getting busted."

"Busted for what? Did the fashion police finally catch up with you for wearing those clearance specials in public? And getting busy with whom?"

"Just a guy, that's all," murmured Vashti, helping Monique removed the garland from the fireplace.

"Who?" Vashti looked away. This was one secret that she intended to keep to herself. "Was it Brentz? Did you get caught by one of his baby's mamas?" Vashti shook her head. "He's the only one I know of that you've been kickin' it with like that except for that little boy you were trying to flirt with the other day." Vashti's failure to deny the accusation sent Monique reeling.

"Vashi, tell me that you weren't letting that li'l boy hit it! I mean he was cute and all, but oh girl!" said Monique, dropping the garland into a plastic sack. "Is it so bad that you've got to start prowling the playground to find a man?"

"Monique, don't get all self-righteous on me. You all but encouraged me to do it. Besides, you've dated younger guys before. What about that rapper, Baby Chris?"

"Baby Chris? Oh, yeah, him. He was twenty, and I did get a diamond bracelet and a free weekend in the Bahamas out of the deal. All you could get from this dude is a reserved space in his yearbook. Who caught you anyway?"

"His mother and his girlfriend. It was awful. I felt like some child molester. The worst part was when he tried to defend our relationship; telling his mother that we were in love and going to move in together."

"Whaaat?"

"I had to set him straight, though, and cut him loose. I felt bad because he was crying and everything, and his girl was crying. I got out of there as fast as I could." Vashti sat on the sofa and drew her knees to her chest, sulking.

"At least, you got a chance to dump him for a change. You were like 1 for 1 in that department," consoled Monique. She tossed the sack into a large box and looked at Vashti with a devilish smirk. "But I have to ask—how was he?"

"I told you—he was devastated."

"No, I meant how was he in bed?"

"Monique . . . ," she groaned.

"Come on, Mrs. Robinson, details. I want the actuals and the factuals." She tapped Vashti for her to scoot over.

Vashti relented and made room for Monique. "He was a virgin, so the first time, he was sort of nervous and didn't know what he was doing, but he soon got over that."

"The first time? How many times was it?"

"Let's just say more than one. We were in the midst of the second time that day when we got caught."

"Dang, girl, that's the most action you've had in months! He must have been all right then."

"He was. Since he was a virgin, I was able to train him. His next girlfriend will really appreciate me."

"Well, now that you've gotten kicked out of Toyland, you should be ready for a real man."

"Like who? Ashton?"

"You should at least go to dinner with him." Monique rose and began detangling the Christmas lights. "If you act right, you might still make that wedding deadline."

"No, I'm straight. I think I need to be by myself for now and get back on track with work. Lewis's daughter's wedding is in a few of weeks and I really need to focus on that."

"How's that coming anyway?" Monique asked, tugging the lights.

"It's coming. I'm really impressed with Lewis. He's been so attentive about this wedding, coming by to make sure everything's on schedule, calling. It must be great for Sabrina and Kirsten to have a dad like that."

Monique turned around, surprised. "He comes by *personally* to take care of the details?"

"Yes, he's like the liaison between Sabrina and me."

"Hmm."

"What?" prodded Vashti.

"Isn't that the sort of thing the mother would do? Men don't usually get into all that."

"Well, her mother's away, I guess. I think that she's somewhere up north. Lewis never talks about her. Personally, I think that it's great that Lewis is taking such as interest."

"Yeah, he's taking an interest all right," Monique replied wryly.

"What's that supposed to mean?"

"Vash, Lewis is a construction worker. What does he know about flower arrangements and dress patterns? He doesn't give a hoot about that stuff; he's just trying to get next to you!"

"Lewis? No, he's like a father to me."

"Well, he certainly is old enough to be. But I've seen the way he looks at you, and it's not a father-daughter stare either. He wants you."

"Girl, you're trippin'. Lewis is my friend—that's all he wants to be."

"Uh-huh," she said skeptically.

"You have way too much time on your hands," concluded Vashti.

"Mark my words. Lewis is starting to hear wedding bells of his own, and it don't have the first thing to with Sabrina. If you want to be a bride by September, you may have to go through him. With the contenders you've been selecting, my grandchildren will probably beat you to the altar."

"Monique, this isn't just about getting married before September. It's also about me finding someone who I want to spend my life with, to grow old with."

"Then cancel out Lewis. He's gotten started on the 'growing old' part without you. Plus, he's so religious. He's more likely to have you screaming 'oh, God' in church instead of in the bedroom."

"Calling on God right now might not be such a bad idea. It looks like I'm gonna need all the help I can get!"

Chapter 17

"I'm bored," sighed Monique, clicking off the television with the remote control. They were spending yet another Friday night at Vashti's house doing absolutely nothing. "We need to get out of here."

"I thought you were waiting for Trent to call you to let you know that he was back?"

"Trent's plane was supposed to land around eight; it's after ten," she retorted bitterly. "Forget it! It's a Friday night, and I refuse to sit here watching *Good Times* reruns with you." She stood up to throw away their empty bag of potato chips.

"You're not my first choice for company either, you know!" snapped Vashti and slumped down into the sofa.

"This is wrong; we should be out somewhere," Monique resolved.

"You go on without me. I'm tired. I think I'm just going to stick around here, maybe clean up a little bit."

"You will do nothing of the such!" denounced Monique. "You should at least go have a drink with me. You *need* a drink with the drought that your love life's been on."

It was true. Vashti had only been on one date since her fling with Tyrell, and that date ended terribly and was more than a month ago. Her date was Maurice Long, a self-abasing accountant who spent most of the night complaining about his life, but with Valentine's Day—and her deadline—approaching, Vashti had gotten desperate enough for male companionship to try to find his phone number. Like a lot of women in and out of the church, instead of waiting on God to fill the void in her life, she was looking to fulfill it with the first male or distraction available.

Vashti yawned. "What is there to do?"

"What *isn't* there to do? This is Miami! We shouldn't be stuck in the house watching T.V. We should be out *living la viva loca*!" Vashti knew that Monique meant business whenever she started speaking in Spanish.

"Fine, what do want to do?"

"I don't know—have some drinks, hit up a few clubs. There's a new reggae club opening tonight. That's where we need to be."

After she'd gotten involved with Kedrick and the church, the club was a place that Vashti no longer frequented. Now that she had lost ties to both, she was a prime candidate to be lured back into the devil's playground.

"I'll go, but can we make it an early night?"

"Sure . . . it'll be early in the morning when we get back home!"

At the club, Vashti was nursing her third drink while Monique, who had abandoned her after bumping into first love Craig Billingslea, twirled on the dance floor. Vashti was quietly enjoying her Amaretto-induced haze and the reverberation of the Caribbean drums when a flannel-clad, slightly heavy-set guy with cornrows sat down next to her at the bar. As he ordered a drink, Vashti prayed that he wouldn't talk to her. She found out that some prayers don't get answered.

"What's up, Slim?" he growled in a deep, raspy voice.

"Are you talking to me?"

"Who else?" he asked, looking around the bar. "What's your name?"

"Um, Vashti." She kicked herself for giving him her real name instead of a "club name."

"Vashti? Your moms must have been high as a kite when she named you!"

"It's a biblical name," she informed him.

"Oh, word? Mine is, too."

"Really?"

"Yeah, it's Ezra, but folks 'round here call me Ol' E."

"Ol' E?" Vashti had deduced a long time ago that whenever a guy nicknamed himself after a brand of malt liquor, things could only go downhill from there.

"Yeeah," he drawled. "That's hot, right?"

"I guess. I kind of like Ezra, though."

He wrenched his head back a little. "Girl, I'm a rapper! I can't go around calling myself no Ezra!"

"A rapper, huh? What label?" Vashti perked up at the thought that he might be somebody important.

"Blunted-out Records."

"Excuse me?"

"Blunted-out Records," he repeated. "Yeah, that's my label, straight-up independent. Forget all that major label garbage. All my money is staying in my pockets."

That was all she needed to hear to conclude that he was, in fact, *nobody* important. "So, it's an upstart?" she inquired.

"Yeah, I run that mother, though; I'm CEO, CFO, COO, president, producer, business manager, and artist."

"That's a lot for one man. Where are your offices located?"

"Man, I'm chillin' for right now; you know, running things out my basement and all."

Why wasn't she surprised? "Well, I guess you have to start somewhere."

"It's gon' blow up, though. I just signed these young cats, man. They like the new Hot Boys and Cash Money."

She nodded and sipped her drink, telepathically summoning Monique to come rescue her.

"Aye, you, what's your number?"

She vigorously shook her head. "Oh, I'm not really dating right now."

"I ain't ask you all that! I just wanted your number." He smacked his teeth. "Y'all females be talking about meeting a good man and stuff and when one tries to holler at you, you got excuses. I know I ain't big time yet, but at least a nigga tryin'. I just wanna call you some time. I ain't tryin' to marry you or nothing."

Vashti wondered who was she to write him off just because he seemed a little "rough around the edges." No, he didn't seem like her type, but who knew what kind of man lied beneath the braids and beer-belly? For all she knew, he could be her soul mate.

"What the heck?" She scribbled her number on a piece of paper and handed it to him. He tucked it into his pocket.

"All right, *Miss Vashti*, I'll get up with you later." He took his drink and walked back out into the lounge area. Vashti looked on as Monique tore herself from Craig on the dance floor. He grabbed her hand for another dance, but she shook her head and headed back toward the bar.

"Sorry it took so long, girl," breathlessly apologized Monique. "But you know how I like to get my two-step on."

"Uh-huh, you better be glad that Trent's not here. I saw you all up on Craig, droppin' it like it's hot!"

"Please, you couldn't pay Trent to come to a club like this." She blotted the beaded sweat on her forehead. "Who were you talking to a minute ago?"

"Oh, that was Ezra, a.k.a. Ol' E."

"Ol' E?"

"He claims that he's a rapper-slash-producer."

"Okay, that's code for *I don't have a job, and I sell weed out my mama's basement.*"

"I don't know, he seems kind of nice—very upfront and honest, which is more than I can say for most men these days."

"A producer, V? Please!"

"I know what you're thinking, but he could be the next Diddy or Russell Simmons. Besides, we both have biblical names. Maybe it's a sign." Vashti was looking for a sign from God when she should have been seeking God himself.

"Yes, V, it's a sign that you've had too many drinks!"

"I'm not going to marry the guy, 'Nique. I just gave him my phone number. He probably won't even call."

"Girl, the broke ones *always* call."

Vashti was about to defend her decision to give him her phone number again when Craig, a thicker, taller version of the guy that Vashti remembered from Monique's prom pictures, walked up with a wide smile and out-stretched arms for Monique.

"Come on, girl, you know this used to be our jam back in the day!" He began to sing "Mr. Loverman" along with Shabba Ranks, loudly and out of tune.

" 'Nique, please take him; he's killing my buzz," pleaded Vashti. Monique slid her hand into his and was soon wrapped in Craig's arms with thoughts of Trent far behind as she swayed back and forth to the music.

"Mr. Loverman!" sang Monique, replaying the song in her head as they drove home with the top down of Monique's Maserati Spyder, fighting the temptation to doze off after too much dancing and too many drinks.

"Speaking of 'Mr. Loverman,' did you ever hear from Trent?"

"Yeah, he's been blowing up my phone since around midnight. He'll be all right, though." Monique continued to hum to herself.

"You and Craig looked pretty cozy back there," noted Vashti.

"Girl, Craig looked plain pretty! I had forgotten how fine he was."

"And, clearly, how *married* you are!"

"Chill out, we were just having a little fun. It was nice to have a man paying attention to me for once."

"That's what your husband is for."

"Try telling him that."

"You're spoiled, you know that? Trent gives you everything that you could possibly *think* you want, and you're here complaining."

"Money ain't everything, V," she grumbled.

"Well, I'm glad that you had your fun. Hopefully, you sent Craig packing so you can devote your attention to Trent." Monique was silent. "Don't tell me that you plan to see him again."

"We're old friends!" she reasoned. "Trent doesn't have anything to worry about. Craig doesn't make enough money for me to be seriously interested in him, so what's the harm in going to lunch, huh?"

"Keep telling yourself that," muttered Vashti. "You're always talking about my unresolved feelings for Kedrick, but what about yours for Craig?"

"Craig and I are ancient history—that was high school!"

"He was your first love, first everything. You were crazy about him!"

"I was crazy about Kwame and polka dots back then, too!" she recalled, laughing. "Craig and I were puppy love. I'm not going to get into anything I can't handle."

Vashti wearily looked on as her friend drove in a daze, humming "Mr. Loverman."

Chapter 18

"Hey, I'm coming over. Where do you stay?" was the greeting Vashti received from Ezra early the next morning. Her head was pounding from Amaretto shots from the night before, and she had no idea who she was talking to on the phone.

"What? Who is this?" she barked.

"Ol' E, Ezra. We met last night at the club." She tried to dredge up the memory. She cringed when his cornrows and sagging pants came to mind.

"Look, Ezra, today's not a good day. Saturday is my busiest day at work."

"Where you work at?"

It was too early in the morning for Vashti to be having this conversation. She hadn't had time to prepare a plausible lie to feed him and was afraid that, in her state of mind, she might slip up and tell him the truth.

"Ezra, look, I've got go." She clicked the phone off and groped her nightstand to find the receiver.

After snoozing for another half hour, Vashti rose and began getting dressed. While she was in the shower, she heard the phone ringing but decided to let her voicemail catch it on the off-chance that it was Ezra calling back.

When she stepped out of the shower, she checked the caller ID. The name Ida Thomas appeared and her phone signaled that she had a message pending.

"That's messed up what you did!" growled the voice on the answering machine. "A nigga is just trying to get to know you. If you didn't want to talk to me, you shouldn't have gave me your number. It's all right, though. That stuff is gon' come back on you. I could have made you happy, girl, but you so quick to judge that you can't even see that. That's cool, though; do you! You can't always judge a book by its cover—remember that!"

Vashti felt bad. Had being around Monique finally turned her into a snob? Here she was dismissing this guy for what—because he actually called her like he said he would? Because he wanted to spend time with her? Wasn't she just longing to meet someone the day before? She looked at the number on the ID box and dialed, hoping that Ezra would still want to talk to her given the way she'd treated him. She recognized his voice when he answered.

"Hi, Ezra, it's me, Vashti."

"What you want?" he snapped.

"I wanted to apologize for the way I acted this morning. I was asleep when you called, and I wasn't myself. I hope you can overlook that."

"It's cool, Shawty," he answered coldly. "Is that all you wanted?"

"No, you said something about getting together today."

"You said that you have to work, remember?"

"I do—have to work, I mean. But I usually close up around four on Saturdays."

"Oh, you got your own business?" he asked with interest.

"Something like that, yeah."

"Aye, look here, I'm free all day today, so you let me know what's up."

"Don't you have to work in the studio?"

"Naw, I laid down some tracks early this morning. Plus, my mom is going to be cleaning up down here today."

"Down where?"

"In the basement—that's where I keep all my equipment."

Monique's words rang in her head. "So, you still live with your mother?"

"For now, yeah, while I'm trying to get my label off the ground. I'm saving up for my own place, but right now, my money is tied up in this music."

Vashti's instincts told her to hang up the phone immediately, but it was drowned out by the voice that rationalized that he at least had a plan and was willing to make personal sacrifices to follow his dreams. She scolded herself for not being more sympathetic to his situation—not everyone can have a successful business handed to them like she did.

"What did you have in mind for today?" she ventured.

"Dang, you're the one with the cheese. You ought to be taking me out!"

She winced at the thought, but he had a point. She

had been blessed, so why shouldn't she share it? Besides, she was liberated enough to treat a man to a meal.

"How about dinner?"

"Yeah, that's cool. Let's go somewhere nice like Nobu or Casa Tua," he suggested. "I don't get to go out that much."

"I'm by no means rich, Ezra. Let's keep it simple."

"A'ight, so what time are you coming to get me?"

"Don't you have a car?"

"Yeah, but it's in the shop. The radiator's busted; it's probably gonna take them a while to fix it."

Vashti rolled her eyes and exhaled. For as long as she could remember, "in the shop" usually translated to "does not exist." But she realized that he probably felt embarrassed about not having a car, so she didn't press the issue.

"So I'll see you around seven?" she confirmed.

"Yeah."

"Where do you live?"

"You can just pick me up over my cousin's house. He stay out in Liberty City."

"Liberty City—isn't that area kind of rough?"

"Ain't nobody gon' try to mess with you. Just come on through." He gave her the directions and hung up the phone.

Later that afternoon, Vashti was still contemplating whether or not she should go through with the date when Lewis entered the store.

"You mind if I help myself to your water cooler?" he asked, perspiring heavily.

"Go ahead," she sighed.

He watched her as he took a swig of water. "What's eating you today?"

"Nothing in particular. I've got a lot on my mind."

"I hope that it's got something to do with Sabrina's engagement party next week. She's looking forward to it; she's been talking about it all week."

"Don't worry—I haven't forgotten. I'm letting Monique help out a lot with the planning. It keeps her out of trouble."

Lewis chuckled. "You know what you ought to do? You ought to come out to the church with me tonight for revival. Maybe then you'll stop looking so sad."

"I would, Lewis, but I have a date tonight."

"Another one? Woman, you keep more boyfriends than anyone I know!"

"He's not a boyfriend; he's not even a friend, really. We just met."

"Well, I hope that he takes you someplace nice and shows you a good time."

"Actually, the date is *my* treat tonight."

Lewis groaned loudly. "Aw, here comes some mumbo-jumbo about how a woman can do whatever a man can do. I don't care what y'all say, there are some things that a man just ought to do, like take his woman out!" he argued.

"Oh, no, I agree, but he's a little down on his finances right now. We've all been there."

Lewis frowned. "You just make sure that he treats you right."

"I will, Lewis. You're so sweet to care." She patted his hand.

"I do care about you, Vashti. I don't want to see no man messing over you."

"That sounds like something my daddy would say."

He squinted his eyes and cocked his head to the side. "Is that how you see me?"

"Of course! You're always looking out for me, and I appreciate it."

"I've got to go," he said gruffly. "You just remember what I said, you hear?" He hurried out of the store before Vashti had a chance to say good-bye.

Chapter 19

Vashti didn't want to label her date with Ezra as *disastrous*, but Monique couldn't think of any other adjectives to describe it after Vashti recounted the details of their date while they were at Monique's home finalizing the plans for Sabrina's engagement party.

"Start at the beginning," instructed Monique, biting into a stalk of celery. "Maybe it sounds better the second time around. Don't leave anything out."

"Well, I pulled up to the house, which looked like it could fall down at any second. There were a bunch of guys outside, blasting music. Broken down Chevys and Novas were parked everywhere. A couple of the guys had guns tucked into their pants. Right away, I was like, 'heck no,' but Ezra spotted me before I had a chance to leave. He was out there smoking weed with the rest of them. I got out of the car, and one of the men actually grabbed my behind! He said that he wanted to know how somebody so little could tote all that," she narrated.

Monique dunked her celery into a small container of ranch dressing. "Go on."

"So Ezra comes over, telling everybody that I'm his girlfriend and pushing up on me. I was really pissed because he had on this dingy T-shirt and some dirty khakis after I told him that we were going to a real restaurant, not some burger joint."

"It sounds like his clothes were the least of your problems."

"So, we go to the restaurant, and he gets mad because they didn't serve Hypnotiq. Then he cursed out the waitress because she got our orders mixed up. I mean she literally ran out of there in tears. The manager came over and threatened to put us out. I was so embarrassed that I started to leave anyway."

Monique had a bewildered expression stamped on her face. "Please explain to me how this was *not* a disaster."

"Well, when we got ready to leave, he told me that he usually doesn't go to that kind of restaurant and that he gets all nervous and starts messing up in that kind of environment. He did thank me for not making him feel stupid, though."

"Vash, you went to Applebee's, not Buckingham Palace! He felt out of place in a restaurant that sells chicken fingers. If this is your standard of a good date, you really are hard up!"

"Monique, we can't be too quick to judge him. I think there's potential there."

"Potential for what—for him to rob you?"

"Society has already counted the brothers out. We can't do it to them, too."

Monique groaned and shook her head. "Vashti, how old is this man?"

"He's 32."

"Okay, so that's 32 years—six more than you've had—to get his life together. I don't want to hear that bull about what *society* is doing. What is *he* doing? What does this man bring to the table?"

"What did *you* bring to the table with Trent aside from maxed out credit cards, student loan debt, and a crazy family?" Vashti fired back.

"That's different!" insisted Monique. "I didn't ask Trent to take care of me; he wanted to. And if he left tomorrow, I could take care of myself." She stretched out on her butter-soft leather sofa. "I just choose not to."

Vashti pushed Monique's feet aside and sat down in their place. "Anyway, I'm not giving up on him."

"Hide your checkbook, that's all I'm saying."

Vashti began spreading sample wedding invitations onto the coffee table. "I think you'll change your mind once you get to know him. The four of us should go out."

"Trent and me with your mangy little friend?" heckled Monique. "I don't think so."

"Then just you. I guarantee that if you met him, you'd see the potential that I'm talking about."

Monique mulled it over. "Well, I was planning to go to The Cellar for spoken word tomorrow night. I suppose you two can tag along."

"That would perfect! Ezra would have a chance to showcase his music."

"It's poetry, V, not rap."

"Same thing—he can adapt it."

Monique mumbled, "whatever," and began sifting through the invitations.

"Just remember to bring your barbeque sauce," Monique reminded.

"For what?"

" 'Cause I'm gon' grill his hide like it's the fourth of July!"

Chapter 20

When Vashti and Ezra arrived at the dimly lit jazz club filled to capacity with young, black professionals and college students, she expected to find Monique there. What she didn't expect to find was Craig seated next to her, rapt in conversation over a glass of Chardonnay.

"You didn't tell me that you were bringing someone," Vashti mentioned casually as she and Ezra sat down across from them.

"Craig is a big fan of spoken word," explained Monique. "He might even get on stage tonight."

"Right," replied Vashti, suspecting that it was more than a love of poetry that brought him there that night.

"Anyway, Craig, you remember Vashti, and this is her friend . . . Easy?"

"Ezra," he grunted. "Just call me Ol' E."

"You're a little old for a nickname, aren't you?" sneered Monique. Vashti kicked her underneath the table.

"I thought you said she was married," said Ezra, taking a crack at Monique.

"She is. Craig is an old friend from high school," Vashti told him.

"So, Ezra," Monique began, clasping her hands together. "I hear that you're in the music business."

Ezra nodded, "That's right."

"That's a very lucrative career move. I guess even more so for you considering that you're living out of your mama's basement. You must save a lot of money that way," Monique added sweetly.

"Business is slow right now—not everybody can whip some little white boy with a football, but I suppose *you* save a lot of money *that* way."

"I have a degree, thank you very much!" she shot back.

"So." He shrugged and added, "A lot of hoes got degrees. That don't mean nothing—they still hoes; they just hoes with degrees."

"Hey, wait a minute," mediated Craig. "I thought we were here to listen to poetry, not a sparring match." Monique and Ezra didn't say anything but continued to glare at each other across the table.

"Baby, why don't you go over there and talk to someone about getting on the mic," coaxed Vashti to ease the tension.

"You need to talk to my man, Skills," replied Craig. "Come on, I'll introduce you." As soon as Craig and Ezra left, Vashti hammered Monique.

"Why are you treating him like that?"

"*Him*? He called me a hoe!"

"You insulted him first with all that crap about living with his mama. That wasn't called for."

"I can't believe you're defending him—I can't believe that you're *dating* him! He's such a loser. And why did he roll up in here dressed like some hood? I don't know how he even got passed security."

"You're being judgmental, which really isn't a good look for you considering that you're out with another man!"

Their argument was interrupted by the emcee's voice droning on the microphone.

"Coming to the stage is a brother straight outta Liberty City. He's the founder and CEO of Blunted-Out Records. Show some love, y'all—Ol' E . . ."

As Ezra strutted to the microphone, a hush fell over the crowd. He cleared his throat and began. "I ain't no poet. This right here is coming off my new album. Go cop that!"

Monique rolled her eyes.

"Give him a chance!" entreated Vashti.

"These hoes make you wanna choke a bi*#@, choke a bi*#@!" he rapped clumsily. "Smack you in your face, hoe—your face, hoe! It's the O to the E, trick—that's me. My rhymes is so tight, hatin' niggas wanna bite. But you can't steal this flow; you can't get my dough—oh no! It's Ol' E, baby, and I'm trill. I'm countin' dough stacks in the mils. Can you handle that? Do I have to get my gat? Bust you right in the face! Trump that thang like you the jack and I'm ace!"

"Oh my God!" gasped Vashti.

She and Monique exchanged horrified looks as he continued to spit nonsense into the microphone. Vashti's mind was racing to find a tactful way to tell Ezra that it was the most appalling performance that she'd witnessed.

"Yeah, yeah, it's Ol' E, baby, Blunted-Out Records! Holla at your boy!" he roared over the microphone.

There were a few sparse claps from the audience,

but there was mostly an uncomfortable silence, broken by the occasional cough.

Discerning their disapproval, Ezra lashed out with a resounding, "Forget all y'all," before taking his seat. "These lames don't know I'm talented!" he lamented, slouching down in his seat.

Vashti rubbed his back to comfort and to calm him down.

"We'll be back," said Monique, excusing herself and Craig.

"Baby, I thought it was pretty good," embellished Vashti. "I really liked the line about trumping him like he was a jack and you were the ace. This type of crowd probably isn't into that gritty, hardcore hip-hop."

"This bougie bull!" he griped. "I don't even know why I let you talk me into it. I got to take a piss." He violently flung his chair back and stomped off.

When he returned, Craig and Monique were behind him. Neither of them said anything, but there was a silent tension between them that Vashti picked up on right away.

She leaned over and whispered to Monique. "Did you say something to him?"

"Naw, naw, we're cool." Monique seemed distracted. Her pensive mood made Vashti even more suspicious.

"I seen enough for today," announced Ezra, cutting his eyes toward Monique. "You ready to go?"

"Um, sure." Vashti grabbed her purse and slid out of her chair. "I'll call you later, 'Nique." Monique nodded but didn't make eye contact with them.

"Did you and Monique have words?" asked Vashti once she and Ezra were in the parking lot.

He smiled to himself. "It's more like an under-standing," he alluded.

"She is my best friend, and I wish you'd make an effort to get along. You didn't have to call her a hoe."

"I call it like I see it. Anyway, I'm sure that she's gon' start treating me with more respect from now on," he predicted.

Vashti started to ask him what he meant by his cryptic prognosis, but she decided against it, positive that she didn't really want to know.

Chapter 21

Vashti finally succumbed to Ezra's overwhelming pressure and told him where she lived and worked, which turned out to be a decision that she soon regretted. He was now taking liberties that clearly demonstrated that he had overestimated the extent of their relationship. He would find excuses to come over to her house and end up crashing on her couch for the night following his jettisoned attempts to have sex with her. There would be times when Vashti would come home from work and find him in the same place that she left him—planted in front of the television after having raided the refrigerator. He had even taken to answering her phone and screening her calls.

"I need to hold your car for a minute," huffed Ezra after walking the five blocks from the bus stop to her store. After a week of throwing hints, Vashti finally managed to get Ezra out of her house, but now he had begun harassing her at work.

"I let you borrow the car last week, and you drove up all of my gas and left food in the car. I was killing ants for a week! I don't think so." She moved to assist a customer.

Ezra trailed along beside her. "Come on now, Vash. I know that I fouled up, but this is important."

His language and disheveled appearance made Vashti's customer uncomfortable, and she abruptly walked out.

"Did you see that?" asked Vashti, motioning toward the women as she sped away. "You need to leave, Ezra. I'm working."

"Just let me get the car. I'll be right back."

"I can't. Sabrina's engagement party is tonight, and I have to go to Monique's as soon as I leave here."

"It ain't even noon yet," he pointed out. "I'll have the car back way before then."

"Ezra, I can't take that chance."

"I'll be back in thirty minutes," he promised. "You know that rap group, Thug 'n' Young? I did a track that I think they can bang out. I need to get it to them. I heard them on the radio. They're in town but just for today. This could be my big break!"

Despite the urgency in his voice, Vashti was still hesitant.

"Come on, Vash, you're the only one in this world who really believes in me. You're the only thing I have to be proud of other than my music. Why would I let you down? I ain't trying to mess you up or mess up your business. I'm trying to get my own so I can be the right kind of man for you."

She saw an intensity and sincerity in Ezra that she had never seen before. Vashti hadn't realized how important she was to him until that moment. She was moved. Perhaps Ezra's problem was not that he couldn't be trusted, but that no would give him a chance.

She handed him the keys. She knew that it was a small gesture, but the proud smile on his face made her feel like she had just saved his life. He thanked her profusely and vowed to be back within the hour.

Vashti kept one eye on the clock as her customers filed in and out of the store. She hadn't heard anything from Ezra since the screeching of the tires as he peeled off. Around five o'clock that afternoon, Vashti was forced to abandon her theory about Ezra only needing a chance to prove himself when she found herself flagging Lewis down for a ride.

"You need to call the police!" he insisted when Vashti explained to him where her car was during the drive to Monique's house.

"I can't do that. He's on probation. I don't want to create problems for him."

"Probation?"

"Don't ask. It's nothing serious."

"You're over here worried about creating problems for him, but what about the problems he's created for you?"

"I have family and friends that I can rely on. He's got nobody."

"Now you see why!" quipped Lewis and piteously shook his head. "Do you love this fellow, Vashti?"

"God no!" she exclaimed. "He's just...I don't know...he needs me, you know?"

"He needs you to do what?"

"To encourage him and be there for him. He hasn't had a lot of breaks in life. I'm trying to show him another way of living."

"He's a grown man, Vashti, and no man wants a

woman who's going to try to change him," he lectured.

"I'm not trying to change him; I just want to help him."

"Are y'all in a relationship?"

"Well, I'm not sleeping with him if that's what you mean," she replied defensively.

"No, I'm just asking if the two of you are planning a future together. Where is this thing headed?"

She stared out of the window to avoid his disapproving gaze. "I don't know yet."

"Well, what do you want?"

"I just want a man who's going to love me, Lewis."

"That's it?"

"For the most part, yes."

"See, that's your problem. You're aiming too low. Any Joe Blow can say that he loves you—that's the minimum. You ought to want more than that—you're *worth* more than that! God wants more for you."

"How much more is there than love?" A sad look came across Vashti's face. With the way she had been spiraling downhill, surely she was on the bottom of God's list when it came to her wants and needs.

"Vashti, you deserve to be with a man who's going to love you and treat you right, somebody with his own money who won't be trying to take none of yours. You need a man who believes in spoiling his woman so that she don't have to want for nothing and who won't hit you or make you feel neglected. You need somebody who knows how special you are," he declared.

She smiled sheepishly, not expecting Lewis to react so strongly. "Gosh, you've really put some thought into this!"

"Well, I care about you, and I don't like to see you getting mixed up with these fools who ain't worthy to wipe your boots!"

"Ezra's not that bad, Lewis. I think that he could be a good catch for someone."

"But not you." She turned away. "If you're not looking for a future with this man, you need to let him know. You shouldn't even be spending time with a joker that you know you ain't seriously interested in. It's not fair to him. It's not fair to you when you think about it. With the time you're wasting with him, you could be with somebody else."

Lewis was playing the role of the concerned father again. "I think I know where this is going," she construed.

He beamed. "You do?" He reached over and laid his hand on her hand. "It's about time! I was about to give up on you, woman."

"This is about Kedrick, isn't it? You think that I'm just biding my time until he comes charging in on his white horse to whisk me away, but you don't have to worry about that. I'm not sitting around waiting for him. I know that future husband is out there, and I know that his name's not Kedrick Wright." Lewis seemed let down, which confused her. He quickly moved his hand away.

"That is what you were worried about, right?"

"Yeah . . . right." There was a hint of disappointment in his voice. He cleared his throat. "I'm glad that you're moving on. I want you to be happy, Vashti."

"I know you do—that's why I love you so much!" She leaned over and gave him a friendly peck on the cheek. He blushed as he pulled up to Monique's gated entrance.

"We're here. Go'n, girl, get outta here," he directed, feigning annoyance.

By eight o'clock, most of the guest had arrived and were nibbling on the exotic collations that the caterers had prepared.

"This is a great party, Vashti," said Sabrina's fiancé, Jason.

"We weren't expecting you to go through so much trouble," added Sabrina. "Everything's so beautiful—the flowers, the food, and this house is amazing! Thank you so much." Sabrina gave Vashti a hug. "You, too, Monique."

"You lovebirds deserve it," Vashti assured them. "Now, go on and have fun. This is your night and you better enjoy it." The happy couple waved good-bye and rejoined their guests.

"Not bad," noted Monique. "You have almost pulled off the kind of party that people would expect me to be hosting."

"I'm assuming that was your misguided attempt at giving me a compliment, so thank you."

"But what's up with your car?" Monique asked. "Have you even heard from that fool?"

"He'll be here, Monique. He left a message on my cell. He's on his way."

Monique was halfway through another diatribe about Ezra when they overheard a commotion in the foyer.

"Get your hands off me!" snarled Ezra to one the greeters posted at the door who had mistaken him for an intruder. His voice echoed through the vaulted ceilings and walls.

"Oh, heck naw!" exclaimed Monique when Ezra stumbled in. His eyes were bloodshot and drooping. His oversized Blunted-Out Records T-shirt was rested sloppily over his sagging jeans. Not even Vashti could ignore his slovenly appearance.

"What? So he's a little . . . scruffy," Vashti admitted begrudgingly.

"He's a little high, Vash! Look at him!" He nearly tripped over a potted plant in his path.

"Hey, 'sup, girl!" Ezra called over to Vashti. She went to him, feebly attempting to shield him from everyone's view. She couldn't help being embarrassed. He reeked of liquor and marijuana smoke.

"Ezra, are you high?" she asked softly.

"I'm just chillin', girl."

"What were you thinking coming up in here like this?" demanded Monique in a loud whisper when she approached them.

"Who you talking to like that, trick?" he slurred.

Vashti tried to quiet him. "Ezra, please . . . People are staring."

"That hoe can't talk to people any way she wants to. You gon' respect me, trick!"

Monique squint her eyes and pointed her finger at him. "You trifling mother—"

Ezra swatted her hand out of his face. "Aye, don't put your hands in my face no more!" he warned.

"Ezra, Monique—stop it! You're embarrassing me, both of you!" admonished Vashti.

"Well, excuse me for being an *embarrassment* to you," mocked Ezra. "I ain't no daggone socialite. I'm just a hard-working man, trying to be a good man for you!"

"Please get him out of here," pleaded Monique. "This is bad for your business."

Vashti looked around at the people gawking at them and at the concerned look on Lewis's face. She grabbed Ezra by the arm and escorted him out.

"Hey, what's wrong with you?" he asked once they were outside. "You ashamed of me?"

She looked at him, struggling to maintain his balance and breathing hot beer into her face. Wedding deadline or not, this was definitely not what she was looking for in a mate.

"Ezra, this isn't working out."

"You letting that hooker come between us?" he asked, raising his voice.

"She's not a hooker, Ezra, and she's not the problem."

"She-she don't want me to start talking," he sputtered. "I saw her, and I'll tell it if she don't watch her mouth and start showing me some respect."

"What are you talking about?" She didn't know if he was just spouting drunken gibberish or if he really had something on Monique. He flung his hand to dismiss Vashti's question.

"Later for that chick, this is about us—me and you. I'm falling in love with you, girl, you know that?"

"Ezra . . ." she began and shook her head.

"I know you might not feel the same way yet. I know that I ain't rich like your friends in there. I don't talk or dress all fancy, but I'm trying to make changes in my life for you . . . for us."

Even though she doubted that she and Ezra had a future together, Vashti felt that her presence in Ezra's life was a good influence on him. She concluded that if a few more weeks with her could make him a better man for the next woman, there was no harm in postponing the inevitable.

"All right, we can give it another shot, but please go home and sober up. My clients are in here, and I can't have them seeing you like this."

He dropped his head. "You're right, you're right. I

guess I did have too much to drink. You go on back." He handed Vashti the car keys.

"Can you make it home okay? Do you want me to call you a cab?"

"I'm straight. I'll walk."

Vashti watched him stumble away. As she was about to go back inside, she was approached by Lewis.

"Is everything all right?" he asked.

She nodded. "It's fine. I'm sorry about all the fuss back there."

"I'm not thinking about that; I'm worried about you." He paused and extended his hands. "Vashti, what are you doing with this boy?"

"What do you mean?"

"We both know that you ain't got no business with a clown like that. Look at you—you're smart—"

"Yeah, Lewis," she broke in. "I'm smart, I'm pretty, and I have my own business. I'm a real catch," she replied sarcastically.

"You are! Can't you see that?"

She shook her head, fighting back tears. "Then tell me why I can't keep a man, huh? Kedrick left me seven months ago, and I haven't had a real boyfriend since. You talk about Ezra, but he's the only guy who's even asked me out since I broke up with Brentz; he's the only one who's paid me any attention. Ezra is the only man who seems to notice that I'm a good catch." The tears began sprouting forth like a geyser. She had been holding her true feelings in for months because she thought that it made her look weak to admit the truth. Now, she no longer cared.

"Vashti, you don't have to settle," he reiterated.

"I'm not. I know that Ezra isn't this tall, dark, and handsome man that we've been programmed to believe in, but you know what? I've learned that love doesn't always come the way you expect it to look. Look at me and Kedrick. Everybody thought that we were so perfect together, but he broke my heart. I just want to be loved like everyone else. Is that so bad?"

"I understand that, but why this guy?"

"Ezra needs me," she answered painfully. "I know that this relationship isn't going anywhere, but sometimes it feels good to be needed."

"He needs you like a parasite needs its host. You don't want to be needed that way."

"I know that you think he's using me." She shrugged, wiping a tear from her cheek. "Maybe he is. Maybe I'm using him a little, too."

"He's not good for you. He doesn't add anything to your life."

"But he's *somebody*. I'm not strong, Lewis. I'm not one of those women who can spend their lives alone. Right or wrong, I want a man in my life. I want to feel loved; I want to matter to someone who isn't a friend or a part of my family. Ezra is not perfect, but he's there and he wants me and he needs me."

"Why is it so important to have him need you, huh?" He moved closer to her.

"I guess a part of me feels like if a man needs me, then he won't abandon me." She stared at the ground. "You know, Monique and I sort of have this bet going about me getting married by September. If I can find a husband, she says she'll pay for the wedding." She laughed to herself. "It's silly, really, but it gave me a reason to be hopeful and to keep trying and not give up on love completely."

"So you would marry this punk just to be married

by some deadline? If that's the case, I'll pay for the wedding if you take the time to wait on the Lord to send you somebody."

"I did that already. I waited for five years with Kedrick, and now I'm alone again. Ezra's not much, but he's a start."

Lewis hugged her and kissed her forehead. "Don't settle. You're better than that. Don't sacrifice tomorrow for gratification today. You deserve more. It's too bad that everybody can see that except you."

Chapter 22

Vashti cursed as she whizzed by the state patrol car on the side of the road. She was late for an appointment with Sabrina's caterers and was driving at least 80 when the officer clocked her. As expected, flashing blue lights soon appeared in her rearview mirror.

"Good afternoon, officer," she sang sweetly and flashed him a seductive smile. She wasn't above trying to flirt her way out of a speeding ticket. The stoic expression on his face didn't offer much hope.

"I need to see your license and registration, ma'am," the officer demanded.

"What's the problem officer?" she asked innocently. Where flirting floundered, naïveté might prevail.

"You were going 86 in a 60 mile per hour zone."

She reached into her purse and handed the officer her driver's license.

"Registration, ma'am?"

"Oh, it's in here." She reached her hand underneath the glove compartment to pop it open. She sifted through the stack of envelopes and coupons that she had tucked away in there trying to locate her insurance card and tag information. When she reached for the envelop containing her insurance verification, a small bag of marijuana slipped out from underneath it.

The police officer spotted it at the same time as she did. "You need to step out of the car, ma'am."

"But it's not mine," she tried to explain, stepping out of the car.

"Hands on top of the car, ma'am." He radioed in on his CB. There, with her hands outstretched on the hood of her heated Camry, she thought of Ezra. Before she had time to think of what to do next, she felt handcuffs being slapped around her wrists.

"You're under arrest for possession of a controlled substance. You have the right to remain silent . . ."

The officer went on reciting the rest of her Miranda Rights. Vashti was in a fog. This could not be happening to her, yet it was. She was shoved into the squad car and taken to the police station, where she was searched, fingerprinted, and booked on drug possession charges.

Chapter 23

Vashti's arrest was easily the most humiliating experience of her life, even more so than the wedding. She was hustled about no differently from the murders and rapists who entered the precinct. After booking, she was thrown into a holding cell, where she was accosted by other criminals awaiting their fate. Monique arrived promptly to bail her out as soon as the amount was set, but Vashti realized that her legal troubles were far from over.

The hours following her release were filled with a range of emotions from jubilation to absolute fury. All of her feelings of rage were directed at one person: Ezra Thomas.

Vashti's heels clanked loudly as she punctured the wooden steps leading to Ezra's basement studio early the next morning. As she approached the last step, she was caught in a cloud of marijuana smoke. Music was blaring, and Ezra was banging out a tune on his keyboard. He was flanked by two teenage boys.

"That's that hot beat right there, boyee!" he exclaimed, bobbing his head to the beat. He took another hit of his blunt and started back-playing. The boys began free styling over his beat.

"Excuse me!" called Vashti over the music. Ezra, who hadn't noticed that she was in the room, motioned her to wait.

"I need to talk to you *now!*" she persisted.

"Hold up a minute, baby. Can't you see I'm busy?"

"I can see that, but do you know what *I* was doing this time yesterday? I was sitting in a police station busted for your drugs!"

He stopped playing and looked at her. "Oh, word? It wasn't the meth, was it?"

"No, it wasn't the meth! It was the weed that you had stashed in my glove compartment. What is wrong with you?"

"Aw, shoot, that ain't nothing. You'll probably get a li'l fine, maybe some community service. That's just a misdemeanor." With that, he resumed playing. Vashti was infuriated. She snatched the keyboard's power cord out of the socket.

"What the heck are you doing?" demanded Ezra, rising.

"Are you kidding me? I was in jail, Ezra—*jail!* I was cuffed, fingerprinted, and charged, and all you can say is that *it ain't nothing?*"

"Well, what am I supposed to say? You're out now."

She shook her head in disbelief. "You don't even care, do you?"

"It wasn't even an ounce in there. It ain't like you're going to have to do any time for it. Just pay the fine and be through with it."

Her eyes widened. "You're not even going to pay the fine?"

"What do you want me to do, Vashti, huh? I just bought all this equipment, mom's trippin' about me giving her rent money; I got to pay for studio time, demos, all that. Is you gon' help out with that?"

Vashti was incensed. She didn't know whether or not Ezra just couldn't comprehend the magnitude of the situation or if he was just that stupid.

"They're going to put me on probation, Ezra," she punctuated slowly, hoping that her words would permeate into whatever sense of morality he had. "If I'm lucky, I won't have to serve any time."

"You'll get first offender status. It'll be like it never even happened."

Vashti threw her hands up. "Ezra, you are missing the whole point!"

"Look, we tryna have a session. I'll have to talk about this later. Aye, yo, Sawed-off, go plug that back in."

The music cranked back up, the boys continued to freestyle, and it was like she wasn't even there. Vashti realized that it wasn't Ezra who didn't see the point; it was she. She decided that it was time to take her head out of the smoke clouds and to get on with the rest of her life, realizing that it wasn't her job to save any man, especially one that didn't want to be saved. She figured that if Ezra was the best there was out there, she was better off being alone. She turned and retreated back up the stairs in defeat.

She drove home that day determined not to look back, but not before dishing out a little comeuppance by giving the police an anonymous tip about where they could find a ton of marijuana and possibly stolen studio equipment.

Chapter 24

"**A** five hundred dollar fine and twelve months of probation—can you believe it?!" wailed Vashti. Her lawyer was able to get her out of serving jail time and secure her first-offender status, but she wasn't able to negotiate getting the charges dropped.

"I told you, girl," cautioned Monique, shaking her head and filing her nails as they stretched across her plush, custom-designed sleigh bed. "You can't go around messing with no broke-behind reefer-chiefers. We're too old for that!"

"I can't believe that I was so stupid."

"Well, believe it!" Vashti buried her head in the pillow. Monique patted her on the back. "Come on, now, worse things have happened. Don't you remember when Allen Payne filed those stalking charges against me? I didn't trip." She examined her nail work.

"But you didn't actually get *arrested*—you just got warned. I was handcuffed!"

"Uh-huh. That's all the more reason for you to come out with us tonight."

"Not Ashton again," groaned Vashti.

"Yes, Ashton! It's obvious that I can't trust you to find a decent man. I don't know what you're complaining about. Ashton is cute, and he's been begging me to hook you two up."

"I don't date white men. That's your territory."

"Sista-girl, my *green* is my territory. I don't give a flip what color the man is who's tending the lawn. Anyway, you need to diversify. Black men and stockbrokers do it all the time."

"Monique . . ."

"Besides, I'm tired of you moping around here. It is a colossal waste of time to be crying over a loser like Ezra, especially when you can be having dinner with a cutie like Ashton."

Monique had a point. To Vashti, the only thing worse than losing a jackass like Ezra was being depressed about it.

"All right—drinks, that's it!" she conceded.

"And an appetizer," pushed Monique.

". . . and an appetizer."

"Monique, over here!" waved Ashton shortly after they entered Prime 112, a popular South Beach steakhouse known for its casual atmosphere and mouth-watering Chilean sea bass.

"Isn't he cute," squealed Monique. Vashti didn't respond. "Okay, you go over there and get acquainted." Monique gave her a slight shove. "I have to make a phone call."

"Monique, don't leave me!" pleaded Vashti in an elevated whisper, but it was too late. Monique had already skated off and Ashton was approaching her.

"Hi, I'm Ashton Mullins." He extended his hand.

"Vashti." She blandly shook his hand and looked him over as they stood awkwardly in the middle of the dining area. His expressive eyes were the same shade of blue as the ocean, and a lock of his sandy-brown hair drooped lazily over his right eye. He proudly sported a tightly ribbed sweater and tarnished jeans, a look that Vashti utterly detested.

"Vashti," he repeated. "That's original. Is it African?"

"I'm not sure. Vashti was the wife of King Ahasuerus in the Bible."

"Wow, you know I've been studying African names myself."

"Really?"

"Yeah, I'm thinking of calling myself Zareb. It means protector. Or I may go with Aitan; it means fights for possessions."

"I'm sure that will go over very well with your parents," Vashti added sarcastically.

"What's your middle name? I bet it's something wild like Boomshonda or Lalamika."

"Actually, it's Marie."

"Oh. Well, come over here at sit down. I ordered us some drinks." He led her to their table.

"So, Monique tells me that you're a photographer," broached Vashti once they were seated.

"Yeah, I've shot for *Vibe, Cosmo, Vanity Fair* . . . I can't even remember all of them."

"I guess you travel a lot then."

"Yeah, it's great to see all these exotic places and people. Being a photographer is like looking at the world from the outside, you know?" She nodded, thankful to see Monique advancing toward them.

"Sorry about that, you guys. I had to take care of something." Monique slid into the seat next to Vashti.

"It's no problem." Vashti leaned over to whisper to her. "Don't leave me alone with him again," she said through her teeth.

"I know how it feels to wake up messed up. Pockets broke as hell, another rock to sell," rapped Ashton to himself.

"Excuse me?" interrupted Vashti.

"It's nothing. That song has been in my head all day. I love Biggie."

"Biggie?" she echoed, amused.

"You know, *Everyday Struggle*—The Notorious B.I.G."

"I've heard of him, Ashton," Vashti assured him.

"Yeah, his lyrics speak to me. Being on the corner, selling rocks, hustling—it's not that much different from what I do."

Vashti was confused. "I thought you were a photographer."

"Yeah, but I still have to hustle."

"Right." She nodded and cut her eyes to Monique.

"Anyway, Monique tells me that you've been locked up."

Vashti abruptly spit out her drink. "Sorry," she apologized, mopping the spill.

"That's all right."

"Did she also tell you that it wasn't my fault? They weren't my drugs," she replied, directing her comments at Monique. "I don't even smoke."

Ashton shook his head sadly. "The Man is always going after the brothers. Now, I see he's starting in on the sisters, too."

Vashti assumed that he was suffering from some form of a racial identity crisis. "Why don't you tell me a little more about yourself, Ashton?"

"Well, I'm from Lincoln, Nebraska, but my heart has always been here in Miami, Liberty City."

"Oh?"

"Yeah. You see, we didn't have a lot of black people in my hometown. I think we had like two in my whole graduating class. Then when I was a freshman in college, I took a Black Studies course. It changed my life."

"How's that?"

"I fell in love with the culture, the people, the whole Black experience."

"I can tell," muttered Vashti.

"Since then, I've read everything I can get my hands on about the Black man's plight—*Makes Me Wanna Holler, Native Son, Malcolm X*. Recently, I've started getting into David Walker's work. Did you know that in 1829, his proposal was considered to be the most dangerous commentary on slavery and liberty?"

"That's fascinating," Vashti replied indifferently, scanning the room for other eligible men.

"Yeah, then when Trent married that fine sister over there, I knew I had to have me one, too. You know what they say—the blacker the berry, the sweeter the juice!"

"So I've heard," she retorted flippantly.

"So what's up?" he inquired, drawing nearer to her.

"What's up with what?" she asked and frowned.

"What's up with you and me?"

Vashti had to stop herself from laughing out loud. "I don't know, Ashton. I mean, do you think that your friends and your family would approve of our dating?"

"I don't care about what anyone else thinks."

"Maybe not now, but you will if there's enough pressure."

"My friends wouldn't care."

"What about your parents? Would they be okay with it?"

"Oh, heck naw! My mom is scared of black people, but I get tired of them judging me and trying to control me. I'm a photographer who's been all over the world, but my parents are pissed because I dropped out of college instead of going to med school like my dad. I'm 25-years-old. Maybe once they see me with you, they'll realize that they can't control me anymore."

"Oh, I get it," she replied. "So this whole Black experience thing is just a way for you to irk your parents, right?"

"Naw, naw. I dig you, Vashti. You're sexy and successful. Truth be told, I've been checking for you since Trent and Monique's wedding."

Craig strode up to their table as Vashti was about to turn Ashton down.

"Craig, hi!" smiled Monique. "What a strange coincidence to see you here!" But Monique's smile was too wide and her voice had gone up too many octaves for Vashti to believe that his presence was merely by chance.

"Craig, we meet again," rejoined Vashti with a hint of sarcasm.

"Yeah, I called in an order, and I'm here to pick it up," he explained.

"Craig, I want you to meet Trent's cousin, Ashton. Ashton, Craig and I go way back. We graduated from high school together." The two spoke and shook hands.

"Ash, can I talk to you for a second?" asked Monique,

motioning her head to a corner in the room. He nodded and followed her with Craig tagging along behind them. After a few intense minutes with Monique, Ashton walked back to the table while Monique and Craig grabbed his order and walked out of the door.

"Where's Monique?" Vashti asked, baffled.

"She left. Her friend's taking her home."

"Why?"

"Because she knew that I wanted some time to be alone with you."

"Did she leave the car keys with you? She was my ride."

"I'll take you home," he offered, but it did little to mollify her. She knew that she had been set up and was heated with everyone involved.

"This is not cool, Ashton. I want to go home—*now*!"

"Vashti, wait a minute! I just wanted to—"

"Don't say nothing!" she said, holding up her hand and cutting him off. "Just take me home. I don't know what kind of game you and Monique are playing, but I don't want any part of it."

After trying to justify his actions and being shot down again, Ashton relented and asked for the check. Vashti grabbed her purse and marched out ahead of him.

Despite Ashton's efforts to initiate conversation, Vashti refused to talk to him during the drive home unless it was directing him to her house. He became frustrated and pulled off to the side of the road.

"What are you doing?" she shrieked.

"We're not moving another inch until you talk to me."

"Fine, I'll walk," she quibbled and unbuckled her seatbelt.

"I can't let you do that. It's late; we're on the highway. I'm not going to let you put yourself in danger no matter how mad you are at me."

"Then take me home."

He punched the steering wheel. "This isn't anything like what I had planned. I really wanted things to go well tonight, and now I've screwed things up so badly that you won't even talk to me. You'd rather *walk* than be with me!"

She sighed and dropped the attitude, feeling a little empathetic toward him. "It's not just you," she granted. "This hasn't been a good day for me. The last thing I needed was to be set up tonight."

"Let me make it up to you."

"There's really nothing you can do, Ashton. All I want to do is go home and forget that today ever happened."

"There's one thing I can do," he suggested.

"What's that?"

He grinned at her and then dove in between her legs headfirst. She slinked back and pushed his head back up.

"Ashton, what are you doing?"

"Just let me taste. We don't have to have intercourse or anything. I just want to go down on you."

Vashti was stunned. She didn't know how to respond to that, but Ashton certainly became a lot more interesting than he had been five minutes earlier.

"Ashton, you can't do that! You don't even know me."

"I know what I like. I just want you to see what you'll be missing out on if you keep dissing me."

The proposition was tempting, and she'd had firsthand confirmation from Monique that what was said about white men was true, at least in that department.

"Come on, Vashti," he beseeched, reclining her seat back.

Later in her bed that night, as she stared up at the ceiling, she rationalized that, after all she'd through in the past 48 hours, she was at least entitled to a little satisfaction.

Despite the fact that Ashton could find his way around the G-spot, he was still looking for himself, and the last thing Vashti needed was a man who was more lost than she was. It would be a sad case of the blind leading the blind. She figured that if a relationship was going to work, at least one person needed to know what direction they were headed. She couldn't see herself being led by a man whom she didn't have enough confidence in to follow.

While she knew that she'd never date Ashton, he did manage to wheedle Vashti's phone number out of her. After making her legs tremble, she thought that she at least owed him that.

Chapter 25

Monique promenaded into Vashti's store and dramatically slammed two invitations down on the counter. Vashti raised an eyebrow and continued watering the bromeliads that bordered the counter. It had been two and a half weeks since Ashton and Monique set her up, and Vashti wasn't thrilled about the prospect of being the victim of another one of Monique's schemes.

"Okay, what is this, Monique?"

"*This* is where we're going to be Thursday night."

Vashti picked up the invitations and gasped. They were for a listening party for Maverick, a neo-soul crooner who was about to launch his sophomore album after a hugely successful debut. He had boy-next-door charm and an incredible singing voice. He had quickly become one of Vashti's favorites.

"How did you get these?" asked Vashti, astonished.

"He sent them to my mama to give to me."

Vashti was taken aback. "Your mama? Loretta needs to hook a sister up because I love him!"

"Girl, you should!" Monique enthused. "That ain't nobody but Travis."

"Who's Travis?"

"Travis Baker! I know that you remember him."

The only Travis that she could recall was a chubby little boy with a chronic runny nose and thick, over-sized corrective lenses for his crossed eyes, who used to come into the shop with his mother and play with Vashti and her dolls.

"Not Trap!" she exclaimed.

"Yes, Travis Baker is Maverick."

Vashti dusted off a place in her memory that she hadn't visited since she was thirteen. She took her fuzzy image of the loud-breathing, snotty-nosed boy and juxtaposed that with the seductive, dreadlocked singing sensation whose picture was imprinted on the invitations. There was no immediate resemblance, but the wide, welcoming smile was the same.

"Oh, my God! I can't believe that's him!"

"Yep," Monique nodded. "His family moved to Philly about ten years ago, but our moms kept in touch. They still talk pretty regularly. His mama even came to my wedding."

"Was Trap there, too?"

"No, he was on the grind out in California trying to get a record deal."

"I still can't believe this. Wasn't he a lot younger than us?"

"Not really, about a year or two. He's going to flip when he sees you."

"Monique, he's a star. His album went double plat-inum, he has millions of fans, and he's traveled all over the world. I doubt that he's going to remember a girl that he used to play with thirteen years ago."

"I don't know," sang Monique. "The last time I

talked to him, he asked me what ever happened to the girl who had all of those dolls and used to eat ants."

Vashti corrected her. "It was *one* ant on a dare."

"Whatever—the point is that he remembered you."

"And when was this? I don't remember you ever telling me that an international sex symbol was asking about me."

"It was about five years ago," she recalled. Vashti groaned.

"Five years ago? He wasn't even fine then."

"Again, you are missing the point. Look, just have yourself there Thursday night, looking gorgeous. I'll even take you shopping on me. Your Target specials simply won't do for this occasion."

"Is Trent coming?"

"Of course. You know he never misses a photo op," she added bitterly.

"Travis Baker," Vashti sighed, still in awe, "Who would have thought?"

When they arrived at the club that Thursday night in Trent's limousine, a crowd had already begun congregating behind the velvet rope trying to get in or at least get a glimpse of Maverick. Vashti staggered out of the car in the four-inch heels that Monique had insisted that she wear. Since Monique had paid for the $490 Christian Louboutin pumps, along with a revealing ensemble by Dolce & Gabanna that showcased her taut figure, she complied. Monique was expensively and flawlessly dressed as usual and could have easily been mistaken for a celebrity herself. Trent lagged behind them, gabbing on his cell phone and signing autographs. Monique sulked while they waited for him to catch up.

Inside, the club was packed. It was an intimate setting with candle lights and Maverick's soothing voice flowing through the speakers. Some people danced while others bobbed their heads and sipped on Bacardi. Someone began snapping pictures as soon as they walked in. Vashti shied away from the camera, but Trent and Monique posed playfully and soaked up the attention.

Twenty minutes later, a thunderous applause erupted as Maverick strolled in on the arm of Kimoni, a stunning model that Vashti recognized from the cover of a plethora of fashion magazines.

They were seated a few feet away from him. Maverick turned in their direction and winked his eye at Monique when he saw them. He was even more handsome in person. Vashti was star struck.

Maverick strode onto the stage as his band and back-up singer assembled themselves behind him. He grabbed the microphone and addressed the audience in his deep, slow drawl that reflected his southern roots.

"How are y'all feeling out there? Miami, my hometown! It feels good to be home!" There was applause and cheers from the audience. "As you know, my album drops on Tuesday, so I thought that I'd come out tonight, play a little something for you, and let you tell me what you think. Is that cool?" He signaled his band and went into his first number.

Halfway through his set, Maverick stepped down to mingle with his fans. He approached their table with his trademark smile and a hug for Monique. "Girl, you still look good!"

"Please—I *always* look good," she jested.

"What's up, Trent?" Maverick shook his hand. "You ready for next season?"

"No doubt, man. We're going all the way this year," Trent replied.

"How's your mom?" he asked Monique.

"She's good. Trent just bought her a new house in Coconut Grove, so she's bringing a little flavor to the suburbs."

"She finally got out of the projects—that's all right! Tell her that I'm happy for her." He turned his attention to Vashti. "And who is this pretty lady sitting over here all quiet and shy?"

"She's your surprise, Trap. You remember Vashti, don't you?"

He reared back and covered his mouth. "Oh, snap! Come here, girl!" He pulled her into a tight embrace.

"I know you don't remember me," she said timidly.

"How could I forget you? You're the only person that I've ever met with the name Vashti. I remember you running around your grandmother's store eating ants." Mentally, she reiterated that it was only one ant, but decided not to debate him on the issue. She had more important things to worry about like trying not to urinate on herself in excitement.

"I never forgot you," he repeated. "I remember that the other boys would clown me because I was sick all the time, but you and Monique looked out for me. That meant something to me. Even now, you're here, still supporting me."

She was impressed with his humility. He was certainly a millionaire by now, but he acted as if he was honored to even be in their presence. He pulled up a seat next to Vashti. "So what have you been doing for the past, what, ten years?"

"You know—school, work. Actually, I run my grandmother's shop now," Vashti answered.

"For real?"

"Yeah, my grandmother left it to me when she passed a few years ago."

"Man, your grandmother was a sweet lady," he recollected, shaking his head. "There were plenty of days when we didn't know how we were going to eat, and your grandma would reach down in that bra and pull out a little something and tell me to give it to my mother. She was good like that."

Vashti nodded in agreement. "She was one in a million."

Travis propped his elbows up on the table, his locks brushing across his shoulders. "So, tell me, Vashti, you got a man?" She smiled and shook her head. She was about to transform into flirt mode when Travis's date tapped him on the shoulder and whispered something in his ear. He nodded and stood up, taking her by the hand.

"Are you all going to stick around for a minute?" he asked.

"Yeah, sure," Monique spoke up.

"Do that. Maybe we can hang out later and reminisce about old times." He and his date disappeared into the crowd.

"What did I tell you!" shrieked Monique, frantically clinging to Vashti's arm.

"Yes, he remembered me," conceded Vashti.

"He seemed to be doing a lot more than remembering. I saw him checking you out."

"Are you kidding me? He has a woman. Look at her! She was just on some magazine's *Hottest Honeys* list last week. I know that I'm not ugly, but I can't compete with that!"

"You can because you have something she doesn't have."

"What—not an eating disorder?" joked Trent. Monique poked him.

"History! You were down with him when he was a crossed-eyed, wheezing, pathetic pound of flesh; she just got in the picture. Do you think she'd be all up on him like that if he wasn't famous? She would have him hemmed up for even *thinking* about stepping to her."

"Yeah, but she's a model," whined Vashti.

"She's the model; you're the real thing."

Vashti looked on as dozens of camera bulbs flashed on Travis as he stood with his arm wrapped around Kimoni's waist, smiling into the lenses.

"No, 'Nique, you're wrong. We may have grown up together, but we're worlds apart now."

Vashti declined Monique and Trent's offer to wait around and have drinks with Travis after the show. Travis didn't speak to Vashti for the remainder of the evening, and he and Kimoni were rarely out of each other's sight when he wasn't performing. He even invited her on stage to be formally introduced to the crowd. It was at that point that Vashti, wallowing in self-pity, decided to catch a cab ride home.

Her phone rang ceaselessly until the wee hours of the morning. Vashti knew that it was Monique trying to lure her back to the club, but spending the night with Puddin was more appealing than watching Travis drool over Kimoni.

Around seven the next morning, Vashti heard someone pounding on her front door as she was dressing for work. Vashti knew that only Monique would have the gall to come visit someone during that hour of day.

"Why didn't you answer your phone last night?" Monique demanded to know.

"Because I knew it was you," Vashti replied, letting her into the house. "I wasn't up for an all-nighter. Some of us do have to get up in the morning and go to work, you know."

"It wasn't me, sweetheart; it was Trap."

Vashti whirled around. "What?"

"He wanted you to hang out with us last night. He left you a bunch of messages."

Vashti picked up the phone and dialed the code to retrieve her voice-mail.

"Hey, yo, Vashti, it's Travis—Trap. I was hoping that you'd come kick it with us tonight. We're still at the club; swing by when you get this message."

She moved to the next message.

"Hey, it's me again. It's been about thirty minutes. We're still here, waiting for you. I'll even throw in a free CD if you get here in the next ten minutes. Bye."

"I know that you put him up to this," accused Vashti.

"I didn't have to put him up to do anything." Vashti checked the next message.

"So you're the kind that wants a man to beg. That's cool. Ahem . . . please, Vashti, don't make me cry . . . don't say good-bye . . . Vashti," he sang.

Monique's voice screeched through the phone on the next message.

"Girl, answer your darn phone! I know that you are laying up somewhere with that cat! You could've been laying up with Trap! He's been asking about you all night. You need to get out that bed and bring your behind back to the club!"

"Dang it," cried Vashti. "I can't believe I missed it!"

"I tried to tell you. He wants you. Can I pick 'em or what? Now, go call him."

"I can't do that."

"Why not?"

"I haven't talked to him since I was fourteen years old. I can't just call him out of the blue."

"I don't know why you can't," countered Monique. "Look how many times he called you!"

"Yeah, but that's different."

"The only thing that's different is that he is rich and talented and honest, which is a step up from the guys that you are used to dealing with." She reached into her purse. "Anyway, here's his number in case you decide to come to your senses."

"Did he tell you to give it to me?" Vashti asked eagerly.

"No, but he didn't tell me not to either."

Vashti declined taking the card. "He was probably just being polite," she reasoned.

"Girl, will you take a chance? Stop being so scary all of the time!" urged Monique.

She sighed and looked at the card again. "He *is* fine . . ."

"And single and available and he's got enough money to pay for his own darn wedding!" added Monique. "So what do you have to lose?"

Chapter 26

"I'll be with you in a second," called Vashti from the greenhouse in the back of the store when the bell signaled that she had a customer.

"Take your time," answered a male voice. She recognized the southern dialect at once.

"Trap?" Her heart pounded so hard that she thought it might jump out of her chest.

"Yeah, it's me. Where are you?"

"I'm in the back. I'll be right there." Vashti stashed the guzmania that she was potting behind a stand and raced to the front of the store to greet Travis.

"What are you doing here?" she asked surprised, wiping the soil from her hands.

"I came to see you. I thought that you were going to come with us last night." A large, burly man in a black suit too small for his massive frame walked in. He was clean-shaven and bald with a complexion the color of molasses. He didn't acknowledge Vashti and walked over to Travis.

"I got rid of 'em, boss. I don't think they'll be creeping around here any time soon." His thunderous voice was as intimidating as his presence.

"Thanks for handling that for me, B," Travis said. The man nodded and walked out of earshot but stood close enough to keep an eye on them.

"Who's that?" whispered Vashti.

"That's my main man, Bruce. He's my bodyguard. You gotta have one these days."

"What was he talking about just then?"

"It ain't nothing, just some little thugs. They saw the limo and followed us. They tried to rush me when we stopped, but Bruce is quick. He's big, but he's quick. He got them."

"How many was it?"

"About three or four."

"Weren't you scared?" she prodded.

"I'm getting kind of used to it now. I used to be able to go hang out and do whatever but after I got robbed about a year ago, I hired Bruce to work full time."

"Does he go everywhere with you?"

"Yep, even the bedroom. You can't trust these women out here. They're more scandalous than the men—present company excluded, of course."

"Of course," she concurred, grinning.

Travis moved about the store, looking around and touching things. "This place hasn't changed much, has it? It even smells the same."

"I've tried to keep it the way my grandmother left it. I'm doing some construction next door, though. I'm expanding."

He nodded approvingly. "This is nice. You should be proud."

"I am." She paused and looked at him. "You still haven't told me why you stopped by. How did you even know I'd be here?"

"You said that you worked at your grandmother's store. Did you think that I'd forgotten the way?"

"Well, yeah," she confessed.

"Naw, some of my best times growing up were spent right here."

She diffidently shifted her weight from one leg to the other. "So what brings you by other than nostalgia?"

"I told you, I came to see you." He skated a finger across her face.

"Yeah, right."

"It's true. I tried to call you last night, but you never answered. So I decided that if the mountain won't come to Muhammad . . ."

"I was tired last night," she lied. "But I got your messages."

He scrutinized her and shook his hand.

"What?" she asked, wondering what he was doing, or worse, what he thought was wrong with her.

He smacked his lips. "I know that I said that this place hadn't changed, but you certainly have! When did you go and get so sexy?"

"Me?" she balked. "You're the hotshot superstar."

"No, *Maverick* is the hotshot superstar. I'm just regular ol' Travis Baker."

She couldn't stop grinning. "I still can't get over it. You're Maverick! Do you know how many times your CD has gotten me through the night?"

"If I have been able to touch you in any way through my music, I'm honored," he professed, placing his hand over his heart. "It's the least I can do after everything you did for me growing up."

"I didn't do anything except maybe make you a target for the other boys by having you back here playing with me and my dolls."

He laughed, remembering all the dolls he had diapered and fed in that room. "The beat downs were well worth it!"

"Did you like playing with dolls that much?"

"Come on, now, don't tell me that you didn't know."

"Didn't know what?"

"Why do you think I kept coming by here?" he asked with a smirk. "What kid do you know is going to spend his summer holed up in some flower shop having tea parties and playing school without an ulterior motive?"

"I just assumed you were going to be gay."

He laughed again. Vashti loved his laugh. It sounded happy and genuine, like it was coming from a place deep within.

"No, I wasn't gay, far from it. I braved being picked on and missing out on bike rides and going swimming for one reason: to be with you."

"Are you serious?"

"Yes, I had the biggest crush on you! I waited all year long for you to visit your grandmother during the summer."

Vashti rolled her eyes. "Stop playing, Trap."

"It's true. I even thought about trying to hook up with you a few years back. I called Monique to get your number and everything, but she said that you had a boyfriend, so I let it go." Vashti thought back. Five years ago was right around the time she began dating Kedrick.

"Yes, I did have a boyfriend back then. It was quite serious, actually. We were engaged for a while, but it didn't work out."

Travis began fiddling with a leaf on a nearby peace lily. "So are you seeing anyone now?"

"Not really, just sort of weighing my options. What about you? I couldn't help but notice you with that model yesterday."

"Let's just say that I'm weighing my options, too."

They looked at each other, both of them blushing. Anticipation hung in the air. "I can't believe that Maverick had a crush on little ol' me," said Vashti. "I guess that'll be something to tell the grandkids, huh?"

"You say that like the crush is over," he teased.

"I would think so. You're into models and actresses now, aren't you?"

"I'm into realness. It's so much fake stuff in the music business that I really crave for something real... somebody like you."

"Whatever, Trap," she replied, desperately wanting to, but not permitting herself to be taken in by his words. "I must say, you've gotten a lot smoother since we last spoke."

"You act like I'm trying to run game on you."

"Well, aren't you?" Before he could answer, his cell phone went off and he excused himself to answer the call. He came back a few minutes later.

"I've got to go, but I want to see you again before I leave."

"When will that be?"

"Tomorrow, maybe the day afterward. I've got to be in New York for a talk show taping on Monday morning."

"You're just all over the place."

"But I want to be at *your* place. How about dinner later on?"

She eyed him curiously. "I can't tell if you're being serious or not."

"I'm serious! We go way back, so why wouldn't I want to see you again?"

"Where do you want to go?"

"Would it be asking too much for you to cook for me? I'm not a chauvinist, and this isn't some woman's-place-in-the-kitchen speech. I just don't want to face a crowd tonight. I'd rather chill out with you and a plate of southern food."

"What about Bruce?"

"I'll leave him in the car or at the hotel. It'll just be the two of us. I do have to ask you not to tell anyone I'm coming, though."

"Okay, what time?"

"Is seven good for you?" She nodded, and he motioned to Bruce. Bruce hurried to hold the door open for him.

"All right, Vashti, I'll see you later on tonight. I trust that you won't be serving ants this evening."

"I guess you'll have to see, won't you?"

He waved and walked out with Bruce behind him. Before climbing into his car, he jogged back to the door and kissed Vashti on the cheek before dashing out again.

"Ouch!" Monique sucked her finger and ran it under the faucet. "I cut myself again. Why didn't you just have this dinner catered? You know that I'm not good at this Martha Stewart mess."

"I'm not having it catered for two reasons. One, I'm not you, and two, he wanted a real, down-home southern meal," Vashti replied.

"So that's what that smell is," mumbled Monique.

Vashti flung an apple chunk at her. "He likes oxtails, all right? Plus, I got collards, black-eyed peas . . . seems like I'm forgetting something . . . ."

"Cornbread?" suggested Monique.

Vashti snapped her fingers and pulled out a box

from the cupboard. "Here, make yourself useful. I can't have you bleeding all over the apples. There are no knives involved with making cornbread." She thrust the box at Monique.

"I haven't seen you cook like this for a man since you-know-who," remarked Monique. "Is there something going on between you and Trap that I should know about?"

"We're just having dinner, that's all. That model is his girlfriend, right?"

"I don't know what she is. She was acting all stank last night after the party."

"How so?"

"The three of us were talking, you know, catching up with each other, and she kept breathing hard and looking down at her watch, tapping her foot like we were supposed to be intimidated by that. Finally, she mumbled something about going back to the hotel and stormed out."

"Did he go after her?"

"Actually, that's when he called you."

Vashti measured her sugar and dumped it into the mixture. "He said that he used to have a crush on me. Did you know that?"

"Yes, didn't you? Why else would a 12-year-old boy hang out in a flower shop?" she asked, stirring the batter.

"I never picked up on it. I always saw him as my little brother; I thought he saw me the same way." Vashti shrugged her shoulders.

"No, you had him all right, but there was no one way I would have let you ruin my reputation by dating him back then."

"Your reputation?"

"Yes, mine. When you went back to Georgia in the

fall, I would have been seen as the girl whose friend was dating Travis, and Travis was a far cry from Maverick. He didn't even get *decent* until he was about 20."

"What was he like in high school?"

"Well, he left during my junior year; he was a freshman, I think. He was pretty lame back then, real quiet and kept to himself, still had that inhaler. He got a little name after he won a school talent show, though. Soon after that, his family moved to Philly."

"It was weird seeing him today. It was almost as if he was flirting with me."

"And I hope that you had the sense to flirt back!"

"I can't! On one hand, I see him as the weird kid that nobody wanted to play with. On the other hand, he's Maverick, somebody who I love as a musician but couldn't see myself trying to date."

"Why not?"

Vashti shook her head and sprinkled cinnamon onto her apples. "It would just be too surreal. Having people taking our pictures and that monster body-guard following us everywhere—I just don't think I could do it. Plus, you know he's got tons of women."

"Are you saying that you would turn him down?"

"I don't know. Besides, it's probably not even an option. Have you seen Kimoni? I'm not trying to go head-to-head with her."

"It wasn't Kimoni that he was checking for last night—it was you. Anyway, you know that he doesn't go for those stuck-up broad types. He likes them slow, country, and simple; like you." Vashti nudged her. "Anyway, I'm tired of being the only one rich and fabulous."

Vashti dotted her apple mixture pieces of butter and licked her finger.

"Will there be any of that going on tonight?" egged Monique.

"Any of what?"

"Finger-licking or anything else licking?"

"No!"

"Come on, V. Don't say you've never fantasized about him like that."

"Yes, but about Maverick, not Travis!"

"Well, then, it can be a ménage a trois featuring both Maverick and Travis."

"I don't know about all that!" she chortled.

"Hmph, mark my words—you and Trap will be doing the do before the sun rises!"

It would be several hours past seven o'clock before Vashti would even see Travis. The grease had congealed on the oxtails, the cornbread was hard and stale, and the greens and peas lukewarm by the time Vashti heard him knocking on her door. She had dozed off on the couch waiting for him to arrive.

"I'm sorry I'm so late," he apologized when she opened the door, bracing himself against the rain that darted him.

"It's almost midnight," she said, yawning. "You should have called."

"I know. Things just got so crazy, and there was one crisis after the other. I got here as soon as I could."

Vashti was perturbed by his lack of sensitivity to the time and effort that she had put into the meal, but he was looking so good that it wasn't worth throwing a tantrum over.

Travis was shivering and wet, looking over his shoulders as if he half-expected someone to leap out from behind one of the trees.

"Come in, and get out of this rain." Vashti moved

aside to make room for him to pass through. He removed his jacket and looked around the house.

"This is nice, real cozy," he noted.

"You don't have to patronize me. I'm sure that you've stayed in places with bathrooms larger than this."

"It's not always about the size." He joined Vashti on the sofa. "When I walked in here, I got this feeling of warmth, like I was at home. You can't get that from a hotel."

"There's not going to be a bunch of reporters or groupies at my door, is there?"

He shook his head. "Nobody knows I'm here; I didn't even bring my cell phone. I can just chill out and be myself for awhile. If anything goes down, Bruce knows how to find me."

"I'm glad that you feel comfortable here. I don't know exactly what it's like to be you, but I did get a glimpse of it last night. It looked like it gets pretty intense at times."

"It does. You hear people saying all the time that they want to be rich and famous, but they have no clue about the amount of bull that comes along with it." He took her hand into his. "Ordinarily, I wouldn't have come by so late, but I really wanted to see you again. Plus, I couldn't stay at the hotel any longer."

"Why? What happened?"

"Some fans found out that I had a room at The Delano. It was crazy! They got into my room, went through my stuff. Three girls were waiting for me in my bed when I got there."

"Stop bragging," she snarled playfully, rolling her eyes.

"I'm not. I'm exhausted. I've been on the road and in the studio non-stop for the past year and a half. I didn't get into bed until five this morning and had to be up to do a radio show at seven. After that, I came to see you. From there, there were more interviews, I had to take a fan to lunch as part of a promo, and I had a meeting with my publicist and my manager. I hadn't been back to the room since I left this morning. I only had about an hour to rest, so I just wanted to sleep, only to get there and find out that they had ransacked my room. I love the fans, I do, but sometimes they can be too much."

"Yes, but doesn't this beat sitting in your dorm room, writing songs that nobody's ever going to hear?" He yawned.

"I know I'm blessed, Vashti. I'm not trying to sound ungrateful, but sometimes I miss that dorm room. At least I had a life then."

"No, *now* you have a life! I mean people dress up and wait in line for hours to see you. That must be such an incredible feeling."

He nodded. "It is."

"And you get to meet all kinds of celebrities. I saw you in a picture with Prince about a year ago— *Prince*! Do you know how major that is?"

"Yeah, I remember that. It was at the Grammy's."

"You see—the Grammy's!" She gestured her hands to illustrate her point. "I can't imagine being in a setting like that with all those famous faces. You get to meet people most of us only dream about, not to mention date them." She watched him for a reaction. She was looking for a loop to broach the subject of Kimoni, and this was as good a way as any.

"All right," he yielded, smiling, "I can see where this is headed. This is about Kimoni, isn't it?"

"She's another perk you get from being famous, I suppose. She's beautiful."

"Yeah, she's beautiful," he replied. "She's a lot of other things, too," he added with inflection in his voice that indicated that there was more to the story.

"How serious is it between you guys?"

"It's not."

"You looked pretty tight at the party," pointed out Vashti.

Travis sighed and shook his head. "It's something our agents sort of hooked up. They thought that it would be good for us to spend some time together. You know, give the press something to talk about. I'm not really that into her. She's not my type."

"Then why are you still seeing her?" He chuckled and shook his head. "What? What's so funny?"

"Do you really want to know why I'm with her?"

"Yes."

He sighed and grinned, looking like the mischievous Travis that she remembered. "She gives good head." Vashti slapped him on the wrist. "I'm for real!" he intimated. "It's like the perfect blend of tongue, lip, and suction. You can't find that everywhere."

"Are you serious, Trap?"

"I'm *very* serious. That's the only thing we have going for us. She's not that bright, Vashti. I can't sit down and talk to her about anything serious or even how I'm talking to you right now. All she knows how to do is smile, pose, and give good head."

"I don't believe this."

"It's true. I'd take a 'round the way girl' over one of these models any day."

"Then why aren't you dating one?"

"It's the business, you know? I've got to keep up an image, and me showing up at the Grammy's with Kimoni is better for business than me showing up with Tamika from down the street. Plus, so many women are only out for the dollar—look at your girl Monique. You know that I love Monique to death, but she's a gold digger if I ever saw one. I bet she came out the womb with a shovel!" he joked. Vashti doubled over laughing, visualizing the image.

"At least I know that Kimoni's not after my money; she's got her own. She's just looking for free publicity like me." He became more thoughtful as he went on. "If I'm to get serious about any woman, she has to be real, somebody I knew before all the money and fame. She would have to be a woman that I can be myself with, who won't give a darn about when my next album is coming out or how I can advance her career. I'm looking for a person who can separate Travis from Maverick and still prefer to be with Travis at the end of the day."

Vashti wanted to scream, "I'm that girl!" but simply stated that the type of woman he was looking for shouldn't be hard to find.

"She's not," he said, looking intently at her. "She thinks I'm playing games, though." Vashti blushed and turned away. "Oh, now you want to act shy," he kidded. "Don't go getting quiet on me now."

She exhaled heavily. "Why do you keep messing with me like that?"

"Why do you think I'm playing? Dang, girl, has it been that long? Don't you think you're worthy of a guy actually liking you?"

He was only teasing, but his words struck a chord with her. Did she really feel like she wasn't worthy of a man like Travis?

"Trap, I'm not stupid, all right? You're a good-looking man. Even without the money and the fame, women would be all over you. With it, you can literally have any woman you want. Why me?"

"Why *not* you? You have no idea how amazing you are. I would consider myself the lucky one if you wanted me."

She smiled and lowered her eyes. She couldn't allow herself to believe what he was saying, no matter how badly she wanted to.

"What about the groupies?" she asked.

"What about them?"

"Don't try to act like that's not an issue. Five minutes ago you were telling me that you had three women waiting for you in your hotel room."

"Yes, but where am I? Okay, I'll admit that when I first got in this game, the groupies became my new best friend. But you can't get sucked into this lifestyle. I get panties thrown at me everyday; sex, drugs, money—whatever. It's real easy to get caught up and lose sight of yourself and what's important. That's why I need somebody like you. You could keep me grounded and be my refuge in all this craziness."

She shook her head. "You're just talking, Trap."

"I get so lonely out there on the road, Vashti," he confessed. "I've got these people smiling in my face while sliding their hands down my pockets. I never know who is real anymore. Then I've got my agent and my publicist saying you can't date *her*, you can't go *there*, you've got to say *this*, say you believe *that*. Think about your image; you've got to appeal to *this* group; you can't isolate *that* group. Sometimes, it feels like it's not even my life anymore. But when I look at you, you remind of a simpler time when things made sense."

"I didn't know you felt that way."

He leaned over and kissed her on the cheek. "Please don't write me off. I'm not lying to you."

"What about all of the things that you were saying

about your image? Kimoni's a world-renowned supermodel; I'm just a florist. How's that for your image?"

"I told you that she doesn't mean anything to me. I
know that it's asking a lot to ask you to play second
fiddle to her, but you wouldn't be second to anybody
in my heart—I can promise you that."

"How can you promise me anything? To let you tell
it, you have to get permission for the kind of drawers
you want to put on."

"I know one thing that I don't have to get their permission for."

"What's that?"

He drew her to him and brushed his lips across
hers. The kiss was very tender and sweet and ended
way before Vashti was ready for it to end.

"What I did I do to deserve that?" Vashti asked.

"I like you. How many times do I have to tell you
that?"

"I guess until I believe it."

He spotted Vashti's grandmother's piano in the
corner of the room and was immediately drawn to it.
"You play?" he asked, tinkering with the keys,

"Sure."

"Let me here something." Vashti followed him to
the piano and sat down next to him on the bench.
She positioned her fingers on the keys and cleared
her throat.

"Stepping up, stepping down, then a skip," she
sang while alternating between middle C, D, and E
on the keyboard. "So what do you think? Can I get a
record deal?" she joked.

"Maybe if we tried this." He placed his fingers over
hers and struck the same notes while adding a chord
to them. "Stepping up, stepping down, then a skip."

"You even managed to make that sound like a hit.

My grandmother would be proud. She tried to teach me to play. I never had the patience for it, though."

"You've got to have that drive. Check me out." He started running his fingers up and down the keys and began singing a ballad to her in his smooth, contralto voice.

"Wow, did you write that?"

He nodded. "It's a cut from the new album. You like it?"

"It's beautiful. Do another one," she implored.

"I will do that on one condition; you have to sing with me."

"I don't know what's on your new album. It hasn't come out yet, remember?"

"Let's do something you know. What about this?" He launched into the first verse of Lionel Richie and Diana Ross's "Endless Love."

"My first love," crooned Vashti, laughing at herself for being completely out of tune.

"Come on," he encouraged.

"You're every breath that I take," she sang, gaining more confidence despite screwing up the lyrics.

"All right, time for the harmony . . ."

They sang the chorus together, gazing into each other's eyes. Vashti was a little flat, but Travis didn't seem to mind. By the time they reached the end of the song, they were locking both eyes and lips.

"Let me stay with you tonight," he whispered. Vashti was hesitant.

"You will always be my endless love," he sang softly. With that, Vashti lost the last ounce of will that she had to resist.

"Do you know what I really want to do right now?"

"What?" she asked with bated breath.

"I want to . . . get a plate of those oxtails you've got

back there in the kitchen." They both broke into laughter at the same time.

"I kind of had an appetite for something else," hinted Vashti.

"I know, but I smelled them as soon as I hit the door." She smiled and shook her head.

"Greens, too?"

"Yes, and cornbread if you have some."

"What southern girl would make collard greens without the cornbread?"

They walked into the kitchen, and he watched anxiously as she heaped mounds of food onto his plate.

"Apple pie, too?" he asked, pleasantly surprised when she pulled it out of the refrigerator.

"Apple pie, too!" She set the plate down in front of him.

"I might have to marry you, girl!" He bit into a fork full and leaned back to savor the taste. "I haven't eaten like this in I don't know how long."

"Please—what's an oxtail when you can be eating steaks and caviar every night?"

"Room service and fast food gets old real quick. This is me right here. This tastes like some of my big mama's cooking."

Vashti watched contently as he cleared his plate. He even let out a hearty belch when he was finished.

"That's just what I needed!"

"I have enough for leftovers if you want to take some with you tomorrow."

"You're too much, you know that? You're going to make somebody a good wife one day."

"I hope so." She stood up to clear the table. He grabbed her hand as she reached for his plate.

"You know, I do have room left to eat a little more," he alluded.

"What—do you want some more apple pie or something?"

"I want a little *Vashti* pie—forget the apples!" He pulled her down onto his lap and kissed her.

"You just finished eating. Don't you want to let your food settle down?"

"I don't know why I should—nothing else on me is settled down." She chuckled. "Unless you don't want to."

"I didn't say that."

He pulled a stray strand of hair out of her face. "Vashti, it's been so good seeing you again. I know that it's been several years but the second I saw you, all of those old feelings came right back. It feels like no time has passed at all."

"Trap, it was only a crush. We were both kids."

"It was more than that to me. I was crazy about you."

"At six?"

"Maybe not at six, but I never forgot you, V. I always hoped that one day we would wind up together."

"Why didn't you say anything to me back then?"

"Who wants to face rejection? I knew that all you ever saw me as was a friend, and I was all too grateful for your friendship."

"What about now?" she asked, fastening her arms around his neck.

"Now, I want a little more than friendship."

"Well, let's just concentrate on tonight for now." She yawned again.

"Are you sleepy," he asked.

"A little," she confessed. "I'm usually in bed way before this."

"All right, then we should go to bed," he proposed.

"We?"

He stood up, lifting her out of the chair. "Yes, *we* should go to bed."

He carried her to the bedroom and gently laid her down on the bed. He propped himself up next to her.

"None of the women in Hollywood can compare to you, girl. You're the real deal."

"I bet you say that to all the oxtail-cooking, apple pie-baking tone-deaf girls," she said, fingering his dreadlocks. She clasped her hands around the back of his head and drew him into a kiss, pressing her body tightly against his frame.

He slipped her shirt over her head and laced her neck with kisses. She snaked her legs around him and ran her hand under his shirt and across his back. She maneuvered the shirt over his head as they engaged in deep kisses. He stopped momentarily, and she could see him gazing at her from the moonlight beaming from her window.

"You're so beautiful," he whispered. He ran his hand down her bare stomach and unbuttoned her pants. He slid her pants from underneath her and kissed her again. Then, throwing her legs over his shoulders, executed every touch, every kiss with tenderness and love. Vashti squirmed in sheer ecstasy. There was no place on her body that his lips and hands didn't explore. He was as gentle with her as if she was a precious crystal that he had been charged with protecting. She didn't feel pressured or rushed, and she knew that she could stop him at anytime and he would be okay with it. She felt safe with him and cherished; a feeling that she hadn't had in almost a year.

Once they were stripped of all clothes and inhibitions, he told her that being with her made him feel like a virgin again, because, in a lot of ways, this would be the first time that he ever felt like he was making love. She held him close to her as she let his body dissolve into hers.

She knew that she was deluding herself—maybe they both were—for thinking that a relationship between the two of them could work. But for one night, at least, she wanted to be his and allowed herself to give in to the fantasy.

Chapter 27

Vashti sat in her window seat, watching the rising sun cast light on the rows of lollipop-plants that lined her backyard. There was a chill in the room. Vashti, wrapped in Travis's shirt, didn't know if it was brought on by the weather or the reality that comes along with breaking of the day. She was so rapt in her thoughts that she didn't even notice him as he sneaked up behind her and snaked his arms around her waist.

"I missed you when I woke up and you weren't there. What's going on?" he asked.

She shook her head. "Nothing, I wanted to do some thinking."

"You can think in the bed," he tantalized, kissing her on the neck. She wiggled out of his grip. "What?"

She sighed and put her head down. "You don't have to do this."

"Do what? What's with you? I thought we had a great time last night."

"We did; it was beautiful, but it's a new day...
back to life, back to reality."

"What's that supposed to mean?"

"It means that you go back to your life, and I go
back to mine. I'm not a kid, Travis. I know the rou-
tine."

"Then explain it to me," he replied testily.

"It's not a big deal. You're a musician; this kind of
thing is probably a way of life for you."

"Are you saying that this was a one night stand?"

"Wasn't it?"

"Is that what it was for you?"

"Travis, I'm not dumb. I know how this works. Yes,
things between us were great last night, but today,
you're going to walk out that door and have another
great night with someone else."

His demeanor suddenly changed. He began
scrounging the floor for his clothes. "So it's like that,
huh?" he asked, stepping into his pants.

"It is what it is."

"I don't believe this," he muttered, buckling his
belt.

"What? I thought that you'd be happy that I'm not
trying to tie you down."

He refused to look at her as he continued to dress.
"I didn't think that you were one of those chicks,
Vashti, one of these chicks that'll jump into bed with
anybody so that they can say that they boned a
celebrity. I guess I had you all wrong."

"What are you talking about? Wasn't it you going
on about the groupies and the head-giving models?"
she fired back.

He slipped his undershirt over his head. "Yes, I
have groupies and a *fine* model back at the hotel, and

she is ready to do whatever I want to do, however I want to do it. If I just wanted sex, I could have gotten that anywhere."

"Then what *do* you want?" she demanded, putting her hands on her hips.

"I want you, don't you get it?" He brusquely pulled her to him. Once he had her in his arms, he spoke to her softly. "I want you. It's always been you."

She broke away from him. "It wouldn't work. You're Maverick for God's sake!"

"Not with you," he answered. "Right now, I'm just Travis. Sometimes, I just need to be Travis, and I know that you accept me being just him." She shook her head. "What?" he prompted.

"How can I believe you? How do I know that you're not saying this to placate me for what happened last night?"

"Do you want me to prove to you that I'm serious? Wait right here." Travis bolted out of the room and returned with his jacket in his hand. He reached into the inside pocket and pulled out an envelope and handed it to Vashti.

She flipped it over. "What's this?"

"It's cash for my plane ticket. I fly to New York tonight. I'll be there for three days."

"Then why are you giving me your money?"

"I want you to buy a ticket. I want you to meet me in New York."

"I don't want some three day romp with you, Trap."

"That's not why I want you to come. I've got a 30-city promo tour coming up, and I want you to come with me. *That's* how serious I am."

"How long would I be gone?"

"About six weeks. You could take that much time off, couldn't you?"

If Vashti could get someone to take over her responsibilities at the store, she could take the time off. She was intrigued by the prospect of going on the road with him, but the voice in the back of her head deemed that it was too much too fast.

"Travis, I don't know. You're just now springing this on me."

"Well, look, keep the money." He folded her fingers around the envelope. "Like I said, I'll be in New York for three days. I'll be waiting for you. If you don't come, I'll know your decision."

"That's fair enough," she agreed. He kissed her forehead.

"Now as much as I would love to stay here with you all day . . ."

"You've got to leave," finished Vashti. He nodded.

"I've got to do an appearance at this charity golf tournament, I still have to pack, and Kimoni is speaking at some teen girls' conference. I'm supposed to be there, too."

"Don't let me keep you," she answered curtly, taking the shirt off and thrusting it at him. Now that she'd slept with him, the last thing Vashti wanted to hear was his plans with Kimoni.

"You know that I'd rather be here with you, don't you?" She didn't answer him.

"What are you going to do about Kimoni if I come to New York?"

"She's not coming on the tour with me. Hopefully, we can let the whole thing sort of die down." His contention did little to sway her. "Vashti, I told you that this relationship with her is nothing for you to worry about; it's just for publicity."

"Yeah, but you're sleeping with her. Is that for publicity, too?"

He exhaled and clasped her hand. "I'll be waiting for you in New York. We can sort everything out then, all right?"

"Will I have a chance to see you before you go?"

"I don't know. I can't make any promises." He saw the look of disappointment on Vashti's face. "I'll try. I have a lot to do, but I will try my best to swing by before my flight." He gave her a peck on the lips. "I'll see you in New York," he anticipated before walking out. She heard the front door close behind him.

"AUUGG!" cried Vashti and fell onto the bed. She had roughly twelve hours to make a potentially life-altering decision, and she had no idea what she was going to do.

"Are you crazy? You need to have your butt on that plane tonight!" proclaimed Monique when Vashti explained her dilemma on the phone.

"I don't know. It's all so sudden."

"V, the most dramatic changes in our lives happen all of a sudden—one minute you're alive, the next you're dead. One minute you're single, the next you've met the man of your dreams. One minute you're having sex, the next you're pregnant. Don't blow this by analyzing it to death. Go for yours!"

"This whole thing could blow up in my face. Then what will I have?"

"Some great memories and the peace of mind that comes with knowing that it wasn't meant to be. Otherwise, you'll always wonder."

"Monique, you know this isn't like me. I have to have a plan. I like order and knowing what's going to happen next. Who can predict what will happen out there on the road?"

"Vashti, haven't you noticed that whenever you try to plan, the plan never works out? Live a little! Go to New York and see the world with Travis. This is a once-in-a-lifetime opportunity. Do you know how many women would kill for this chance? Probably a few men, too!"

"I have a business to run," she rationalized. "How can I just up and leave spur of the moment for six weeks like that?"

"Well, do you have any weddings coming up?"

"Not for a few weeks."

"I'll tell you what. I'll run the store for you while you're gone," propositioned Monique. "Monique, are you sure about that? You know how you are when it comes to doing work."

"I covered for you last year when you had the flu, and you're still in business. Besides, it's for a good cause; you getting a life! I'll do dang near anything to see that happen."

Vashti mulled it over. "Well, if you're covering the store, I really have no excuse *not* to go, do I?"

"Vashti, you have spent the better part of the year whining about meeting someone special, getting married, and falling in love again. Well, this is it! Don't let him slip away."

"I hear what you're saying, Monique, but the thought of putting my heart out there again and having it broken is more than I can handle right now."

"Trap isn't like that. You know he wouldn't try to hurt you."

Vashti was still a little shaky. "Do you really think that Trap could be the one, 'Nique?"

"It makes sense, doesn't it? You've known him all your life and in all this time, he never stopped thinking about you. On top of that, he's a celebrity, and he's rich, not to mention thank-you-Jesus fine. How often does that come along?"

"But you aren't factoring in the risks and uncertainties involved. What if he changes his mind about me or if this thing with Kimoni is more serious than he's letting on."

"Just go," pushed Monique. "I can't say with a hundred percent certainty that he's the one for you, but I do know that there's only one way for you to find out."

Vashti still hadn't made her up mind when she walked into the store that day, but she tidied up and filed important things away just in case.

"Hey, Lewis," she yelled over his hammering when she walked over to the newly-constructed part of the store. "About how much longer do you think it'll be before you guys are finished over here?"

"Probably about another week or two. All the rain we've gotten in the past few weeks has put us behind schedule a little bit. Why? You ready to kick us out?" he kidded.

"It's nothing like that," she said, inspecting the freshly painted walls. "I may be going away for awhile, so I'm trying to get things in order."

"Going away?"

"Yeah, my flight leaves at eight."

"Where are you going? When will you be back?"

"Well, it's not a done deal yet, but I may be going on tour with Maverick!" she squealed.

"Who's that?"

"He's a singer. Don't tell me you've never heard of him."

"Girl, I don't keep up with all this new stuff. Give me The O'Jays or some Luther Vandross. So, what, did you enter some kind of fan contest?"

"No, we're old friends. We grew up together and played right here in this store. Anyway, he's in town this weekend. We ran into each other at his listening party the other night, and now he's asked me to go on tour with him."

Vashti waited for a response, Lewis simply shook his head and began hammering a plant shelf into the wall. "Let me guess—you don't approve."

"I just can't understand why you've gotta go from one man to the other. You need to settle down."

"Lewis, you say that like I'm just sleeping around with everybody. I'm not! And I know that this thing with Maverick may seem impulsive, but I trust him."

"How long will you be gone?"

"He says about six weeks."

"And what are you supposed to do while he's in rehearsals and performing?"

"I don't know—hang out, maybe do a little shopping, read."

"You're willing to leave your business to hang out and shop?"

"Monique is going to run things for me."

He shook his head again and continued hammering. "I sho' hope that you know what you're doing."

"I do, Lewis. Just be happy for me."

Vashti's flight was to depart from the airport at 8:00 p.m. She was sitting on her bed amid the plethora of shirts, bras, dresses, and shoes still contemplating her decision. She glanced over at her clock, which read 6:42 p.m., and at the unzipped suitcase on the floor. She knew that she should have packed hours ago, but she kept finding reasons to delay it—taking more time than necessary to assist a customer, indulging in a leisurely lunch during the day, taking the scenic route, which added an additional thirty minutes to her drive home. She had to be packed and on her way to the airport within the next 18 minutes, but she couldn't move. She felt paralyzed and overwhelmed.

So much was riding on the next 18 minutes. She tried to envision her future with Travis. Would it be a storybook romance where she could wake up in Paris for breakfast and cool her feet in the waters of the Rivera at night? Or would it be a house full of material possessions and loneliness? Was Travis her last chance at happiness or was he just the forerunner for what was to come? Could she handle thousands of women fawning all over her man? Could she trust him to be faithful—to be there, period?

She eyed the plane tickets on her dresser and ran her hand over the spot in the bed where he had lain just hours ago. Being with him felt so right, and he wanted her. He wanted *her*!

She smiled to herself. It was crazy and spontaneous and all of the things that she had been taught never to do, but she didn't care. She had a chance at happiness and was not going to let it slip away again!

She scuttled about the room, frantically stuffing her clothes into her suitcase, not bothering to fold or organize anything. She didn't have time to decipher what was essential and what she could go without, so she just crammed everything within reach into her bags. She left a quick message on Monique's voicemail telling her that she'd be back in six weeks and where to find the store's key. She checked the clock again—7:10. There was still time to make the flight. She took in a deep breath, looked around her house one last time, and locked the door behind her.

Vashti collapsed into one of the hard plastic chairs lining the airport lobby. She had gotten there in record time, only to hear that the flight was being delayed an hour. She pulled out a copy of *Big Mouth*, the gossip magazine she'd picked up for her travel reading on the plane.

She casually flipped through the hordes of candid shots of the glitterati walking their dogs and shopping at the grocery store, oblivious to the spying cameras that stalked them. She turned to a spread entitled, "The Hottest Celebrity Hook-Ups." It featured the customary grungy rock star paired with the glamorous supermodel and the beautiful, somewhat emaciated, actors and actress who fell in love on the set of one movie or another.

Vashti's eyes immediately zoomed in on one couple in particular. It was Travis and Kimoni seated outside underneath a patio umbrella at a cafe with a caption that read, SUPER-HOT INDUSTRY COUPLE, R&B CROONER MAVERICK AND SUPERMODEL KIMONI STOKES, SHARE LAUGHS AND BRUNCH AT LA'S NEWEST SPOT FOR CELEBRITY SIGHTINGS. In the picture, Kimoni was smiling and feeding Travis what looked like a slice of cantaloupe.

Vashti stared at the picture a long time before closing the magazine. Even though she had no right to, she felt betrayed and as if she had been stampeded. She had been wondering what her life with Travis would be like, and this was it. Their relationship would always be scrutinized and tracked by the media, or worse, never acknowledged at all. The tabloid reports would become commonplace, so would the constant wondering of whether the rumors of sexcapades and other women were true. There would people who had greater influence and authority over him than she ever would, people who could dictate when and if she saw him and for how long. There would be late night recording sessions and month-long promotional tours that didn't include her. There was his image to be maintained and all of the drugs, back-stabbing, and ambiguity that came along with the music business. There would be his depression when his album didn't sell or if he was passed over for a coveted award. Everything would revolve around him, and she'd have no real life of her own.

She realized then that she couldn't go to New York. As beautiful as the fantasy was of a life with Travis, the reality would call for more sacrifices than she was willing to make. She wasn't willing to settle anymore.

Vashti returned to the same empty house that she had left two hours earlier, a part of her wondering if she'd made the biggest mistake of her life. She called Monique over to commiserate while downing Vodka-spiked smoothies.

"You know you could've been sipping this on a balcony overlooking the New York skyline," noted Monique, propping her feet up on the coffee table.

"I know, but he wasn't the one," Vashti concluded.

"Do you ever think that this belief in 'the one' is over-rated?"

Vashti pondered the question and shook her head. "No, I still think he's out there."

Monique took a long sip from her drink. "So despite everything you've gone through, you still believe in happily ever after?"

"I still believe that I can find the one I was meant to be with." She walked over to the window. "I know he's out there, and he's looking for me, too. And I'm going to be right here waiting for him to find me."

Chapter 28

Vashti spent the next several weeks vacillating about her decision to stay in Miami instead of touring with Travis. Some days, she was sure that staying was the best choice she could have made, especially when she saw him kissing other women in videos or spotted pictures of him on the red carpet with Kimoni. It was the lonely nights that really made her question that decision. She couldn't remember the last time that she'd met anyone interesting, and she had all but given up hope of being married by summer. She submerged herself in her work, and on that end, she was more productive than she'd ever been, but no flower or beautifully planned wedding could replace the ache in her heart that longed for companionship.

Vashti was still sulking when she logged on to her computer. Virtual retail therapy would have to satiate her for now.

As she was conducting an online search for new shoes, an ad for Meet 'n' Mates popped onto her screen. It had happened for the second time during her twenty minute search. Not that she was one to ever stoop to surfing cyberspace for a date, but she figured that there was no harm in checking out the website—for laughs, of course.

She clicked the site's icon and skillfully airbrushed African-American singles flashed across the screen. Once she entered the site, she filled out a questionnaire about herself and her preferences, and a search was initiated for registered singles in her area that had checked off interests similar to hers. Vashti clicked and deleted her way through a superfluity of men, none of whom had pictures that looked like the delicious male models she was promised on the homepage.

After dismissing Greg, who was cute but admittedly had a fear of commitment, Rod, who only dated women who fit the "brown bag" complexion rule, Javious, who had an obsession with cleaning, and Darren, who longed for a woman who reminded him of his mother, Vashti concluded that Internet dating was all of the disappointment that she had expected it to be. This was further confirmed when she saw Brentz's picture and profile posted.

Just as she was about to log off the dating site and continue her shoe search, she saw a listing for a man named Fletcher. He was a 31-year-old writer from Torrence, California, who enjoyed roller-blading, cooking, and traveling. He was seeking friendship but was open to a relationship if he met the right person. Vashti was intrigued enough to check out his picture. He was handsome, almost pretty, and his eyes had sort of an enigmatic look about them, like one never quite knew what he was thinking. Vashti wanted to know more.

When she opted to email him, she was stonewalled by the site's broiler plate message that separated the merely curious from the serious—the $30 monthly fee to officially enroll as one of the site's "mates." It was only by becoming a member that she could actually contact any of the other listed members.

Vashti rationalized that $30 wasn't much, especially if things worked out between them. On the other side of the coin, though, there was the possibility that he was a sociopath preying on lonely, shoe-obsessed women. At the very least, he could have lied about who he was. She needed reinforcements. She picked up the phone and dialed Monique's cell.

"Would you ever go out with someone you met on the Internet?"

"What?"

"I'm online at Meet 'n' Mates. There's a guy I want to email, but I have to pay thirty dollars."

"The guy is charging you to email him?"

"No, it's a dating site. You have to pay to become a member."

"I wouldn't if I were you. My cousin met someone on one of those sites. The guy told her that he was from Texas and was Will Smith's trainer. It turns out that he was a 300 pound degenerate from Mississippi. His son was actually the gardener for Willard Smith, some rich white guy. You can not trust these Internet people."

"I doubt that they're any shadier than the people we meet in real life. Besides, people meet their soul mates in chat rooms all the time."

"Girl, you don't even have to do all that. Give Ashton another chance. He's still asking about you."

"No thank-you for the thousandth time." She

glanced at Fletcher's picture again and slammed her hand down on her desk. "I'm going to do it!"

"Talk to Ashton?"

"No, pay the thirty dollars to meet the guy!"

"All right, it's your thirty dollars, not to mention your life—and I mean that literally!"

"Monique, you're being melodramatic. You act like I'm going to hook up with some stalker or something."

"You might!"

Vashti ignored Monique's caveat and took a leap of faith. After agreeing to the site's terms and conditions and paying for her membership, she was able to email Fletcher. She started to use her regular email address until Monique's words began echoing in her head. She decided that it was safer to use another one under a different name.

It only took her a few minutes to open a new email account under a different moniker. She chose the name Donna Morgan for her web listing at Meet 'n' Mate and for her email. She thought that the name sounded believable and non-controversial.

She stared at the blank screen trying to think of something witty yet friendly, flirty yet sincere, and unique yet approachable to write Fletcher. She took a deep breath and began typing:

Dear Fletcher,
I was just about to write Meet 'n' Mates off as a site for the perpetually disturbed and lonely when I saw the listing for a caring and sensitive writer named Fletcher in search of new friends. Like you, I'm not necessarily looking for someone to lead down the aisle as much as I am for someone to share a good

laugh and a strong cup of coffee. If this sounds
feasible, write me back and we can go from there.
Donna Morgan

She smiled to herself, pleased with the tone of
email and the prospect of meeting someone new.

The next day at work, Vashti anxiously checked
her email, hoping to find a reply from Fletcher. She
scrolled down the screen and stopped when she
spotted a reply to her message from a Demetrius
Fletcher. Apparently, Fletcher was his last name. She
clicked on the message and read his reply.

Dear Donna,
I read your email with great interest. I read your
profile. I know that you're 26, you run your own
business, and you enjoy gardening, dancing, and
wedding-planning, but I would like to know more
about you. How much more are you willing to share?
Fletch

Her heart flipped and a smile spread across her
face after reading his email. He seemed to be as interested as she was. She carefully crafted her reply
back to him, careful not to appear over-eager but not
giving the impression that she wasn't interested either.

Dear Fletcher,
Thank you for responding to my email so quickly. I am
willing to share as much about myself as you are.
What do you want to know? You can ask me anything
you want, but you must answer the same question
about yourself.
Donna

She clicked the "send" button and checked her inbox two minutes later, disappointed to find no response. She went on to be disappointed 15 more times within that hour. If Lewis hadn't shown up to take her out for lunch to finalize the wedding expenses for Sabrina, she would have gone on checking.

"This wedding is killing me!" exclaimed Lewis, looking down at the final tally for his daughter's dream wedding.

"Well, we can cut back a little on the catering. There was another company that was a little cheaper, but the caterer that we went with is providing tablecloths, china, and servers. I've seen some of his work. He's good, and Sabrina was very impressed with him when they met last week. But, like I said, the other caterer is still an option."

Lewis sighed and tossed the bill onto the table. "Well, the dress itself cost me two mortgage payments. What's another five grand?"

"And don't forget, this includes the cake. That alone could run you several hundred dollars, especially with the kind of cake she wants."

He leaned across the table. "Tell me, Vashti, is all of this worth it? Is it really that important? I mean, I got married at the courthouse for about the price of a tank of gas."

"Yes, it's that important, Lewis! A girl spends her whole life dreaming about her wedding day."

"All of this catering and flowers and candles and lace just ain't me. If I ever get married again, it's going to be something simple with me, the pastor, and my wife. I want her to have on a nice dress, maybe a flower in her hair. I don't like the veil; I want to be able to see her face. And I don't want no fancy dinner either. I'm a big country boy. Some fried chicken and collards would do me just fine."

"Lewis, please! I don't know where you're going to find a woman like that. Every woman wants at least one day that she can feel like a queen."

"I'll make my woman feel like a queen everyday."

"You know, I believe you would." He pretended to be annoyed by her flattery. "I never figured you for a romantic, Lewis."

"Oh, I'm a big sucker for love—champagne, picnics, weekend trips. I love doing all that stuff. My daddy was this big 280 pound man who could tear a man limb from limb, but he was a big pussy cat for my mama. She was his queen, and he was her king. They were married for 44 years, and they never left the honeymoon. That means something to me."

"Wow," said Vashti in awe. "My parents have been together 28 years, but they lead totally separate lives. Their honeymoon ship sailed a long time ago."

"You can't ever let the romance die. You remember that the next time you get involved with one of those knuckleheads you keep chasing."

"I'll remember that." She leaned back in her seat. "Actually, I need all the advice I can get with this new one."

"Oh, yeah? Who is he?"

"His name is Demetrius Fletcher, at least I think it is."

"You think?"

"Yeah, I met him online." Lewis groaned loudly. "What?"

"Online? Do you know how many crazy people are on the Internet? I read about some fool the other day—a 40-year-old man, luring 12- and 13-year-old girls to his house by pretending he was a 15-year-old boy. The girls would come out there, and he'd rape them. The daddy of one of those girls blew his head off."

"I know all the risks, Lewis, but it's just e-mails. I probably won't even meet him in person. Even if I did, it would only be after I've checked him out first."

"Just don't let me read about you in the paper being found somewhere."

Vashti began packing her belongings. "Don't worry. I'm a big girl. I can take care of myself."

Lewis reached out and touched her hand. "But you shouldn't have to. You're too nice and too pretty a girl to not have some man taking care of you."

"That's sweet, Lewis, thank you."

He slid his chair closer to hers. "Let me ask you this—what do you know about Queen Vashti?"

"I know that her husband dumped her and married Esther," Vashti retorted.

"No, no, you've got it all wrong," said Lewis, shaking his head. "The king was all drunk and partying with his friends, and he wanted Vashti to come out and parade around for his buddies so they could see how pretty she was. But Vashti wasn't having it! She wasn't gon' let no man, not even the king, degrade her and treat her any which way. She knew who she was and didn't settle. That's the legacy of Vashti, not that King Ahasuerus divorced her and married Esther. That's how I want you to be. You don't have to settle for a man who can't treat you right or one that you've got to find on the Internet."

"That's a nice speech, Lewis, but where are they, huh? Where are all of these men that are waiting in line to sweep me off my feet and treat me like royalty?"

"Believe me, they're out there."

"Well, please point them out to me!" she replied, looking around the terrace. "The men I meet seem like they are out for themselves. A good man *really is* hard to find!"

"One might be closer than you think." Lewis observed her inquisitively with a gleam in his eye then changed the subject. "Well, I best be getting on. I want to get that electricity wired today. Are you going to be all right getting back by yourself?"

"It's just across the street, Lewis."

"I know that. I'm trying to be a gentleman. Obviously, that's something y'all young girls ain't used to."

"No, I think that I'm going to sit here for awhile and enjoy the sunshine."

"All right, Miss Hunter. I'm going to pay for the lunch, and then I'm heading back."

She thanked him for lunch and waved as he darted across the street. She thought about what he'd said and wondered if she was selling herself short by trying to hook up with Fletcher. She dragged herself away from the warm sunshine and into the shop, determined to block all future e-mails from Fletcher if he hadn't responded by the end of the day.

With her new resolve in place, she no longer had the urge to check her e-mail as often as she did before and didn't check it again until she was ready to go home. A reply from Fletcher was in her inbox. Though she'd never admit it, she was thrilled to see it and to know that she wouldn't have to follow through on her threat.

Dear Donna,

I guess the first thing I should ask you is whether or not you've been completely honest with me. I know that a lot

of people tend to fabricate when filling out these per-
sonality profiles. I was pretty upfront on mine because
I have a high regard for honesty. I think that we should
clarify this issue before moving forward. Also, is that
really you on the picture? If so, you're gorgeous!
Fletch

She was tempted to give him her real name, but
she thought about Lewis's story and countless others
like it and decided against it. She did, however, decide to keep writing him. After all, Lewis had also
said that the man of her dreams could be closer than
she thought.

Dear Fletcher,
I've been mostly honest. I wasn't honest about my
name, but that is because you never know what kind
of people will reply. I did it for my own protection. If it
is okay with you, I would like to continue to use
"Donna Morgan" until we get to know each other
better. Aside from that, everything else is true and,
yes, that really is me on the picture!
Donna

She felt a twinge of guilt about the picture seeing
as how it was taken when she was a sophomore in
college, when having regularly manicured hands
and stylishly trimmed hair meant something to her.
These days, a lack of time and finances often dictated
that her nails would be done at home and her hair
tied up in a ponytail with only the occasional trip to
the beauty salon for retouches.

She checked her inbox before climbing into bed
that night, not really expecting a reply from him so
soon, but was happy to see one nevertheless.

Dear Donna,
I understand your wanting to use caution, so you can
continue to be "Donna Morgan" if you'd like. Just so
you know, that really is me on the picture, too. And my
first name isn't Fletcher, it's Demetrius, but Fletcher is
a little more "boardroom friendly" if you know what I
mean. Everybody calls me Fletch. You still haven't
told me anything about you other than that Donna is
not your real name.

His email meant two things: one, that he was understanding and patient; and two, that he probably
had a nice, white-collar job, especially since they
didn't take too kindly to his very ethnic-sounding
first name. She didn't want to appear overly anxious
and desperate, so she made her reply short.

Fletch,
I told you to tell me what you want to know.

"Isn't that beautiful!" gushed Monique over a
Birkin bag when she and Vashti were out shopping
the next day.

" 'Nique, it's $5,000! Why would you spend that
much on a purse when you already have a closet full
of them?"

"But I needed this one. Where else am I going to
put all this?" She pulled out a wad of hundred dollar
bills clipped together.

"Girl, did you rob a bank? Where did you get that?"
gasped Vashti.

"Where do you think I got it?" She stuffed the
money back into her purse, and they careened the
store for other luxuries that Vashti would never be
able to afford.

Vashti shook her head in disbelief. "Trent must really love you!"

"Love my foot! It's the least he could do after blowing me off on our anniversary." She absently examined a pair of diamond-studded sandals.

"I thought that you all were supposed to fly down to Anguilla for the weekend to celebrate?" Vashti's eyes popped when she noticed the $700 price tag on the shoes.

"So did I. I was all packed and ready to go; then his personal assistant called and said that Trent had to postpone the trip because he had to make an appearance at some charity auction in Chicago. He left me a fat envelop full of money, though, and said that I could fly down without him and that he'd *try* to meet me there on Sunday. There was no way that I was going to go down there alone, though."

"You should have called me. We could have hung out or something. I wouldn't have wanted you to be by yourself on your anniversary."

"Oh . . . I wasn't alone," she murmured, placing a discarded shoe back on its stand.

"What—did your mom come by?"

"Dang, V, do you think that you and my mom are the only people I can hang out with?" she snapped.

"Nooo, I know that you have other friends. What I don't know is why you're being so weird about my asking."

"Did it ever occur to you that maybe I didn't want to discuss it with you? That maybe I don't have to tell you every single detail of my life?"

Vashti was taken aback. "What's with the attitude? You're the one walking around here with a purse full of money, looking at $700 shoes. I would think you'd be happy."

She rolled her eyes. "You would."

"Wait a minute, what's that supposed to mean?" Monique didn't answer. Vashti repeated the question as Monique's cell phone rang. Hearing the voice on the other end put a smile on Monique's face. Vashti assumed that it must have been her husband.

"Hold on a minute." Monique cupped the phone with her hand and addressed Vashti. "Look, I have to take this. I'll catch up with you later."

"But you're my ride!"

Monique smacked her lips and shoved a hundred dollar bill into Vashti's hand. "There . . . now, are you happy? Take a cab; that should be more than enough." Monique whirred around and sashayed off, leaving Vashti behind in the department store.

Vashti was still vexed about her encounter with Monique when the taxi dropped her off at her house. She and Monique had had their quarrels in the past, but it wasn't like her to shut Vashti out completely like she'd done that day. Even when they had their rift about Brentz, it was because Monique didn't want to see Vashti making a huge mistake. This new estrangement was totally unprovoked.

She checked her phone messages hoping to hear a message from Monique apologizing or explaining her behavior, but there wasn't one. She set the laptop on her bed and logged onto her computer. A message from Fletcher would be just the thing to pull her out of her funk.

Dear Donna,
Okay, I want to know what makes you tick. What turns you on? What turns you off? Are you seeing anyone? What do you do for fun? Have you had your heart

broken? Have you broken many hearts? What do you
do when you're not growing flowers? Where are you
from? I could go on, but I don't want you to think I'm
stalking you.

Yes, his e-mail was just what she needed! Puddin'
crawled onto the bed and curled into Vashti's lap. She
tickled his ears and began eagerly writing Fletcher
back.

Fletch,
I will answer your questions as best I can. What
makes me tick? My cat, for one . . . romance . . .
love . . . shoes! What turns me on? A well-groomed
man, who is caring, sweet, and knows how to appreciate
a woman. What turns me off? The complete opposite!
I'm not seeing anyone right now, but I'm open to the
possibility that love could be just around the corner. I
haven't broken many hearts, but I have had mine
broken a few times. I was engaged a while back, but it
didn't work out. It was a very painful break-up, but I'm
getting over it. I hardly want to kill him anymore (that
was a JOKE!). I run a floral shop that I inherited from
my grandmother. I was born and raised right here in
the south. Remember, you agreed to answer anything
that you asked me.

Just as she hit "send," the phone rang, startling
Puddin, who had dozed off in Vashti's lap.

"Did that phone wake the baby?" she coddled to
her cat. She reached over to her nightstand to retrieve the phone. "Hello."

"Hey, what's going on?" asked a perky Monique on
the other end of the phone.

"Oh, you're talking to me now?"

"You're my girl! Why wouldn't I be talking to you?"

"Was I your girl earlier today when you left me stranded at Nordstrom's?"

"Oh, sorry about that. I was in a bad mood."

"Obviously! I suppose Trent's phone call straightened all that up."

"Huh?"

"The call from Trent. That was him who called you, right?"

"Um, yeah . . . that was him."

"So, I take it that you all have worked everything out? You seemed bummed about the anniversary trip being cancelled."

"Everything is great! I'm happy, and I had a wonderful, relaxing afternoon. Life is good," she boasted.

Monique sounded happy, but something in her tone drew suspicion from Vashti.

"Are you sure that everything's okay?" asked Vashti skeptically.

"Yes, V. Aren't you the one who said that I have every reason to be happy?"

Vashti sighed and shrugged her shoulders. "I guess. So do you and Trent have big plans for tonight?"

Monique rolled her eyes. "Please—he's at one of his teammates' houses playing cards."

"Do you want me to come over? I'm not really doing anything here."

Monique suddenly seemed uneasy. "That's okay. I have to go get ready anyway."

"You going out?"

"No, I meant ready for bed," covered Monique.

"You have to get dressed up to get ready for bed?"

"Oh—that's my other line. I'll call you back tomorrow." Monique clicked over to the other line so quickly that she was gone before Vashti had time to say good-bye. Something definitely was going on with Monique, and Vashti had the feeling that nothing good could come of it.

Chapter 29

Dear Donna,

I am more than happy to oblige your request. I am the Arts & Entertainment editor for the *Tribune*. I like a person who's open-minded and willing to try new things. I believe that it was Samuel Johnson who wrote that in life there are "many shows to be seen," and I try to live by that principle. I enjoy doing everything from skating to scoring antiques at yard sales to studying the poetry of Tupac Shakur and taking long strolls by the beach. I guess the answer to "what turns me on" is LIFE. I love life; I embrace it! I'm looking for someone who does the same. A person that turns me off is one who is motivated by traditions and pre-conceived notions of what's right and wrong. Maybe that's the reason that I'm not in a steady relationship. I like to go out and meet people, make new friends. I've encountered many fascinating people since I've been here, but not anybody that I want to settle down with and commit to. Don't get me wrong—when I meet that special person, I will be

totally committed. I would tell you that I'm sorry that
things didn't work out between you and your fiancé,
but then we wouldn't have met, would we? I am sorry
that you were hurt, though.
Fletch
P.S. I have a confession to make: I look forward to
checking my email everyday to see if there's
something from you. I hope that we can continue this.

So it wasn't just her. As strange as it was, Vashti
was completely infatuated with a man that she'd never
met in her life. The more she learned about him, the
more he appealed to her. His zest for living was exactly what she needed in her life. Between Monique's
increasingly secretive behavior, planning Sabrina's
wedding, the store renovations and running the shop,
Fletcher's e-mails were a welcomed diversion. She
decided that it was time to take an important step
with him.

Dear Fletcher,
I have a confession also: I look forward to your
emails, too. And I really like your outlook on life. I'm
not really a risk-taker, but I'm trying. You have no idea
what a big deal it was for me to even try meeting
someone online. But there is one risk that I'm willing
to take with you . . . my name is Vashti Hunter.

In the days since they'd been communicating,
Vashti found herself spending more and more time
thinking about Fletcher. She had a general idea of
what he looked like from his picture, but she also
imagined what his voice sounded like and how
they'd feel once they saw each other face to face. She
wondered if they'd take one look at the other and

know that they'd found their soul mate. Then a
daunting thought fell upon her: what if they saw
each other and there was no chemistry at all? What if
that wasn't even him on the picture? Her face was
still livid from this thought when Lewis came in from
next door with some new alterations for her to approve.

"I sho' hope it ain't me making you frown up like
that!" he mused.

"Oh, hey, Lewis. I was just thinking about Fletcher."

"Who?"

"Fletcher—you remember, the guy I met online."

His face dropped. "Oh . . . you're still talking to
him?"

"Yes, everyday."

He grunted. "How's that going?"

"Great! He's fascinating. I really like him."

"What's with the frown then?"

"Well, we haven't met yet, and I was thinking
about the first time we meet in person. I mean, you
brought up some interesting points before. What if
he is psycho or what if I find out that I'm not attracted to him after all?"

"You could always end things now before you get
in too deep," suggested Lewis.

"Actually, I have gotten in a little deeper since the
last time you and I talked. I told him my real name."

"Vashti, no!" he scolded. "What did you go and do
that for?"

"Because he said that he appreciated honesty. He's
been very forthcoming with me, so I thought that I
should do the same."

Lewis shook his head. "And just how do you know
that he's being honest with you? What proof do you
have?"

Vashti was stomped. She hadn't seriously considered that Fletcher might be deceiving her. She had been so desperate for a man that she had thrown all caution to the wind. Now that she had given him her real name, she realized what a vulnerable position she'd put herself in.

"Oh my God, you're right, Lewis. What have I done? He can find out where I live, where I work," she panicked.

"Hold on now." Lewis put his strong arm around her to console her. "He should be easy enough to track down assuming that Fletcher is his real name. You've got a computer back there, don't you?" She nodded. "Then we ought to be able to look him up as easily as he can look you up. What else do you know about him?"

"I know that he's a journalist—an entertainment writer, I think. He said he writes for the *Tribune*."

Lewis appeared leery. "I read the paper everyday. I can't recall anybody named Fletcher."

"His first name is Demetrius. He's a new writer."

"Well, we can settle this right now. You got any change on you?" Vashti plucked four quarters out of the register.

"Where are you going?" she asked when Lewis started heading toward the door. He didn't answer. Instead, he returned about two minutes later with a newspaper in his hands. He sifted through the stack to find the entertainment section.

"All right—arts and entertainment." He handed a few pages to Vashti. "You look in that pile, and I'll look in this one." She began sifting through the papers. "See anything yet?" he asked, scanning his section.

"Nope . . . wait a minute." She leaned down for a

closer look at the headline. "MIAMI NATIVE IS BREAKOUT STAR ON HIT REALITY SHOW by Demetrius Fletcher. It's him! It's Fletcher!" She waved the paper at Lewis. "Look!"

Lewis took the paper from her. "Oh, I've seen his articles before. I was a little thrown off by the name." He folded the paper back up. "Of course now," he began in a fatherly manner, "this doesn't mean that this is your same guy. He could have just picked this fellow's name out of the paper."

Vashti snatched the newspaper out of his hand. "Lewis, you worry too much. I'm sure this is him."

"You better pull up that computer and do a little investigating." He pointed toward her lap top.

They logged onto the newspaper's website. There was a directory listing for all writers and editors.

"There's his name," said Vashti, pointing it out on the screen.

"Check out his biography."

Vashti highlighted his name, and his picture and background information emerged on the screen. The picture was the same one that he'd posted on the dating site, and his credentials and personal history were very similar to what he'd already told her.

"See, Lewis? You were worried for nothing!"

"The jury is still out on that one."

"Well, while the jurors deliberate, I'm going to keep e-mailing him. He seems like a lot of fun. You know better than anyone how much that has been lacking in my life lately."

"I just hate to keep seeing you get hurt. The past months have been very hard on you."

"I'll be okay, and if I get hurt, I always have you to fall back on, right?" she teased.

"Yes, you do," he answered solemnly. "You will always have me."

"Don't look so serious, Lewis! I will be fine."

"You better," he issued. "I don't know what I'd do if anything ever happened to you."

"You'd say, 'That crazy broad finally got what she deserved!'" finished Vashti, laughing.

Lewis was troubled. "Vashti, if only you knew . . ."

"Knew what? What's wrong?" He didn't reply. He only shook his head and bolted from the store.

Chapter 30

Dear Vashti,
Now that's much more interesting than just plain ol'
Donna. Thank you for trusting me enough to tell me
your real name. If you want verification that I've given
you my real name, you can verify it with the paper. It
also has my email address in my by-line.

Hi Fletcher,
I already did that. I even took the liberty of "googling"
you on my computer and a friend helped me find you
in the paper. Everything checked out. That's why I feel
comfortable giving you my name.
Vashti
RE: So you've been checking me out, huh? What do
you think about doing it in person?
Fletcher
RE: So what are you trying to say?
Vashti
RE: I think that it's time that we met face-to-face or at
least a phone conversation.

Fletcher
RE: Where would you like to meet?
Vashti
RE: How about lunch one day next week?
Fletcher
RE: I would love to, but I'll be busy with a wedding
next week. I'll be free next weekend, though.
Vashti
RE: That's great! Actually, I'm doing a review for the
play Ragtime next Sunday. You interested?
Fletcher
RE: I LOVE that play. I'm very interested!
Vashti
RE: Great! I guess this is where it gets awkward
again—I'm going to have to ask you for your phone
number.
Fletcher

At this point, Vashti was in too deep to back out
now. She emailed him her number and instructions
to her house, putting herself in the hands of fate.

Chapter 31

Vashti was in the throws of preparing for her date with Fletcher when Monique arrived at her house unannounced. Vashti's attempts to shuffle her out only made Monique more suspicious, so she parked herself on Vashti's bed and refused to move until Vashti came clean.

"His name is Fletcher, and he's a reporter for the *Tribune*," briefed Vashti, smearing blush onto her cheeks.

"I don't know, girl—you met him on the Internet. How safe is that?"

"I met Brentz at a bank. How safe was that?" She rubbed her arm.

"True," acknowledged Monique. "What do you know about him?"

"Well, he's from California, no wife, no kids. He's been here about eight months, and he says that he is looking for exciting, new experiences with new and exciting people."

"Open to new experiences could mean anything.

At the very least, it means that he's seeing other women."

Vashti fluffed her hair in the mirror. "He's just checking his options."

"Whatever."

"Anyway, he'll be here in a few minutes, and I want you to be gone by then," she instructed to Monique.

"You need me here to check him out for you."

"No," she disputed, strategically spraying on her perfume. "What I need for you to do is leave."

"V, if I didn't know better, I'd swear you were kicking me out."

"Run with that! Now, will you go home and tend to your own man?" She waved Monique in the direction of the door.

"Who, Trent?" Monique smacked her lips.

Vashti rubbed lotion onto her legs. "I thought he was in town this week."

"He is, but he's doing some big endorsement-promotional thing. I probably won't see him until some time tomorrow." Monique looked sad for a moment but perked back up. "Don't worry about me, though. I'm sure that the alligator-skinned Barranda clutch that I've been bitching about and a dozen roses will be waiting for me when I get home."

Vashti shook her head. "You are so lucky."

"Anyway, I'd much rather be here interrogating your date. Where is he taking you?"

"We're going to see *Ragtime*."

"The musical?"

"Yes. I've read it, but I've never actually seen it. Fletcher is doing an editorial piece on it. It should be a lot of fun."

"I don't know, V. I'm not comfortable with you

going out with some dude you met on online. Maybe you guys could come out to my house instead. Marta could put something together real quick or we could throw some steaks on the grill out by the pool. What do you say? It's a lot safer than you going off alone with this guy."

Vashti checked herself out in the mirror one last time. "It sounds good, but he has to go the musical in order to write about it. Besides, you're just looking for an excuse to show off your big, pretty house."

"I'm not, really. I could use the company." Monique lowered her head. "That big, pretty house can get lonely sometimes."

"Girl, you're trippin'! It wasn't that long ago that you were sneaking over to my grandmother's house because your apartment was too crowded. You remember that?"

Monique chuckled. "Do I?! It was me, my mama, my grandmother, my sister, her two kids, my brother, my aunt and cousins—all of us cramped up in that tiny apartment. I remember wanting to get away from them so badly, just wanting some peace and quiet and a room to myself. Now, I have all the rooms and quiet I want, but sometimes I miss the noise . . ." Monique was about to say something else when the doorbell rang.

"Okay, you need to leave. You can go out the back," instructed Vashti, loading makeup and loose bills into her purse.

"Monique Delvonne Holmes-Channings does not go out the back, Mrs. Jim Crow. She will meet this man, give her approval, and exit from the front door like any other citizen."

Vashti knew that it was pointless to argue with her, especially whenever Monique referred to herself in third person. Vashti nervously opened the door. On the other side stood Fletcher, immaculately dressed in a pin-striped suit draped over his chocolate-brown skin, brandishing a wide smile and perfectly-formed teeth. He smelled good, too. She noticed that he had hazel eyes and thick curly eyelashes, almost like a girl's. He was so striking that she was willing to overlook the manufactured waves that covered his head.

"Fletcher?"

"Vashti?" She nodded and smiled, and he surprised her by giving her a hug.

"Hi, Fletcher." She pulled away from him and led him into the house. "Fletcher, this is my friend, Monique. She was just leaving."

Monique shook his hand. "It's nice to meet you, Fletcher." He was mesmerized by her.

"You have such beautiful skin!" he remarked. "What is your secret?"

"Thank you. I try to get a facial at least once a month, but my real secret is this little $20 jar of exfoliating crème I found at a kiosk in the mall. It works wonders."

"Well, you certainly are working it!" He turned to look at Vashti. "And you look scrumptious yourself. Turn around, let me get a good look at you, girl." Vashti playfully modeled for him and laughed. Already, she felt at ease with him.

"Absolutely gorgeous!" he asserted. "And that color really brings out your eyes."

"Thank you!" She turned her head and smiled back at Monique as if to say, "I really like this one!"

"So, Fletcher, Vashti says that the two of you are going to a musical," Monique commented.

"Yes," he answered, settling onto the couch. "And there are going to be some people from work there. I hope you don't mind if I introduce you to them," he said to Vashti.

"No, I wouldn't mind at all!" replied Vashti, flattered that he'd want to introduce her to his colleagues.

"Yeah, they'll be really surprised to see me with a pretty girl like you on my arm." He looked down at his diamond-encrusted watch. "I guess we better get going if we're going to make the show on time."

"Of course." Vashti grabbed her purse then looked over at Monique. "Actually, Fletcher, why don't you go on and give me a second to tell Monique goodbye?"

"I guess you girls need a minute to talk about me behind my back, huh?" he joked, standing up.

"Exactly!" affirmed Monique. He nodded and left. Both girls looked at each other and squealed.

"Girl, he's so fine!" exclaimed Vashti.

"And he seems so nice, too!"

"And he wants me to meet the big wigs at work!"

"And I smelled him—that was Unforgivable. Brother's got some money somewhere!" Monique's countenance dropped a little. Vashti's excitement died down, too, when they realized what had to be acknowledged.

"Of course, we can not ignore that S-curl," disclosed Monique.

"Maybe it's not an S-curl," reasoned Vashti. "Even if it is, he probably just wanted to look good for our date and left the wave cap on too long."

"Well, mission accomplished because he did look good!"

"And did you see his pretty eyes?" babbled Vashti, locking the door as they walked out, Monique to her car and Vashti to Fletcher's.

* * *

Vashti was still misty-eyed, moved by the incredible production and climatic death scene at the end of the play, when she and Fletcher walked out into the lobby and bumped into some of his co-workers.

"Fletcher!" called a rotund, balding white man who was accompanied by another man and a woman, both black.

"Mr. Lundy, hi!" He shook the man's hand and spoke to the people with him. "Did you all enjoy the play?"

"Splendid! What about you, little lady?" he directed at Vashti. "Did you enjoy it or did this creep talk through the whole thing?"

"Oh, I'm sorry," Fletcher apologized. "I want you all to meet my date, Vashti Hunter." Vashti shook Mr. Lundy's hand.

"Date?" hissed the woman with a twinge of jealousy.

"Yes, Tamia, she is my date," Fletcher repeated.

"I didn't know that you were seeing anyone, Fletcher," added the man quietly, staring into Fletcher.

"Vashti, this is Dexter. He's one of the copy editors in my department." Vashti nodded and smiled.

"Have you two been seeing each other long?" Dexter asked.

"Actually, it's our first date," she confessed.

"But we've been talking to each other for awhile," Fletcher elaborated, returning the man's intense stare. "I think that things may work out for us, at least I'm hoping they will."

"Oh, I see," said Dexter, dropping his eyes. Vashti looked at the two of them curiously.

"You better watch this one, uh, what did you say your name was?" asked the woman.

"Vashti—Vashti Hunter."

"Yes, Vashti, you need to watch him," she warned playfully, but with an iota of truth. "Fletcher here had all of us thinking that he was available and then he shows up here with you. I guess I never had chance with you, did I, Fletch?"

"No, Tamia, you didn't," he answered, annoyed. The woman glared at him. Fletcher cleared his throat to ease the tension. "Well, we better be on our way. We've got dinner reservations. I will see all of you tomorrow."

"Good night, Fletcher," bid Dexter. "It was nice meeting you, Vashti. You're very beautiful. Fletcher is a lucky man."

"Thank you. It was nice to meet you, too," Vashti stated.

Fletcher quickly grabbed Vashti by the hand and almost dragged her out of the lobby. The whole exchange struck Vashti as being bizarre. She bombarded Fletcher with questions as soon as they were seated at Tantra, a Moroccan restaurant that Fletcher had assured Vashti that she was going to love.

"All right, what was that?" she inquired.

"What was what?" he asked innocently.

"Did you two used to date?" she asked. "It's that obvious somebody's a little scorned, and I guess you're the culprit."

He looked tense and uncomfortable. "Vashti, I don't want you to get the wrong idea. I mean, we weren't in a relationship or anything like that. We only went out for drinks a couple times. I ended it when I realized that it was going to be a problem."

"Why would it be a problem? Because the two of you work together?"

"Yes, and you know how closed-minded some people can be."

"Well, a lot of employers look down on office romances." She skimmed the menu of lobster, snapper, and seafood stew. "Personally, I don't see anything wrong with it as long as you don't let one interfere with the other."

He exhaled and smiled. "You're being really cool about all of this. I was worried for a minute there. A lot of women would be freaking out by now."

"Why?" she asked, folding the menu. "I mean, yes, Tamia seems like a handful, but I'm not threatened by her."

"What?" He looked baffled.

"Tamia—that's her name, right?"

"Yeah, that's her name." He fidgeted in his seat and loosened his collar.

"Are you okay?"

"I'm fine. It's just . . . I know that she can come on a little strong, that's all."

"Her friend didn't seem too pleased to see us together either. They must be pretty close?" she asked.

"Why do you say that?"

"Well, he seemed to be more interested in our relationship than she was. I guess he was just looking out for her. That's kind of sweet."

Fletcher digressed. "Hey, you ready to order?" he asked, opening his menu. "The seafood stew is really good."

"Hey, what's wrong? You seem sort of jumpy."

"Nothing's wrong!" he answered defensively. When he heard his tone, he apologized. "I'm sorry. Tonight was supposed to be special. Have I completely blown it with you with all of my craziness?"

Vashti reached out and touched his hand. "You haven't blown anything," she assured him. "I'm having a great time. Yes, running into your co-workers was a little strange, but I know that you had a life before we met. Jealous exes don't faze me. Believe me, I've run in to more than a few, some a lot more intimating than Miss Tamia!"

"You're not just saying that, are you?"

"Come here, let me show you." She leaned over the table and gave him a peck on the cheek.

"All righty, then!" mimicked Fletcher, grinning. "You're too good to be true, Vashti."

She blushed. "I was just thinking the same thing about you." Her disposition plummeted when it dawned on her that she had thought the same thing about Brentz.

"What's the matter?" asked Fletcher, seeing the change in her expression. "Did I say something to upset you?"

"No, it's not you, Fletcher. It's my ex."

"Oh." Now his face dropped. "The date must be going worse than I thought if you're over there thinking about your ex-boyfriend."

"No, I wasn't thinking about him like that," she clarified. "It's just that when we first met, we hit it off right away. Everything was great. We were even planning a future together. Then I found out the truth about him, and it all fell apart. If he'd been upfront with me from the beginning, we could have avoided a lot of hurt and confusion."

"I would hate for anything like that to happen to us," he replied tenderly.

"So would I. That's why we have to be honest with each other about everything, even if it's something the other person may not want to hear."

Fletcher turned away and bit his lip like there was something he wanted to say.

"Is there something you want to tell me, Fletcher?" Vashti asked, noticing his demeanor.

"You said that you wanted to be honest, right?" She nodded. "All right. I don't know if I'm ready to be in a committed relationship at this point. I mean, I like you and I know that we've been communicating for a while, but I'm not ready to be tied down to one person right now." Relaying that seemed to allay his anxiety.

"I understand. I've been burned a few times by rushing into things. Anyway, we just met, and we don't know where this thing between us is headed. We don't need the added pressure of putting a label on what we have."

"Right!" he interjected. "It's not that I don't think that we could be great together. I just want to take things slow."

"Okay, I'm glad that we're on the same page with that." She took a sip from her glass. She didn't want him to know that she was a little disappointed, but she was grateful for his honesty.

Fletcher's spirits were revived. "Now, that we have gotten that out of the way, what would you like to do after dinner?"

She shrugged her shoulders, still a little perturbed by his commitment to remaining uncommitted.

"I know the perfect thing!" he exclaimed.

"What?"

"You'll see. I want to surprise you!"

After they dined on lobster and stuffed crab, Fletcher surprised her with a trip to Target to purchase roller blades. As he laced up his own skates, he alluded to the fun they were going to have roller-blading through the park. Vashti reluctantly agreed to it after he reminded her e-mail stated that she was willing to take chances and try new things. She dug her nails into his arms, clinging for dear life, as they skated through the park.

"Vashti, you're never going to learn how to do it this way," he warned. She vigorously shook her head and clamped her hands around him even tighter.

"I don't care. I'm not about to fall and bust my butt on this pavement; not in this dress anyway."

"You can't always be afraid to fail. If you think like that, you'll never try anything new."

A strong breeze whizzed by, sending the tail of her dress soaring. She shrieked, but would not release him to pull it down.

"It's just a little wind! They ain't gon' see nothing but some panty," he ribbed. "And that nice onion you've got back there." She was glad that he noticed it. Her strong clinging began to make Fletcher loose his balance.

"You're going to make both of us fall!" he predicted, trying to stand steadily.

"I'm scared," she wailed.

He looked at her. "It's like love—you can't be afraid to fall."

With his words, Vashti found the courage to let go and skate on her own. She promptly skated directly into a line of bushes and landed on the ground. Fletcher laughed as he helped to peel leaves and twigs off of her.

"I thought you said it was like love," she whined, pouting and frowning at the scratches on her bare legs.

"Hey, love hurts!" He let her use his arm for support as she staggered up. "But it's not so scary when you have someone to lean on."

She smiled. "This is nice, and you're really nice, too, Fletcher. Meeting you has been everything that I'd hoped it would be."

"Even better, to be honest, but I get the distinct feeling that you'd rather be doing anything other than being out here skating."

"I have a feeling that you are right," she concurred, chuckling.

"All right, we can just travel the normal way."

They took off their skates, and he slipped his hand into hers as they walked through the park barefooted, taking in the balmy breezes and clear sky. She rested her head on his shoulders and thought to herself, *Who says you can't find love in all places, including cyberspace?*

A few weeks later, Vashti found herself bonding with Fletcher on a level that she never thought was possible with any man. She loved being in his company whether it was catching a movie or enjoying an intimate dinner. He was always introducing her to things that she hadn't tried before, whether it was attending a wine-tasting, the opening of a new art gallery, horseback riding, or attempting surfing. Fletcher was always very patient with her and never belittled her for not being accustomed to such activities. His philosophy was to try everything at least once, and he seemed as excited to expose Vashti to his lifestyle as she was to experiencing it.

"Can you imagine it—me, Vashti Marie Hunter, surfing out in the middle of the ocean?" she recalled, laughing as she detailed her latest adventure with Fletcher to Monique.

"Well, it certainly seems like you and this Fletcher have experienced everything," Monique stated dryly, helping Vashti water the plants in the greenhouse.

"I guess you're tired of me talking about him, huh?"

"You think?"

"I can't help it! I like him so much. Spiritually, we're completely in sync with each other, but it doesn't get boring because I never know what he has planned next."

"Yes, you've told me all about the bike-riding and the golf and all that other bull, but I haven't heard anything about the real adventures. Basically, is he putting it down in the bedroom or what?"

The smile on Vashti's face vanished and she turned away, busying herself with a vibrantly colored peacock plant.

"Don't try to dodge the question! I have listened to you ramble on about this Negro for the past month; now, all of a sudden, you want to get quiet."

"Because there's really nothing to tell," replied Vashti.

"I knew it!" proclaimed Monique. "He's wack in the sack! I could tell. All of that running around and skating is just to compensate for the fact that he's lacking in other areas."

"No, it's not that," objected Vashti.

"It's bad technique, huh? I kind of thought that." Monique nodded matter-of-factly. "That explains why he has to go online to find women. Clearly, all of the other women know what he's like. You're probably going to have to dump him, too."

"A relationship is not just about sex, Monique! We have something deeper than that."

"Every woman says that until she finds herself

making out her grocery list while her man is trying
to do her. Believe me, I know. Why do you think me
and Patrick didn't work out?"

"No, Monique, what I'm saying is that I don't know
whether or not the sex is bad. We haven't slept together."

"Wait a minute—you actually got on a horse for
this man, and you haven't even had sex with him?
Honestly, I thought that the only reason that you
were doing all of this was because he had put it on
you!"

"He *has* put it on me, but not in the way that you
mean. Our connection is mental and spiritual. We
don't need sex to validate what we have."

Monique put her hands together and clapped in an
affected manner. "Bravo, Miss Hunter! Bravo! That
was an excellent sermon. Now, try giving it to someone who doesn't know you because I know better.
Yeah, all of this explorer crap may be fun, but I know
what you really want."

Vashti broke her moral stance. "All right—yes! Yes,
I want to get to know him on a more intimate level,"
she confessed, "but it's nice to be with a man who's
not trying to get in my pants every five minutes. We
have fun together, and I like him. I'm not going to
make a big deal about whether or not we have sex."

"Has he said anything about it?"

"Not really. We've kissed, and sometimes it seems
like it's headed that way but then nothing. Take for
instance two days ago—he was teaching me to make
soufflé. I had no idea what I was doing and got what
was supposed to be soufflé all over my clothes, and
he lent me some of his to put on. He came into the
room while I was changing and kissed me. Things
started to heat up, and I know that he was as turned

on as I was but he just stopped, saying something about having to clean up the mess before it hardened and left."

Monique assessed the situation. "Hmmm, are you sure he's not gay?"

"Monique!"

"I'm just saying . . ."

"No, he's not gay!" she scoffed. "He just wants to take things slow, I guess."

"There's slow and then there's *slow*. Is he seeing someone else?"

That was a possibility that Vashti hadn't considered, but she couldn't completely dismiss it. He had told her in the beginning that he didn't want to be committed. She just assumed that once they began seeing each other, it was understood that they were to be exclusive.

"Do you really think there's someone else?"

"How many men do you know who won't at least *try* to hit it? He's hiding something, girl, and you better find out what it is."

Chapter 32

"Is this your first time ... in a cooking class, I mean?" asked Fletcher, twenty minutes into the cake decorating class that he'd signed him and Vashti up for. She nodded her head. "What's the matter, gorgeous? You seem distracted."

It was precisely as he was squeezing a pink rose onto their cake that Vashti blurted out the question that had been nagging her all day. "Why don't you want to sleep with me?" she asked in a loud whisper.

Fletcher laughed. "Huh?"

"I'm serious, Fletcher. Why don't you want to have sex with me?"

"Right here?"

"Anywhere!" she answered, exasperated.

"All right, hop up on the table, and I'll do you right here," he joked.

His laughter only infuriated her as she saw nothing humorous about the situation. "Aren't you attracted to me, Fletcher?"

Fletcher sighed and set down the squeezer. "Would I be standing here in a cake decorating class where I am the only male if I wasn't?"

"Then what's the problem?"

"I didn't want to come at you like that until we had established our relationship. I guess the time has come for us to talk about that."

"Okay, so let's talk about it."

"I don't want to do it here, Vashti." He began turning out roses on their cake again. "Why don't you come over tomorrow night? We'll order in, have some drinks, and hash everything out."

"Tomorrow's no good for me. I've got a rehearsal dinner that I've got to attend. I'm free Sunday, though."

"All right, then, Sunday."

Vashti felt relieved. The fact that he wanted to talk about it was reassuring. With that burden lifted, she was able to enjoy the rest of the class.

She was assisting a customer the next day when Fletcher blew into the store. He seemed edgy and tense when he insisted on speaking to her.

"What's wrong, baby?" she asked concerned.

"I'm having a small crisis and if you can help me out, I would really appreciate it."

"The last time a guy told me that, I ended up in handcuffs."

"It's nothing illegal, I promise. I just need for you to run to my house, get a flash drive out of my computer, and bring it to me at the newsroom. I would get it myself, but I have an interview scheduled in about twenty minutes. There's no way that I can go to my house and make it to the interview on time, and still make my noon deadline for that article."

"Sure, that's no problem. Just let me finish up a few things here, and I'll be on my way."

He hugged her. "Thank you so much, baby! Oh, wait, here's my key." He slid it off of his ring of keys and handed it to her.

"So, do you want me to leave the key at your office with the disk?"

"No," he said, closing her hand with the key in it. "I have a spare. Why don't you hang on to it for a while." He gave her a quick kiss and left.

"He gave me his key!" dished Vashti on her cell phone to Monique while driving to Fletcher's house. "This is big! This is big, right?"

"Yes, now you finally get to see what it is he's hiding."

"Monique, you're missing the whole point. The fact that he gave me a key proves that he's not hiding anything. I think it also means that he wants to take things to the next level."

"If that is the case, then it is even more of a reason for you to get over there and go through his stuff."

"Looking for what, Monique?"

"Evidence! Pictures of old girlfriends, letters, STD medication, credit reports, police records—you can't be too careful these days. It probably wouldn't hurt to listen to his answering machine while you're at it."

"I can't invade his privacy like that!"

"I know you can't—that's why I'm coming, too. Where does he live? I'll meet you there."

"Monique, we are not going through this man's things," she resolved. "It's not right, and we're not going to do it."

Twenty minutes later, with Monique in tow, they were carefully inspecting every item that wasn't nailed down in the living room of Fletcher's beach-front bungalow.

"I feel guilty; we shouldn't be doing this," lamented Vashti.

"Look at this!" Monique held up a credit card statement that she found while rummaging through one of his drawers.

"It's a bill, so what?" Vashti stated.

"Do you know how much information you can get from one of these bad boys? Now, look." She laid the statement out in front of them. "Let's check out his balance . . . $3,000. That's not too bad. It looks like his limit is $10,000, so he must have pretty good credit." Monique scrolled down to his itemized purchases. "Here's something charged to Kenneth Cole, good choice! This looks like some kind of Internet purchase here . . . Pier 1—that's suspicious."

"Why?"

"Most guys haven't even heard of Pier 1 Imports, much less go shopping there. And, look, he made a $150 purchase there. This could mean that some other chick has been using his card." Vashti was disturbed by this new development.

"What else is on there?"

"Gas purchases, some concert tickets . . ." Then Monique's eyes grew large and she gasped.

"What is it?"

"According to this, he was at the Marriot a month ago. Was he with you?"

"No," she answered sadly.

Monique affectionately patted her on the back. "Let's just keep looking. He might have been there for work. We don't want to jump to any conclusions yet." Monique placed the statement back in the drawer and moved on to the refrigerator.

"What do you expect to find in there?"

"You can learn a lot about a person this way." She

opened it and began her evaluation. "For starters, it's clean, which is good; most bachelors have disgusting refrigerators. There is a lot of fruit in here, which tells us that he's health conscious." She pulled out a bottle of Merlot and inspected it. "This is a good year, expensive, too. Of course, if he had any real class, he'd have a cellar to keep this in." She put the bottle back in its place. "Ohh, chocolate syrup and whipped cream—you might have a little freak on your hands!"

"Monique, look at this." Vashti handed her a program that she found in his armoire. Monique read it and flipped it over.

"I don't get it. Why is this important?"

"This is where we went on our first date; he saved it. And look . . ." She opened it. "He wrote my name in it and put a heart around it," she burbled. "This is all the evidence I need right here!"

"Don't get excited yet," cautioned Monique. "We still have to check the bedroom."

"I don't need to check the bedroom or any other room. I trust him, and I trust what we have."

"Trust has to be earned, not given just because the guy's sentimental."

"Fletcher has been very upfront with me since the beginning. Besides, going through his stuff like this feels wrong."

"So does being lied to and made a fool out of, remember?"

"Monique, if he's hiding anything, I'll find out eventually." Vashti slipped Fletcher's flash drive into her purse and grabbed her car keys. "Let's go."

"At least break into his email account before we go. You at least owe yourself that much."

"Monique, there is no other woman!" she stated emphatically. "I believe that Fletcher is everything that he says he is; now let's get out of here." As they were about to walk out, his phone rang. Vashti and Monique looked at each other then at the phone as it rang a second time.

"I shouldn't . . ." said Vashti, tempted to answer it.

"I would!" The phone rang again. Fletcher's answering machine began playing.

"Come on, Monique. Let's get outta here."

"Ignorance is bliss," mumbled Monique, closing the door behind them as the voice on the other end on the phone spoke into the answering machine saying, "Hey, it's me . . . Dexter."

Chapter 33

"I thought that you had plans with Fletcher," reminded Monique over the intercom when Vashti showed up at her security gate.

"He's sick. He sounded terrible on the phone." The gates flung open, and Vashti pulled onto the stately premises. Monique met her at the front door and escorted her to the backyard.

"This could be a great opportunity for you to score some points with him," mentioned Monique as they waded their feet in the pool's clear water.

"How?"

"Why don't you go over there and play nurse? Help him sweat out that cold."

"I can't do that! We said that we'd wait until after we had our talk."

"Girl, saving it is so high school, as you've already experienced first-hand with Tyrell, I might add. You need to find out what you're working with before you mess around and fall in love with this cat. I have a little nurse's uniform if you want to borrow it. Trent's all into that role-playing stuff."

"You are crazy!" she declared, but pondered the possibility. "You really think I should just show up over there?"

"Well, I wouldn't go empty-handed. Take him some soup or something."

A couple of hours later, armed with plastic containers of vegetable and chicken noodle soup that she and Monique quickly whipped together, Vashti, barely covered by Monique's skimpy nurse's uniform and an over coat, marched up Fletcher's walkway. She was a little nervous, but was also electrified by the thrill of it all. She used her key to open the door because she didn't want to awaken him if he was asleep.

"Fletcher," she called softly, lightly tapping the opened door. No one answered. The house was quiet and still.

She made her way into Fletcher's living room. It wasn't as clean as it had been before, and she spotted Fletcher's robe lying on the floor. Then she heard a noise as if someone was groaning in pain.

"Fletcher?" she called again, going in the direction of the sound. As she walked toward his bedroom, she heard the noise again and picked up her pace, worried that Fletcher was vomiting or too sick to answer her.

"Fletcher, are you okay?" She flung open the door, and her jaw dropped, nearly dropping the soup as well. Fletcher was there, doubled over but, as far as she could make out, he was not in pain. He was being mounted by a well-built mahogany man wearing only a tie that hung loosely from his neck. Vashti recognized him; he was Fletcher's co-worker, Dexter.

They didn't even notice that she had entered the room.

"Ahem," she coughed. The two men looked up surprised. "What the heck is going on here?"

"Vashti!" spluttered Fletcher as the two sprang apart.

"You're gay!" she shrieked.

He glimpsed back at Dexter then to Vashti. "No—I mean, I don't know. Look, I told you that I was experimenting," he defended.

"Yeah, but I thought it was with women!"

"I never actually specified that, Vashti."

Vashti turned away from the despicable sight, disgusted more with herself for being duped once again. "I'm outta here," she muttered.

"Vashti, wait—"

He covered himself with a shirt that was tossed on the floor and ambled over to her. The thought of his trying to apologize or rationalize his behavior rattled her ever more. "What, Fletcher—are you going to tell me how sorry you are? Or how this is all some big misunderstanding? That you really care about me and that it's not what it looks like?" she baited.

"Actually," he stated, removing the soup from her hands. "I wanted to tell you that I need my key back."

Enraged, she threw the key at him and stormed out, but not before overhearing Dexter say, "Bring that soup over here—we can do something with those noodles!"

Chapter 34

"I knew it! I suspected him all along!" exclaimed Monique when Vashti broke the news about Fletcher at Vashti's store the next day. "What straight men go antiquing?" She popped a piece of chewing gum into her mouth.

"He seemed so nice, 'Nique, and we had so much in common," Vashti whined.

"Yeah, like the fact that you both like men!" taunted Monique. Vashti tossed a pencil at her. "Girl, why don't you let me set you up with one of Trent's friends? A heterosexual white man has got to be better than a gay black one."

"I'm not ready to do the swirl thing like you."

"You might as well, seeing as how your man isn't ready to do the girl thing!" pointed out Monique.

"Do you think that he knew he was gay when we met?"

"How could he not know, V? You know that you like men, don't you?"

"I'm so tired of getting my heart broken that I don't know what I like anymore," she griped.

"These DL brothers make me sick!" complained Monique. "If you know that you want a man, admit that and let the women get on with their lives! Either you like it in the front or the back—make up your mind."

"Whoa—what did I just walk in on?" broke in Lewis. He handed Vashti a catalog. "Sabrina asked me to give you this and a big thank you."

"Thanks," said Vashti dryly.

"Now, what was all that about liking something in the front and the back?" he asked.

"Vashti caught her boyfriend . . . with his boyfriend," filled in Monique.

"Well, I knew something was up with all that antiquing business." Lewis turned to Vashti. "How did you handle it?"

"I didn't—I just I ran out of there like I stole something!"

He had a hearty laugh as he propped his hulking body up against the counter.

"Now, let's see—you've had a queer, a thug, a baby's daddy, and a fool that left you at the altar," listed Lewis with his fingers, unaware of her tryst with Tyrell. "Why don't you try a real man for a change?"

"Do you know any?" Vashti asked coyly.

"Matter of fact, I do. I'd like to put my name in the ring if that's all right with you." Monique's mouth flew open.

Vashti sighed. "Come on, Lewis, stop playing. I'm depressed enough as it is."

"I'm serious, Miss Lady. Why don't you let me take you to dinner, show you a real nice time."

"I don't need charity, Lewis."

"Yes, she does!" Monique interrupted.

Vashti rolled her eyes. "Anyway, I was thinking that maybe I should be by myself for awhile. I've been doing some soul-searching and coming to some decisions about my life. You were right—I've been settling, and I don't want to do that anymore. I like myself," she declared, brimming with confidence. "I have so much going for me and so much to offer. Why would I waste all of that on someone who doesn't appreciate it? I think that I'm going to take some time to re-evaluate my life and find out what I'm doing wrong when it comes to dating."

"The only thing you're doing wrong is choosing the wrong kind of people. You need a man who knows how to treat you like the queen you were named after."

Vashti studied his face. "I can't tell if you're joking or being serious."

"Oh, I'm very serious. I've been watching you for awhile now, waiting for you to get tired of running after all of these men that weren't right for you. I've seen you grow up a lot during the past few months. Yeah, you've messed up every now and then, but you never gave up. Whenever life knocked you down, you didn't stay there. Meanwhile, I just sat back and observed and prayed to God that He would cover you and keep you safe. Now that you've gotten all of that out your system, I think you're ready."

Vashti was thunderstruck. "Lewis, I don't know what to say."

"Say, 'Lewis, what time are you coming to pick me up tomorrow?' " finished Monique.

"Lewis, what about . . . I mean . . . ," stammered Vashti.

"Yes, I know that you're 26, and I'm 47. I'm old enough to be your daddy, but guess what—I'm *not* your daddy, don't wanna be! I just want to take you out and show you a good time."

"It can't be any worse than the other dates you've been on lately," noted Monique.

Vashti thought about it and smiled. "What the heck? Lewis, what time are you picking me up tomorrow?"

Chapter 35

Vashti's first date with Lewis didn't take place at an exclusive restaurant like she had expected. It took place at their church that Wednesday night.

"I can't go in there, Lewis," she insisted when Lewis revealed that their date would be held at Bible study. "I haven't been to church in almost a year."

"Girl, don't nobody care about that! They want to know that you're all right and that you haven't forgotten about the Lord."

"Yes, but I've added a lot more sins to my ledger since the last time I was here."

"You haven't done anything that half the church hasn't done and that the other half hadn't thought about. We've all fallen short of the glory. Nobody's here to judge you."

The ounce of confidence that Vashti had faded once they pulled into the packed church parking lot. The church looked a lot bigger and more intimidating than Vashti remembered it being. The image of

the congregation's admonitory whispers and searing eyes burning holes into her was terrifying.

"If it gets that bad, we'll leave," Lewis assured her. "But I don't think you have anything to worry about." He tucked his Bible under his arm and let her out of the car. Before they reached the front doors, they bumped into elderly Sister Ingram, an infamous busybody in the church who had a propensity for stirring things up.

"Evening, Brother Brown," she croaked, leaning heavily on her walking cane for support.

"How are you doing, Sister?" asked Lewis. Vashti simply smiled and waved. The woman peered into Vashti's face trying to figure out who she was.

"You're Mattie's grandbaby!" she exclaimed after staring at her a few seconds.

"Yes, ma'am. It's good to see you again," Vashti replied.

Sister Ingram summoned another woman over to where they were. "Look here, Myra. Look who Brother Lewis done brought back to church." She turned back to Vashti. "We ain't seen you in years!"

This was what Vashti had been dreading. As she scrambled to make excuses for her absence, Lewis came to her defense.

"Now, Sister, it's hasn't been years. It hasn't even been one! Miss Vashti just needed to take a little time to herself to work some things out. Thankfully, she realized that she couldn't do that without the Lord."

"How have you been, baby?" asked Myra. "I heard about the wedding and all. I can understand why you stayed away so long. My Renee stayed out six months after she had her son, Jerome, ashamed because she wasn't married. You can't hide from the Lord

though, that's what I told her, and she came on back. Don't you hide anymore either. We're your family, and we love you."

"Thank you, Mrs. Clemmons," replied Vashti, encouraged by her words.

"Now, that wasn't so bad, was it?" posed Lewis once the women walked away.

"Not Myra, but what about all of the people who think like Sister Ingram?"

"For every Dorothy Ingram, there are ten Myra Clemmonses," he affirmed.

The amount of love and support Vashti received from the congregation was indescribable. More than half of the church came up to her, hugging her and welcoming her back. She felt the sense of belonging that she'd been missing. Even Pastor Carey made a special effort to welcome her back to the fold.

During the drive back home, Lewis proclaimed, "You see, you were all uptight for nothing!"

"You were right, Lewis. It felt good to be back. I didn't realize how much I'd missed the church until today."

"Now all we have to do is get your friend, Monique, to come back. Is she still going to that Catholic church over on Vining?"

"Monique might be a harder sell. Something's going on with her. She's been sort of distant lately, and we haven't talked as much as we usually do."

"Did you have another fight?"

"No, not really. I mean, she wasn't all that thrilled about the whole internet thing, but it was nothing like when I was dating Brentz."

"Will she be at Sabrina's wedding on Saturday?"

"As far as I know she will." Vashti shifted in her

seat to face him. "Tell me, Lewis, was this a real date or just your way to get me to come back to church?"

"A little bit of both, I suppose," he admitted. "But I'm hoping that you'll let me take you out again."

Vashti smiled. "I would like that."

"You know, Vashti, I don't have a date for the wedding this weekend," he hedged.

"Neither do I."

"You reckon we can go together, keep each other company?"

"I reckon we can," she mocked him, laughing. "You're so country, you know that?"

"Don't let the country in me fool you," he teased.

"You make me laugh, Lewis. I think I'm going to like this."

He reached across the seat and pat her hand. "That's the plan, girlie. That's the plan."

After a late supper, Lewis walked Vashti to her front door and bid her goodnight, insisting that it wouldn't be right to come in and visit with her so late. As she walked down the hallway toward her bedroom, she happened to glance up at the mirror—the same mirror which nearly a year ago reflected a lost and confused soul in an ill-fated wedding gown. She could barely look at that woman, but she took pride in the one that was smiling back at her now. This was a woman who'd learned more about life and love in a year than most people learned in their whole lives. The jilted bride needed someone to love her; the new woman knew that it was enough to love herself. The old Vashti was willing to settle for "good enough"; the new one settled for nothing less than the best. A year ago, she thought she'd never be happy again; now, she knew how to create her own happiness and would never again allow any man to take her smile away.

Yes, she had flaws—she was short and somewhat neurotic and, yes, she was still single, but she could finally see herself for the person that Lewis had been telling her she was all along. She was a queen.

Chapter 36

"No, the candles go over there," directed Vashti to the staff she hired to assist with Sabrina's wedding. "And where's that runner? It was supposed to be here twenty minutes ago!" She scanned her list to see what else still needed to be done. "Where is Monique with that guestbook?" she thought aloud.

"I'm right here," answered Monique and handed Vashti the book.

"Thank you." She looked up at her friend. She could tell that Monique had been crying. "Monique, what's wrong?"

Monique lowered her voice to almost a whisper. "Can we go somewhere and talk?"

"Sure." Vashti called one of her assistants over and handed the guestbook and list to her, issuing guidelines for completing the remaining tasks. Monique then followed Vashti to one of the conference rooms in the back of the church.

"What's wrong? Is it Trent?"

Monique sniffed and wiped her eyes. "It's Trent. it's Craig. It's Ezra."

"Ezra?" repeated Vashti. "What does he have to do with anything?"

Monique faced the wall. "Do you remember that day we were at the poetry session?"

"Yes."

"Well, Ezra saw something." She turned to look at Vashti. "He saw me . . . with Craig."

Vashti groaned and shook her head. "I was afraid of that."

"He never said anything to you about it?"

"Not really. He threw some hints, but I thought he was just spouting off at the mouth. You swore to me that nothing was going on between you and Craig."

"It's not like I planned it, Vashti! We were just hanging out, you know? Then things got out of hand."

"Monique, how could you be so careless and—" She stopped and took a deep breath, taking Monique's feelings into account. "Okay, so Ezra saw you. Is he blackmailing you?"

"It's more like extortion. He comes off as stupid, but he was smart enough to capture the moment on his camera-phone. I must have given him at least $5,000 already. Now, he's demanding that I bankroll his idiotic record label or he'll go to Trent with that picture, maybe even the tabloids."

Vashti covered her face with her hands. "This is unbelievable."

"I can't lose Trent, Vashti, not over this!"

"What were you thinking? How could you let things get so out of control?"

Monique shook her head. "I don't know. Ezra is a loose cannon right now. He could ruin everything for me."

"But, why, Monique? Why would you cheat on Trent? You have the perfect life and the perfect marriage!"

Monique was quiet at first then began shaking her head. "No, Vash, what I have is a husband who's never home and women calling my house all times of the night and in-laws that wish I would disappear. My life is a joke!" Monique sank down into one of the chairs, whimpering softly. Vashti realized that underneath the jewels and the designer clothes and tough exterior, Monique was every bit as lonely as she was.

"Monique, I didn't realize . . . You and Trent always seem so happy."

"We were for awhile. I guess maintaining a marriage is a lot harder than we thought it would be."

"Are you going to tell him about Craig? It would be better if he heard it from you than from Ezra."

"I don't know. I know my husband. Once he finds out, it's over."

Vashti spoke to her quietly. "Would that be such a bad thing? You obviously still have feelings for Craig. What is he saying about all of this?"

"Craig thinks I should divorce Trent. He wants us to be together." Monique stamped her foot in frustration. "But he's a manager at Foot Locker, V!"

"And?"

"And my husband is a national sports hero! And I have a cook and a pool, and I go shopping in Milan."

"And you're miserable," finished Vashti. "Look at you, you're miserable." Monique buried her face in her hands. "Do you love Craig?"

"Vashti, I've always loved Craig, but I grew up poor. I know what it's like to struggle. I'm never going back to that."

"It couldn't be worse than this. You have to know

that Ezra is going to take you for every dime you've got, and, in the end, he still might tell Trent."

"I know. I know that it was wrong. I know that Ezra's going to keep blackmailing me and that Trent's going to leave me once he finds out. I know that Craig loves me and wants me to walk away from my marriage. What I *don't* know is what I'm going to do about any of it."

Vashti embraced her. "I wish you had told me earlier. I wouldn't have wanted you to face this by yourself."

"I know, but you were going through enough with your gay boyfriend and all. I'd hoped that the problem with Ezra would go away once I gave him the money."

"Do you want me to talk to him? He owes me for the whole weed incident."

Monique shook her head. "No, I think that would only make matters worse." They heard voices outside in the hall. Lewis and his family had arrived.

"I've got to go talk to Lewis and Sabrina, but I don't want to leave you like this. Why don't you hang out back here until I get everything in order."

"No, you go on. They're not paying you to stay here and baby-sit me. I'll be fine. I'm not going to stay for the wedding, though. Give Lewis and Sabrina my best."

Vashti rose and smoothed out her gown. "I will. It shouldn't be too hard considering that Lewis is my date."

"Date?!" Monique yanked her back down. "Start spilling."

"I'll tell you about it later."

"You're going to tell me about it now!" She wiped

away a tear that was streaming down her cheeks. "I'm never too upset for gossip."

"How about I give you a full report once there is something to tell?" Monique smiled faintly, and they both stood up to leave. She squeezed Vashti's hand and sighed.

"Thank you for not giving me a hard time, V. Your support means so much to me."

"Are you kidding me? This was me a year ago, remember?" She brushed a tear from Monique's face. "You were the one who helped me to pick up the pieces when Kedrick left. I'm only trying to do for you what you did for me."

Chapter 37

Vashti waved good-bye to the jubilant couple as the limousine whisked them away from the cheering throng of well-wishers and rice-throwers. Vashti scanned the crowd for Lewis. He wasn't rooting with the rest of them but was off a distance. His expression was a mixture of pride and anguish. She walked over to where he was.

"Hey." She reached up and touched his face. "What's with the long face?"

"She's not my little girl anymore, is she?" Vashti shook her head and rested her head on his arm. "Kirsten will be marrying off in a few years, too. It's not an easy thing for a father to deal with."

"She looked happy, though, didn't she? I don't think I've ever seen a more stunning bride."

"The ceremony was beautiful!" complimented Lewis. "You really know your stuff. And when I saw my baby standing at the altar, looking like an angel, I almost cried."

"But you are happy for her, right?"

"Of course I am. Jason's a good man. I know that he'll be a good husband to her. It sort of hurts a little knowing that I won't be the man in her life anymore, that's all."

"You're still the man in my life," she reminded him. He pulled her closer to his side.

Vashti smiled up at him. They were approached by Lewis's teenage daughter, Kirsten, who seemed less than pleased to see her father coddling Vashti. She hoisted up her satin bridesmaid gown to keep it from dragging on the ground.

"Is it all right if I ride home with Damon?" asked Kirsten, pointing to her boyfriend.

A scowl outlined Lewis's face. "You've been around him all day. Don't you think you've had enough of each other?"

"He just wants to take me to get something eat, Daddy." Kirsten nodded her head toward Vashti. "You look like you're busy anyway."

"Wait a minute, I don't think I've even formally introduced the two of you yet. Baby, you know Vashti, don't you? She goes to the church, and she helped put all of this together for your sister."

"I've seen her," snarled Kirsten

"Vashti, this is my daughter, Kirsten," Lewis introduced.

"Hi, Kristen. You make a beautiful bridesmaid." Vashti attempted to extend her hand, but Kirsten ignored her altogether.

"Can I go?" Kirsten asked impatiently.

Lewis crossed his arms in a defiant stance. "You can go when you stop being so rude!" Kirsten shot Vashti a fake smile and mumbled "thank you." She jetted off before officially receiving Lewis's permission to leave.

"Well, that was interesting," stated Vashti.

"That was just Kirsten being Kirsten. Every since she got this new boyfriend of hers, she's been smellin' herself."

"I'm sure it's just normal teenage angst."

"I hope so." Lewis turned his attention back to Vashti. "Let's say we get outta here!" he suggested.

"And go where?"

"Home." He took her by the hand. "I want to take you home."

Chapter 38

Lewis flipped the light switch to illuminate his family room. The house felt like Lewis with its warm and inviting mahogany woods, quirky bric-a-brac, and masculine plaid-covered living room set.

"This place looks like I imagined it would," said Vashti. She picked up a framed picture on the mantle of the stone fireplace. It was of a small child with her mother's arms draped around her. The young woman in the picture was sporting an afro and a wide smile.

"Who's this?" Vashti asked.

"Oh, that's my first wife, Sandra. Sabrina was around three in that picture."

"You never really talk about your ex-wife. Where is she?"

"She died about two months after she took that picture." There was a breaking sadness in his eyes as he looked down at the picture. "Car accident. I ended up with this scar on my chin; she never made it out. She was three months pregnant with our second child at the time."

"Oh, Lewis, I'm sorry." Vashti had often wondered where Sabrina's mother was during all of the wedding preparation. Now, she had her answer. "That's so sad. How old was she when she died? She looks so young in this picture."

"She was a little younger than you, twenty-three."

"How long were you married?"

"About four years. We were both 18 when she got pregnant with Sabrina. We were young, but we were in love. When she told me she was pregnant, I popped the question right then and there. She said yes, and we were married two weeks later. Right after that, I joined the army so I could take care of my family." Lewis laughed a little to himself. "Didn't have a dime to our names, but we didn't care. I suppose if it wasn't for the accident, we'd still be married today." He returned the picture to the mantle.

"Lewis, I'm sorry for bringing all this up. It has to be hard on you to think about her."

"There's not a day that goes by that I don't think about my Sandra, but it doesn't hurt now, not like it used to."

"What about Kirsten's mom? Where's she?"

"Oh, Brenda—that's a real piece of work there!" He sat down on the sofa.

Vashti joined him. "Tell me about her."

"Do you have a few years you can spare?" he asked, chuckling. "I met Brenda about eighteen years ago. She was just a freelance writer then, but she was a spitfire, sassy, kind of like Kirsten. She was a real challenge, but I was young and I wanted to break her. I knew that up under all that mouth and attitude was a real person." He sighed and clapped his hands down on his thighs. "I was wrong."

"Come on, Lewis, she couldn't have been that bad."

"Well, you know, we had our good moments. I guess what it boils down to is that we wanted different things. I already had Sabrina, so I wanted to settle down and do the family thing; she was on the fast track and didn't want to slow down long enough to be a wife and mother. After she found a company that was interested in producing her stage play, she left. They let her direct it, and she's been in New York writing and directing plays ever since. I guess the simple life was just too simple for her."

"Raising two girls by yourself must've been hard on you."

"It wasn't that bad. I love my girls. Plus, Sabrina was nearly fifteen when Kirsten was born and eighteen when Brenda left. She basically took on the role of being Kirsten's little mother."

"But I'm sure it got lonely for you. Has there been anyone special in your life since the divorce?"

He shrugged. "I go out when I can, but I decided a long time ago that my priority had to be God, my girls and my business. There wasn't much time for chasing women after that."

"You seem to be making time for it now," she hinted.

"That's because I've found the one I want." She blushed. "What are you smiling about?"

"Me, you, this whole scenario. A month ago, you couldn't have paid me to believe that I'd be here with you."

"Well, you know what they say; the Lord works in mysterious ways."

"So you think this is divine intervention?"

"I'll put it like this—I prayed and asked God to send me the woman He wanted me to have as my wife. The very next day, you called asking me to fix up your store for you. If that ain't divine intervention, I don't know what is!"

Chapter 39

Vashti could always tell that summer was approaching by one event: the annual birthday cookout at Loretta Holmes' house during the first weekend in May. Loretta was Monique's mother and self-appointed surrogate mother to Vashti. She represented everything that Monique had spent her life trying to get away from, and Monique didn't dare invite her new affluent associates to Loretta's annual soiree despite the fact that it had relocated from the projects to prosperous Coconut Grove.

"You're going to love Loretta," promised Vashti as she unbuttoned the top button of Lewis shirt. "She's a real character."

"Is she anything like her daughter?" he asked.

"She's *nothing* like Monique. She's crazy and a lot of fun. She wears these tight, tight clothes and big, fake jewelry. She's even got a gold tooth, and her hair is usually dyed some wild color. When we were kids, she threw loud parties at her apartment every weekend and would let us sip the beer. She's a sweetheart, though, but she will let you have it if provoked. She doesn't believe in holding back."

Lewis looked a little uneasy. "What do you think she'll say about us?"

"Nothing, I guess. If there's one thing I can say about Loretta, it's that she's liberated." Vashti went over to the mirror and adjusted her spaghetti-strapped sundress.

"Well, are you nervous? This is the first time that we've really been out around your friends."

"No, I'm excited. I told Loretta that I was bringing someone that I wanted her to meet. Besides, I can't wait to show up on the arm of the most handsome and debonair man there." She spun around and kissed him.

"Watch yourself now, girl!" he warned, grinning.

"Do you want to invite Kirsten to tag along with us?" suggested Vashti, secretly hoping that Kirsten would decline if asked.

"Better not—she's in one of her moods. She ain't said two words all day."

Vashti smiled. "I kind of wanted to have you to myself anyway." They kissed again, unaware that Kirsten's disapproving eyes were closely guarding them.

Vashti and Lewis slipped behind Loretta's backyard gate hand-in-hand. The brightly-colored helium balloons and streamers hanging from the trees were a telltale sign that Monique had no hand in decorating. People armed with plates of barbeque ribs and generous helping of Loretta's famous potato salad swarmed the backyard like bees, and Marvin Gaye's "Get it Up" blared from the stereo speakers set up outside.

Vashti soon spotted Loretta two-stepping her way over to them, gripping a plastic red cup and wearing a fitted floral sheath dress with big plastic hoop earrings that Monique detested. Monique lagged behind her trying to pin the portion of her hair back into place that had come undone from too much dancing.

"There's my baby!" Loretta called to Vashti.

"Hey, Mama Retta." She dropped Lewis's hand to give her a hug. "Happy Birthday!"

"Thank you, baby, and you're looking as pretty as ever, keeping that weight down."

"Thank you."

"Not like ol' Niqua here. I told her she can't sit 'round the house all day doing nothing. Her hips are spreading like the Red Sea."

"Mama . . ," groaned Monique.

"Aw, hush, girl. I'm just trying to help you keep that man of yours." Loretta noticed Lewis standing at Vashti's side. "Well, who's this?"

"Mama, this is Vashti's friend, Lewis," replied Monique.

Loretta extended her hand and smiled up at him. "It's good to meet you, Lewis."

"Likewise, Ms. Holmes. This is a nice place you've got here," observed Lewis.

"Oh, please, call me Loretta. I'd be happy to give you a tour of the place." She smiled again, protruding her chest and butt.

"We may take you up on that," he answered, inching closer to Vashti.

"Don't worry about Vashti; she knows this place inside and out. She doesn't need a tour. She helped me get this garden together. You and me should take a little stroll to look at my flowers." Vashti raised an eye at Loretta. The smiles were too bright and her tone too contrived. Loretta was clearly flirting with her man!

"You'd be wasting your time doing that," informed Lewis. "I don't know a daisy from a dandelion. There's not much use for flowers in my line of work."

"What do you do?"

"I'm a contractor. We usually trample flowers, not plant 'em."

"Oh, you're in construction. I must say that I'm a sucker for a man that knows how to use his hands." Loretta seized his hand and caressed it into hers. "And I must say that these are big, strong hands at that." Lewis laughed nervously and graciously slid his hand from her grasp. Vashti shot Monique a threatening look.

Monique shrugged and mouthed, "I don't know."

"Ahem," coughed Vashti. "Lewis, I'm a little thirsty. Do you mind getting me some punch?"

"Sure will. Would you ladies like something?" he asked Monique and her mother.

"Nothing for me," answered Monique.

"I could use a cold beer from the freezer in the house," replied Loretta and smiled.

"Mama, don't you think you've had enough to drink?" Monique asked.

"Hush up, Niqua. It's a party and *my* party at that!" Lewis nodded and walked toward the house.

Loretta grabbed Vashti and threw her arms around her. "Girl, he is perfect! Thank you—you knew exactly what mama needed! All this ol' thang over here got me was a scarf."

"It was a Chanel scarf, thank you very much!" verified Monique.

"And he's so handsome, too. Does he know?" Loretta grinned.

"Know what?" asked Vashti, confused.

"Does he know that he's here to meet me or were you trying to make it seem like a coincidence?"

Vashti shook her head. "I don't understand."

"Vashti, you don't have to play dumb with me. I'm sure that 'Nique has told you all about her father remarrying and how lonely I've been lately. While I don't appreciate her telling all my business . . ." She glared at Monique. "But you're like family, so I guess it's all right, especially since you brought me such a fine man to take my mind off her daddy. Of course I wouldn't mind letting him take off a few other things, too," she added salaciously and took another sip from her cup.

"No, mama, I don't think you understand," began Monique.

"Aw, girl, I'm just fooling around. I don't intend to let him take off nothin' 'til I get to know him better. But I'm sho' gon' have fun getting to know him— whew!" She shook her head and gulped down another mouthful.

"No, mama, you see Lewis is Vashti's date."

"Yes, I know that, Moniqua. She brought him here to meet me, ain't that right, baby?" She kissed Vashti on the cheek.

Vashti was in an awkward position and didn't know what to say. "Well, of course I wanted him to meet you. It's your party, and beyond that, you're like a second mother to me, but Lewis is my date. We're seeing each other. He's my boyfriend."

Loretta sprung back as if she'd just been bitten by a snake. She squint her eyes at Vashti and twisted her mouth into a frown. "Well, don't this just beat all!" she jeered.

"Ms. Holmes, I'm sorry if I misled you—"

"Vashti, that man's old enough to be your father!"

"I know, but he's really sweet, and we don't let the age thing bother us at all."

"I'm sure you don't! But it's dang sho' bothering me!"

Monique tried to quiet her mother and pry the drink from her hand, but Loretta snatched away from her grasp and invaded Vashti's space.

"I don't see why you would have a problem with it," stammered Vashti.

"I know you don't because you're young and you don't know nothing! You see, I'm 45 years old, Vashti. Believe me, when you get to be my age, the pickings get real slim. Most men my age are married, crazy, strung out, or just plain no good. So when I see a man like Lewis, it gives me hope." She put her hands on her hips. "And you have the nerve to come dangling your man under my nose for me to look at and be reminded of what I can't have because he's too busy chasing after young gals like you!"

"Ms. Holmes, I didn't know . . ."

Lewis walked up clutching the drinks, having no idea of the storm that he was about to be swept up in.

"Here you go, ladies. One punch for you." He handed Vashti the drink. "And one beer for you." Loretta snatched the bottle from him and rolled her eyes, puzzling Lewis.

"Baby, maybe we should get out of here," urged Vashti.

"Did I interrupt something?" Lewis inquired.

Vashti shook her head, but Loretta intervened. "Yes, but perhaps you can clear this up for me, Lewis."

"I will if I can," he offered.

"What's wrong with *me*, huh?"

"I beg your pardon?"

"What's wrong with me?" Loretta raised her voice, and the meddling crowd began to gather around them to see what was going on. Vashti stood timidly at Lewis's side as curious eyes burned holes into them.

"Mama, stop it. You're drunk and you're causing a scene." Loretta raised her hand as if she was going to hit Monique. That was enough to make Monique retreat back to her corner.

"Now, I want to know what the problem is," Loretta ranted. "I've got a good job, got my own house. I can clean; I can cook. Now, I've known Vashti for twenty years. I know for a fact that this heifer can't even boil water!" A few people "oohhed" and heckled at what she said. "And I look good. Fact—I look darn good! Got some good lovin', too. *And* I got a little money in the bank, and my son-in-law plays in the NFL, so why her? Why this li'l scrawny thang here and not me?"

All eyes turned to Lewis, awaiting his response. "Well, Loretta, I'm sure—"

"Call me Ms. Holmes!"

"Ms. Holmes, I'm sure you're a wonderful person and that any man would be lucky to have you, but I want Vashti. I'm not trying to be a player or recapture my youth. I'd want her old or young. It's about the person she is inside. And, frankly, Ms. Holmes, I don't have to defend my relationship to you or nobody else."

"Mm-hmm," Loretta groaned and smacked her lips. "You just wait, you hear? Just wait until ten years from now and you're old and tired and want to go to bed early, and she's raring to go to the club. What about when you come home from work and you want your dinner and she gives you some bull mess about women's lib? Or when she wants a baby while you barely got energy for your grandkids, or when you catch her in the bed with a man her own age 'cause you can't satisfy her like some young buck can. You think about that!" entreated Loretta. "Look at her. It hasn't even been a year since she was supposed to marry that other fellow, and she's been going through men like socks, one after the other. A woman like me—I'm settled. I don't mind waiting on my man, cooking his dinner, washing his clothes—"

"Amen, sista!" cheered one of Loretta's friends.

"Taking care of a man when he's sick, ironing his suits and things for him. You think she gon' do that? These young girls don't know nothing 'bout how to take care of no man. All they know how to do shake their tails in your face and take your wallet behind your back. And my kid's are grown—I don't give a dang 'bout no 'biological clock' ticking. Shoot, my alarm went off back in '91!"

Loretta turned to Vashti. "What you know about life, huh? What you know about picking up your man when he's down? What you know about running a household or tending to him when he's sick? You don't know nothing; you just as crazy as Monique here but at least she had enough sense to pick a man her age so they can be crazy together. You just a child. You don't know nothing about nothing! Men like him are scared of a real woman, so they go get somebody like you, somebody that they can run over and who'll fall for anything. A woman like me knows all the tricks and that scares y'all to death!" Tears swelled in Loretta's eyes and one of her friends came and wrapped her arms around her for comfort.

"It ain't fair, Deanie!" Loretta cried on her friend's shoulder as she dragged her into the house. "It ain't right! How we supposed to compete, Deanie—how?"

There was an uncomfortable silence as the circle that had formed around them began to disperse. Vashti could hear rumblings about how she and Lewis should be ashamed of themselves for flaunting their relationship in front of Loretta. Others contended that maybe Loretta would have a man if she ever sobered up long enough to get one.

"Girl, I'm so sorry," apologized Monique. "You know how mama gets when she's drinking. She probably won't even remember this tomorrow."

Vashti nodded. She was too hurt and embarrassed to speak without succumbing to tears herself.

"Come on, baby, let's get out of here," said Lewis, guiding her by the waist.

"I'll call you," called Monique as they disappeared behind the gate.

Aside from answering a few of Lewis's questions with one word answers, Vashti and Lewis rode silently on the ride home. It was only when he had walked her to her door and was preparing to leave that Vashti started talking.

"Why me, Lewis?" she demanded. "Why me and not Loretta?"

"What are you talking about?" he asked, turning around.

"Why me? Am I your trophy to walk around with to show that you've still got it? Are you looking for someone to raise your daughter? Do you think that I'm some naïve little girl that you can sweet talk and run game on? What's going on here?"

Lewis sighed and held Vashti's face in his hands. He planted a soft kiss on her lips.

"I'm with you because you're beautiful and you make me laugh and you're smart and sexy. Why wouldn't I want to be with you at any age? And you know me—I don't get caught up in trying to prove I still got it. I ain't never had it to start with!"

"Then why not Loretta, someone who's settled and experienced?"

"Vashti, I'm sure that Loretta is a nice lady beyond all that mouth and liquor, but I wouldn't want her even if I wasn't with you. She's bitter. I like my women sweet like you. It's not about age; it's about compatibility. I know that I wouldn't be compatible with her, but I'm very compatible with you." She reached out and hugged Lewis, grateful for his reassurances.

"Now, if you want me to go out and find someone else . . ."

Vashti playfully punched him. "Are you crazy?" she teased. "I know I'd be a fool to walk away from you and all you've brought into my life. You make me so happy, Lewis."

He pulled away from her and looked her in the eyes. "Now, Vashti, that's probably not the last time that we're going to have to deal with something like that. People are going to always say that I'm too old for you or that you're just looking for a father-figure. I need to know that you're going to be able to handle that."

"I can handle it. And I know that some people might also say that I'm on the rebound, but none of it is true, right?" Her nervous laugh at the end of her statement indicated to Lewis that there might be a problem.

"None of it is true on my end, but I can't speak for you."

"I'm not looking for a father, and I'm completely over Kedrick, really," she reaffirmed, determined not only to convince Lewis, but her heart as well.

Chapter 40

Vashti soon found herself doing something that she never imagined: she was falling for Lewis. What was more surprising to her was that he was more than just a man that she was dating, he was becoming one of her best friends.

Aside from the occasional references to arthritis and the differences in their tastes in music, their age gap had no impact on their relationship. To her, Lewis was attentive and knowledgeable. To him, she was invigorating and exciting. The only damper in the relationship was Kirsten's increasingly sullen attitude toward their budding romance. They both attributed it to her aversion to sharing her father with another woman and concluded that the best recourse would be to wait for her to come around and accept the relationship on her own as opposed to forcing it on her.

"You certainly don't kiss like a 47-year-old man," purred Vashti as she and Lewis sneaked in kisses under the moonlight as they strolled on the beach following Bible study that night.

"What's a 47-year-old man supposed to kiss like?"

"I don't know," she answered and laughed. "They're supposed to have dry, cracked lips and kiss with no passion."

"Girl, what misguided soul have you been talking to? We old folks can do anything y'all young folks can do and do it better!"

"Oh, really?" She paused before going on. "When will I get to see what else you 47-year-olds can do?" She gazed at him. A strong breeze whipped between them.

"What do you mean?"

She moved closer to him and gripped his hands. "You know . . . ," she sang. "We've been seeing each other for almost three months now. Don't you think it's time to take that next step?" She placed her lips on his.

"Vashti . . ."

"Yes," she whispered, nibbling on his ear.

"We can't do this."

"No, not here. I was thinking that we should go back to your place."

"That's not a good idea."

She pulled away from him. "You're right. Your daughter's probably there, and that's the last thing she needs to catch us doing! Let's go to my house."

"We can't go to your place either, not for that."

She shook her head. "I don't understand."

He sighed. "I can't have sex with you, Vashti."

"Why not?" she asked, cozying up to him. "Don't you want me?" She tried to kiss him again, but he spurned her.

"I said no," he repeated. "I need for you to respect that."

She fumed and walked away from him, kicking up sand in her path. He jogged to catch up with her.

"What's the matter, baby?"

"Nothing," she answered bitterly. "I just didn't expect rejection from you, too."

"I haven't rejected you."

"Well, Lewis, I believe that's what they call it when you make it clear that you don't want the other person! Here I am practically throwing myself at you."

"You weren't throwing yourself at me, and I'm not rejecting you."

"Please don't be condescending right now, Lewis. It only makes it worse. You don't want me—I get it."

"No, you don't. Let me explain."

"I don't need your explanation. I'm going home." She started up the beach again.

"How are you going to get home?" he called after her.

"Don't worry about me," she shot back. "I can take care of myself."

Chapter 41

"Lewis is gay!" announced Vashti and fell back onto her sofa. She'd called Monique the minute that her cab dropped her off in front of her house.

"Gay?"

"What else could it be? He doesn't want to have sex with me. Isn't this how Fletcher started out?"

"Vash, Lewis isn't gay. He probably just couldn't get it up," rationalized Monique.

"You think he's impotent!" she gasped

"Well, he is up there in age, but I wouldn't worry about it. With Viagra and all kinds of pumps out there, he should be fine."

Vashti swung her head around in response to someone knocking on her front door.

"Someone's here. I'll call you back." She hung up the phone and found Lewis standing on the other side of the door.

"What are you doing here?"

"I wasn't happy with the way we left things," he

explained, absently wringing his cap in his large hands. "Can I come in?"

"Sure." She stepped aside and allowed him to pass through. Once he entered into the living room, she folded her arms across her chest and stood in front of him, still visibly upset.

"There's something I need to tell you, Vashti, and it's only right that I tell you this before we go any further with this thing."

"I'm listening."

He went on, gesturing his hands and pacing nervously as he tried to explain himself. "Now, I know that you are an . . . active young woman. I know that you have certain needs, and you're used to having those needs met.

"Yes," she snapped.

"I know that you're probably used to having sex on a regular basis—"

"I'm not a whore, Lewis. I don't sleep around if that's what you're implying!"

"No, no, just let me finish." He cleared his throat. "When two people are attracted to each other, the issue of sex is always bound to come up sooner or later."

She softened her stance and took his hands into hers. "Lewis, if this is about your age or any physical problem you may have, it's not a big deal. There are all kinds of medical options available. Impotency doesn't have to be a problem."

"Oh, believe me—it's not!" he quickly affirmed then grew very serious. "But pre-marital sex is, at least for me."

"So what are you saying, Lewis?"

He gently squeezed her hands. "I don't believe in pre-marital sex, Vashti." She slid out of his grasp and turned away from him. "Now, I'm not trying to condemn you for what you do or come off as 'holier-than-thou.' I'm just trying to do right by God, and I can't go against His will, not even for you."

"I see," she replied. "So you're completely celibate?"

"Yes, ma'am, been that way for the past six years."

She turned around and faced him. "So what does that mean for us?"

"It doesn't have to mean anything. We can go on dating and getting to know each other like we've been doing or . . ." He paused before continuing. "Or you can say that you want to be intimate with your man in a relationship and that we would be better off as just friends."

She moved closer to him. "You're right, Lewis—I do want intimacy in my relationship. I want to feel that connection, that oneness with another person." Lewis nodded, signaling that he understood her position. She wrapped his face in her hands. "And you give me that. You touch me—not with your hands—but with your heart and your words. The intimacy that people look for in sex is what I've already found in you without it."

A relieved smile creased his face. "So you're all right with this then?"

She nodded. "Did you honestly think that I was going to let you slip away?" She stood on the tips of her toes and pecked him on the lips. "I don't mind waiting. I was just worried that you weren't attracted to me that way," she confessed.

"The fact that I'm *so* attracted to you makes it that much harder—no pun intended," he jibed.

"So can we kiss? Can we still hold hands and hug each other?"

He pulled her close to him and locked his arms around her waist. "We can still do all of those things. We just can't get carried away with it, that's all."

"Okay." She sighed happily. "I can do that."

"We can do this, too," he added and brushed his lips across hers.

". . . and this," she smiled, returning his kiss.

"See, now, you're trying to get me into trouble!"

"Then we better stop. I really want this to work, Lewis. I think we have something special here, and I want to protect it." She took a deep breath. "I love you, Lewis."

"As your brother in Christ?"

"No." She squeezed his hands and looked him in the eyes. "I mean the way a woman loves a man."

"Baby girl, I ain't been shy about how I feel about you." He beamed and added solemnly. "I love you. I hope you know that."

She embraced him. "I do know that, Lewis. Even without you telling me, I could feel it."

"Well, who woulda thunk it?" he asked, withdrawing himself from her.

"Not me! All of this time, the man of my dreams was right in front of me. I guess that this is what they mean about not seeing the forest from the trees, huh?"

"Aw, I wasn't worried about you. I knew you'd come around, and I wasn't going to give up on you 'til you did!"

Chapter 42

"Make a wish!" commanded Lewis after serenading Vashti with "Happy Birthday" and presenting her with a decadent chocolate cake when she opened the front door.

"Baby!" she cooed. "Come in." She fastened her robe and pulled her fingers through her uncombed hair. "I'm sorry that I haven't dressed yet. I usually don't receive company this early in the morning."

"It's a big day! You're 27-years-old," he reminded her, setting the cake down on her coffee table. "Go on—blow out your candles." She blew out all 27 candles in a single breath.

"You've got a set of lungs on you, girl! So how does it feel to be a year older?"

"I'm all too glad be finished with the 26th year. I've had so much drama during the past year. This feels like a fresh start, a new beginning."

"I suppose in a lot of ways it is."

Vashti looked a little morose. "I only wish I was able to go to Savannah this weekend with tomorrow being Mother's Day. Besides, I really wanted you to go with me so you could meet my parents, but I have a wedding today; it's not going to be possible."

Lewis sat down next to her and put his arm around her. "You know that I can't have my girl looking all sad, which brings me to gift number two."

"Number two? What happened to number one?"

"You'll see in a minute; be patient." He reached down in his pocket and pulled out a small velvet box. "I guess I don't have to tell you what this is."

Vashti's eyes widened, and she placed her hand over her heart. "I think you better."

"Well," began Lewis, looking her squarely in the eyes. "I love you, Vashti, and it's no secret that I'm a lot older than you or that I ain't getting any younger." He shifted in his seat. "I've watched you grow up a lot this past year, and you've grown into a woman that I admire and respect. You've grown into the kind of woman that I want to spend my life with. I get down on my knees everyday to thank God for sending you into my life."

"Lewis!" she gushed.

"Wait—let me finish. You know, a couple of years back, I had given up on this love thing. I thought I was too old and too comfortable with my life to start over again. But when I look at you, I don't feel that way. You give me hope, like anything's possible. You make me excited to wake up every morning, and I want to wake up every morning with you by my side. I've prayed about it, and I want you to be my wife."

"I think I'm going to cry!" exclaimed Vashti.

He took both of her hands into his hands. "I know that this is your third time hearing these words and my third time saying them, but, Vashti Marie Hunter, will you marry me—but don't answer yet!"

"What?"

"That brings us back to gift number one. I know how much you want to see your parents, and I didn't want to ask you to marry me without your daddy's permission, so I arranged for them to come down here this weekend."

"Really, Lewis?"

"Yes, Monique got me in touch with them. I let them know how important this weekend was to you and even offered to spring for the plane tickets. They turned down the tickets, but they agreed to come."

Overcome with emotion, Vashti reached over and hugged him. "I love you so much, Lewis. I don't deserve someone like you."

"You deserve everything this world has to offer, including me."

Vashti sighed and smiled as she and her mother, Joyce, were putting away the dishes from brunch following her parents' arrival around ten that morning. Lewis had taken her father out under the pretext of fishing so that he could ask him for Vashti's hand while Vashti and her mother lagged behind to "play girl," as her mother called it.

"Isn't it great how well Daddy and Lewis are getting along? He was never like that with Kedrick." Her mother nodded. "Can I tell you something else?" Vashti didn't wait for her to answer. "Lewis asked me to marry him! Now before you say anything, I know that this is, like, my third engagement this year, but this time it's right. I love Lewis. I haven't accepted yet, but I want to. He'll make a wonderful husband, don't you think?"

"Sure . . . wonderful." Joyce pursed her lips together, a sure sign that she wanted to say more.

"If it's so great, why are you looking like that?"

Joyce put down her dishtowel. "I think that it's terrific that your father and Lewis get along, I do. And I love that he makes you so happy."

"But . . ."

She sighed and looked up at Vashti. "When was the last time that you wanted to hang out with your father and me?"

"What do you mean?"

"The reason why your father and Lewis get along so well is because they are practically the same age. They have the same interests."

"What's wrong with that?"

"There's nothing wrong with that if you're 47. There's *a lot* wrong with it if you're 27. You're young, Vashti. You're going to want to go to parties and hang out with your friends, and Lewis isn't going to want to do any of that."

"Ma, we've discussed all of this. I'm really a homebody, and I've outgrown the club scene. Plus, Lewis is very energetic for his age. We go to church together, we work out together, we go to the—"

"What about sex?" interrupted Joyce.

"Mama!"

"Honey, I just want you to be prepared. Your father isn't the man he used to be, let me tell you!"

Vashti shook her head and held up her hand. "I *really* don't need to hear this."

"I know you don't want to hear it, but these are the kinds of things that you need to think about." She resumed. "What about children?"

"What about them?"

"You want them, don't you?"

"Maybe in a few years but not now."

"In a few years, Lewis will be in his fifties. Do you

think that he's going to want to start a family at that point in his life?"

"If it meant that much to me, he would. But honestly, mama, I don't know for sure that I even want kids. Besides, we have Kirsten."

"Who you've already told me you don't get along with. Teens are a handful when they like you. They can be a nightmare when they don't."

"Lewis loves his daughter, but he asked me to be his wife. He wouldn't have done that if he thought there would be a problem with the three of us living together."

"You don't want to put him in the position of feeling like he has to choose between you and his daughter," warned Joyce.

"Mama, I'm happy! Why are you trying to ruin that for me?"

"I'm not. Vashti, I like Lewis, but ten years from now, I don't want you to say that you wish that someone had told you."

"I consider myself forewarned. You don't have to worry about me."

"Come here." She hugged her. "You're my baby— I'm *supposed* to worry about you."

"Look at me, mama." Vashti stood out in front of her. "I'm fine, and I know that Lewis will take good care of me."

"I don't doubt that he will, and I truly believe that he loves you. But you are going into this thing with so many strikes against you, baby."

"I went into my marriage with Kedrick with no strikes against us, and you see what happened."

"That's true," she conceded.

"But I can go into this marriage confident that Lewis would never hurt me like that."

"I don't want you to marry him just because you think that he won't hurt you."

"That's only a small part of it. I want to marry him because he makes me feel good about myself. He knows every stupid and reckless thing I've done, but he loves me anyway. He supports me; he inspires me. He makes me feel loved and wanted, and he adds so much to my life. He makes me laugh, and he doesn't treat me like a child." She paused and took a deep breath. "But the main reason that I want to marry him is because I love him. I love him with everything I have in me that can love. And I trust him with my heart."

Her mother was moved hearing Vashti's poignant plea. "With a love and commitment that strong, you can get through anything." She flung her arms around Vashti. "You and Lewis are both wonderful people. I just don't want to see either of you get hurt, especially my girl."

"Mama, we're going into this with our eyes wide open. I don't want you to worry."

Joyce pulled away from her. "Now, I'm not going to lie to you, Vashi—it won't be easy. They're going to be plenty days when you wish you had left that man where you found him!"

"Is this your idea of encouragement?"

Joyce put her arm around her. "But most days, you're going wonder how you found such favor with God to be blessed with a good husband. And you be good to him, too. Just remember that this is forever. If you're having second thoughts, do something about it before it's too late."

Chapter 43

"He knows," began Monique, standing in Vashti's doorway. "It's over." Vashti hugged her as Monique whimpered softly on her shoulder. Vashti led her into the house.

"What happened? Was it Ezra?" Monique shook her head.

"Not really. He didn't tell Trent, but it was only a matter of time before he would have."

Vashti offered her a seat. "So how did he find out?"

"He found out from me. I told him. I wasn't going to keep letting Ezra blackmail me, and I didn't want to keep living a lie either."

"I guess Trent took it pretty hard, huh?"

"I'd never seen him so angry. But after a while, he said that he understood. He even forgave me."

"Monique, that's great. You two can probably work things out now."

She shook her head. "I don't think so."

"Monique, if he's willing to forgive you—"

"That's not it. I . . . I don't want to be married to him anymore."

Vashti was stunned. "I didn't realize that things between you and Craig were that serious."

"They're not. Vashti, I'm not leaving Trent for Craig; I'm leaving him for *me*."

"But what about the money and the shopping sprees . . ."

Monique sighed. "It isn't enough anymore. I want something real; you taught me that."

"Me?"

"Yes, you and Lewis. When I look at the two of you together, I say, 'That's what I want!' You have the kind of love that people only dream about."

Vashti was humbled by her words. "Thank you, Monique. You have no idea what it means to me for you to say that, especially with everything you're going through." Vashti squeezed Monique's hand. "So what happens now? Where do you go from here?"

"I don't know. Trent left last night for pre-season training. He won't be back for another week. That'll give me some time to think about my next move. I've already decided on one move I'm going to make. I'm coming back to church."

Vashti beamed. "Really, Monique?"

"Yeah, I need to be in a religion that I can understand and in a church that has more than three Black people. Plus, I miss having that relationship with God, you know?"

"Monique, I think it's wonderful that you're coming back. Lewis is going to be thrilled when I tell him."

Monique readjusted her position to face Vashti.

"Speaking of which, what's going on between you and Mr. Brown?"

"I don't want to talk about my relationship when you're hurting this way."

"You better! You're my best friend; your happiness makes me happy."

Vashti braced Monique for the news. "He wants me to marry him, 'Nique."

Monique squealed in excitement. "Girl, you weren't kidding about that year deadline! When did he propose?"

"This weekend. He arranged for my parents to come down, and he asked them for my hand."

"Ohhh," cooed Monique.

"He didn't want me to accept until he'd gotten my father's permission. Now that he's gotten that, he's waiting on me."

"Waiting on you? Didn't you accept?" Vashti shook her head.

"Monique, this is a big step. It'll be my third engagement. I want it to work this time."

"Do you love him?"

"Of course I do!"

"Does he treat you right?"

"He treats me like a queen."

"Can you see yourself spending the rest of your life with him?"

"It's all I can think about."

"Does he have good credit?"

"Monique, come on. . . ."

"Hey, I had to ask! Well, do you think that Lewis is the one God meant for you?"

"Oh, yes! I know he is."

"Then what's the problem?"

She shrugged. "I don't know. I'm afraid, I guess. I want everything to be perfect."

"V, there's no such thing as perfect, but what you have is the real thing. You'll probably never walk around in designer sandals or live in a mansion or drive a Bentley, but Lewis loves you; anyone can see that. Don't let it go."

"But what if—"

"What if you lose him because you were afraid to be happy? You know you love him. Girl, go ahead and tell that man yes!"

" 'Nique, I do love him," she gushed. "He's so good to me and so good *for* me."

"Then what are you waiting on?"

"You're right!" Vashti let out a shriek. "I'm getting married!" Monique gave her a hug.

"All right, I'm going to get out of here and let you go get your man. Call me and tell me how everything went," instructed Monique, standing up to leave.

"And you think about your decision. Things can still work out for you, too, you know." Monique gave Vashti a quick hug and left.

Vashti looked in the mirror and pressed her lips together to refresh her lipstick and brushed her hair back.

"You finally got it right!" she commended herself. Smiling as she pictured Lewis's reaction to her acceptance, she opened the door to leave, but her path was blocked. Standing there with his fist ready to knock on the door was Kedrick Wright.

Chapter 44

"Kedrick?" It was like seeing an apparition. Vashti wasn't even sure whether or not he was real or a figment she had conjured up in her mind.

"Hey, baby. It's so good to see you!" He bent down to pull her into an embrace. She was too shocked to react.

"Kedrick, what . . . what are you doing here?"

"I had to see you. You look great, even more beautiful than the last time I saw you."

She closed her eyes to take it all in. He still wore that same cologne that used to send her hormones raging. The dimple below his left cheek was still there and so were the pouty pink lips that used to drive her crazy. His pecan complexion seemed to have darkened a shade, and she noticed that he was about ten pounds lighter. Other than that everything about him was the same, including the rush she'd get whenever he walked into the room. The impulse to swathe herself in his arms was clouded by the indignation at seeing him again.

"If you think I'm beautiful now, you should have seen me on my wedding day!" she delivered with fire. "But I guess you were too busy hatching your escape." She had overcome her initial shock enough to be angry that he'd have the nerve to show up on her doorstep after so long.

"Vashti, I'm sorry for hurting you like that. Leaving you was the biggest mistake of my life. I know that now."

"What convinced you, huh? When did you realize that leaving me at the altar was a bad idea?"

"When I lost fifteen pounds because I couldn't eat for missing you. And when I broke down crying whenever I heard one of our songs on the radio. When I had to have your picture next to my pillow in order to sleep at night and when Rosario Dawson walked into a restaurant while I was out in California and all I could think was that she wasn't half as gorgeous as my Vashti. I knew then that I had to come back. My heart is with you, Vashti, and it always will be."

She was too emotional to process what he was saying. She hated him, yet she had never been so happy to see anyone in her life. Five minutes earlier, she was prepared to spend the rest of her life with Lewis, and now Kedrick was saying all of the things that her heart had ached to hear him say for the past year.

"Kedrick, I can't talk about this with you right now. I have to go."

"Okay, can I come over later on tonight? I just want to talk to you."

"Fine, just . . . I need to go!" She whizzed passed him and locked herself in the safety of her car. Her head was spinning, and she felt nauseated. She thought that she was having an anxiety attack. Her

hands were clammy and her whole body was quak-
ing. She wanted to cry, scream and laugh all at the
same time. All in a matter of minutes, Kedrick
Wright had managed to turn her world upside down
once again.

Chapter 45

Vashti drove to Lewis's house having no idea what she was going to say once she got there. She knew that she cared very deeply for him but, as always, there was Kedrick. She knew that she couldn't deny that there were still feelings there, too.

"I came here to tell you that I wanted to be your wife," she began once Lewis let her into the house.

"You don't have to sound so sad about it," teased Lewis, but she didn't return his smile.

"I was quite happy about it, actually. But as I was leaving, Kedrick showed up, right there on my door step." Lewis's cheerful mood immediately turned pensive. He slumped down on the couch, staring at the floor.

"Kedrick, huh? What did he say?" But he already knew what Vashti was going to say before she got the words out.

"He said that he still loved me and that leaving me was the biggest mistake of his life." Vashti's voice was cracking and tears began rolling down her cheeks.

"Well, I can't say that I blame him, can I?"

"Lewis . . ."

"So how do you feel, Vashti?"

"I don't know. I mean, I love you, and I was excited about coming here and accepting your proposal."

"But you've changed your mind," he surmised.

"No, I . . . I just need a little more time."

He nodded. "I understand. Take all the time you need. I'll be right here waiting for you."

"This doesn't mean that I don't love you. I want you to know that."

"I know that you love me. Now, you need to figure out whether or not you still love him."

Later that evening, Vashti walked over to the window, watching the rain pound the concrete. Kedrick had returned to her house to talk. She was no closer to a resolution than she had been before, but it did feel good to be around Kedrick again. He pulled up behind her and circled his arms around her waist.

"What does this remind you of?" he asked, staring out of the window.

"What *should* this remind me of?"

"Senior year—we were coming back from your parents' house after Christmas, and the car broke down on that back road. Then it started raining, and we almost froze our butts off."

"Oh, yeah," she said, smiling as she recalled the incident. "You and your shortcuts!" She shook her head and giggled. "Man, it was about 20 degrees that night."

"But if memory serves me correctly, we managed to stay warm all night long," he hinted playfully.

"See, why'd you have to go there?" she asked and poked him in jest.

"I never left there," he answered somberly, taking her hand into his. "I never left you either, not in my heart."

"No, but you did leave in every other sense of the word." She dropped his hand and walked across the room.

"I know that look. You're upset."

Vashti didn't respond.

"You think I don't know you after five years together? I know what every look, every sigh, every smile, every expression means. Now, admit it—you're still angry with me." He walked over to her and looked her in the eyes. "Talk to me. What's going on?"

"Kedrick, I don't even know where you've been all of this time."

He blew out a stream of breath. "Everywhere, but no place felt like home without you there. Initially, I went to California and stayed with a frat brother of mine 'til my money ran out. Then I took an account executive position at a radio station out in Atlanta. A couple of weeks ago, I got hired to head up the advertising division at a major station in Tampa, and I started moving today. The first thing I did when I came to Florida was to come see you. You're the reason I took the job in the first place. I would've agreed to scrub toilets all day if it meant I could be closer to you."

She exhaled and gathered her thoughts. "It's been really good to see you again, Kedrick. I mean *really* good."

"But?" he prompted.

"But there's also tremendous pain when I see you,

too. I was devastated when you left. I didn't get off of this couch for a week. I . . . I wanted to die." She lowered her head and fought back the tears. "You don't know how badly you hurt me."

"Shhh," whispered Kedrick, drawing her into his arms. She buried her head in his chest and wept softly. "I know that I hurt you. I was so stupid, baby, so immature. But you're the one, V. You're the woman that's supposed to be my wife."

"Then why, Kedrick?" she wailed. "Why didn't you marry me? Why did you leave me like that?"

"I was scared. I tried to call you and talk to you about what I was feeling, but no one would let me talk to you."

She pulled away from him. "You couldn't call back? You couldn't have made me listen? Was humiliating me in front of everyone the only way to get your point across?"

"No, that's why I wrote you the letter."

Vashti was befuddled. "What letter?"

"The letter I left in your mailbox. I knew that you were coming back here after leaving the beauty shop, so I put it in the box. Didn't you get it?"

"No," she answered thoughtfully. "I never checked the mailbox."

Her mind flashed back to the day that Monique came over after the wedding. Vashti remembered her bringing in a stack of mail, but she never did sift through it. In her wrecked state, she threw everything away.

"So you never read my letter?"

"I remember there being some letters and stuff," she said slowly. "But I threw everything out before I even looked at it."

"You must have overlooked it," reasoned Kedrick. "Baby, you know that I wouldn't have left you hanging like that."

"What did it say?" she asked, still in shock.

He held her hands. "It said that I loved you and that I wanted to marry you one day, but that I needed more time. I didn't want to be tracked down, so I got a new cell number. I gave you my number in the letter, though. I told you to call me if you understood and thought we could still have a future together, but that if you didn't call, I'd know that you wanted nothing else to do with me. When I didn't hear from you, I assumed that you couldn't forgive me."

"Why didn't you call me? Didn't you think that I'd want to talk to you? Didn't you think that you at least owed me an explanation?"

"I wanted to call you, but when you didn't call me, I figured that you'd made your decision. I was trying to respect your feelings. I thought you didn't want me."

"Didn't want you? I ached for you!" she cried passionately. "I felt like I was dead inside. Do you know how many times I prayed for a phone call, a letter, something?"

"I wanted to be with you, too!" he insisted. "Everything that you were feeling, I was feeling, too—the pain, the loneliness, the void that is never quite filled. At least you had your family. I knew that I couldn't show up here and face your family or mine after the whole wedding situation. I couldn't risk seeing you and have you not talk to me or seeing you with another man. I had to get out of here."

"I thought that you didn't love me," she replied meekly.

"Vashti, I love you more than I love myself. That's why I couldn't stay away."

"But why now? Why not six months ago or right after the wedding?"

"I told you; I thought that you didn't want to be with me when you didn't call. I didn't know what else to do, so I gave you your space. I would have gone on doing that, but it was killing me. I had to see you again even if it was just for a moment."

"I need some time to think," she said abruptly. "This is too much to process at once. Yesterday, I was ready to accept a proposal from someone else, and today, I find out that you never stopped loving me."

"A proposal?" he repeated, caught unawares.

"You've been gone a really long time, Kedrick. How long did you expect me to wait before falling in love again?"

"Did you ever stop loving me, Vashti?" he asked over her shoulder.

"I don't know." She shook her head. "I've been spent so much time convincing myself that I didn't until I just didn't know anymore."

"Then look into my eyes and tell me what you see, what you feel." She looked at him for a moment then turned away, shaking her head.

"I can't, not now. It's too soon."

He backed away from her a little. "I understand, and I can be patient."

"Thank you."

"But first . . ." He lifted her chin and placed his lips on hers. There was a comfort in the familiarity of his kiss. She allowed him to kiss her again.

"Do you want me to go?" he whispered. "I could stay if you want."

"Do you want to stay?"

He nodded. "I want to be right here with you to hold you and kiss you . . . make love to you."

"Kedrick, I told you. I'm seeing someone. I can't just—"

"I know, I know. You want to settle things with him first. You're not the type to betray anyone, which is part of the reason I love you so much. Just let me show you how much I've missed you. It's been too long as it is."

"Kedrick—"

"Come here, sit down." He led her to the sofa and cradled Vashti in his arms, braiding his fingers into hers. "Doesn't being here with me like this feel right? This is how it is supposed to be—you and me, together always."

"What makes you so sure?"

"Do you remember that day we met?" Vashti laughed a little, conjuring up the memory. "I was running for student president and passing out flyers to everybody."

She rolled her eyes. "Please! You just used that campaign as an excuse to talk to women," chided Vashti.

"It worked, didn't it? It got me you. I can still remember the very first time I saw you."

She smiled. "Do you remember what you said to me when you handed me your flyer?"

"No, but I remember what I was thinking! I knew right then that I had to have you, just like I know it right now."

Vashti looked up at him and sighed. "Kedrick, as easy as it would be to pick right up where we left off, life doesn't work like that."

"Says who?"

"Says everything that's happened—the tears, the hurt. I have a whole other life now that you know nothing about. I'm not the same person that you left at the altar."

"You look like the same pretty girl to me," he teased.

She didn't return his jovial mood. "I've changed a lot over the past year, Kedrick. I know who I am now."

"I do, too—you're my woman. That's who you'll always be." He tried to embrace her again, but she rejected him.

"There was a time when that would have been enough, when all I wanted was to know that I *belonged* to somebody, but that's not the case anymore. I'm a whole person with my own dreams and my own life. A man is just icing; I'm the cake all by myself!"

"Then why don't you let me eat you . . ." he added, trying to bite into her neck. She pushed him away. He finally gave up. "Okay, so you're Miss Independent now, but all the seminars and affirmations and Oprah segments in the world won't erase what we had. We completed each other."

"I was already complete," she weighed in. "I just didn't know it yet."

He gave her a long, hard look. "I guess this is the new you, huh? Funny—I kind of liked the old one. I hope that some parts of her are still there."

"Hmm . . . a few," she admitted, revealing a coy smile.

"Hey, do you remember—"

"I'm sure I do, Kedrick," she cut in. "We shared

some great times, but I can't afford to live in the past, and we can't build a future on memories alone. It's not enough."

"There's five years of history between us. You can't ignore that."

"I can't live on it either. Honestly, I don't want to go back to the way things were—me being so needy and clingy all the time, you controlling every aspect of our relationship. I like who I am now."

"Why are you trying to make it seem like our relationship was so wrong. We loved each other, and we were happy."

"Were we really, Kedrick? If things were so perfect, you wouldn't have walked out on me."

"That was a mistake."

She shook her head. "I don't think so. Whether or not you wanted to admit it to me or to yourself, you knew that something about us wasn't right, something that I was too blind too see."

Kedrick leaned back on the sofa and exhaled. "Look, I'm exhausted. I drove darn near twelve hours to see you. I'm tired, I'm hungry, and all I wanted to do was come here and chill out with my girl. Can I at least have that?"

"We can talk, we can chill—we can do all of that. I just need for you to understand that you can't pop up after a year and expect things to be the way you left them."

"You're right," he agreed. "I guess I was so caught up with what I wanted and seeing you again that I didn't think beyond that. It never dawned on me that you wouldn't feel the same way."

"Don't think I'm not happy to see you, because I am, but I need for you to respect the changes that I've made in my life."

He nodded. "Do you want me to stick around or would it better if I left?"

"You can stay—I *want* you to stay, but don't expect—"

He held up his hand to quiet her. "I'm not expecting anything. I just want to go to sleep holding you in my arms like I used to. Is that okay?"

The offer was tempting, and she was too drained emotionally and physically to resist. Vashti stretched out on the sofa with him and closed her eyes. Lying safely in each other's arms, they dozed off as the rain pelted the rest of the world.

Chapter 46

"Is it morning?" yawned Kedrick, stretching. He and Vashti were awakened by the sun piercing through the windows.

"Yep," she answered and sighed. "I'm hungry."

"What are you in the mood for—steaks, pancakes? My baby can have whatever she wants," he offered, stroking Vashti's arm.

"Is this the same Kedrick that used to ask me to order from the kiddie menu to save a dollar," she joked.

"I told you, I'm a changed man. That childish stuff I used to do is over. I realize that a woman like you deserves to be treasured, and I want to spend the rest of our lives spoiling you."

Vashti had longed to hear those words from him for the past year but somehow, they didn't strike the same chord with her that she thought they would.

"I believe cereal and coffee will suffice, thank you," she stated.

He secured his arm around her shoulders. "Yeah, I guess I better conserve my money. I'm going to need it for the down payment on the house."

"What house?"

"The one I want to have built for us in Tampa."

She sat up. "Kedrick, don't you think that's rushing things a bit? I mean, we're not even officially back to-gether."

"Baby, as far as I'm concerned, we never broke up. I never stopped loving you, and I never will. You just say the word, and it'll be like this past year never happened."

"But it did happen, Kedrick, and I suffered a long time because of it."

"And I want to fill your life with happiness for every second that I made you suffer." He kissed her hand. "We can do this, Vashti. We can still have the life that we dreamed about having."

"Yes, but what about Lewis?"

"What about him?"

"I told you, Kedrick, we're involved. I really care about him, and he wants to marry me."

Kedrick reclined back with his hands behind his head. "I think I know what this is about."

"You do?"

"Yes. When I was away, you hooked up with him, and now you feel guilty. Look, I'm not mad. You didn't think I was coming back, so you moved on. I forgive you."

She blinked, taken aback. "*You forgive me?*"

"Yes, because I love you."

His amnesty was almost laughable. "Kedrick, I don't think you understand . . ."

"I believe I do." He caressed her hands and spoke

softly. I get it, Vashti. You slept with him, so now you feel like you cheated on me. I don't like it, but I can get passed that."

"No, you don't get it!" she admonished, standing up. "Lewis and I are in a relationship."

"Okay, so you have a *relationship*, but it ain't like you and me. We put in five years together. You and this cat been together, what, five minutes?"

"We've gotten very close, Kedrick."

"But do you love him, Vash? Does he make your heart race like I do? Can he make you scream out his name like I can? I don't think so," he answered smugly.

"No, my heart doesn't feel like it's about to jump out of my chest and we don't have wild nights of unbridled passion, but what we do have is real and enduring. I trust him with my life, my body, and my heart, which is more than I can say for you. I never have to question his love or his loyalty to me. We have a connection that's deeper than anything I ever felt with you. He's my soul mate." As she spoke the words, she realized that she truly meant them.

"So, what are you saying, Vashti? Are you choosing him over me? It didn't feel that way when you were in my arms last night."

"I may have spent the night in your arms, but I finally know what's in my heart. Last night was about closure and ending this chapter of my life," she explained. "Yes, Kedrick, a part of me will always care about you. Actually, I'm grateful to you. If you hadn't dumped me, I never would have fallen in love with Lewis. And if you hadn't come back, I would have always wondered if you and I could have made it work. Now, I know that truth. I love Lewis, and I can marry him without reservation."

"You're kidding me, right? I see what this is; you want to get back at me for not marrying you." He stood up and wrapped his arms around her waist. She tried to disengage herself, but he wouldn't release her. "All right, Vashti, I'm sorry. What I did was cowardly and wrong. I hurt you. Now, please, forgive me and let's get on with the rest of our lives."

"I forgive you, Kedrick. I forgave you a long time ago, but that's not what this is about." She pushed him away from her. "And although I never thought it would happen, I'm over you. There are no hard feelings, and I hope that one day you find the same kind of happiness that I've found with Lewis. But as far as the two of us are concerned, we're finished."

"So you're saying it's over, five years just like that?" he stated in disbelief. She nodded confidently, knowing in her heart that it was true.

"This is it, Vash. I'm not going to beg you for another chance. If I walk out, it's over—for good this time."

"It was over when you walked out a year ago. I just couldn't accept it until now."

He feverishly tried to reason with her. "Vashti, we belong together. You're making a huge mistake. You do know that, don't you?"

"Kedrick, the only mistake I made was leaving Lewis for you last night."

"But I love you, Vashti."

She walked up to him and kissed him on the cheek. "Then I guess you'll have to get over that."

"Vashti, wait . . ." He grabbed her arm. "I've come too far to lose you again." Then he kissed her like it was his last day on earth.

Chapter 47

"Hi," squeaked Vashti, standing in Lewis's doorway. He leaned his large body against the frame.

"I've missed you," he confessed, burdened with sadness.

"I've missed you, too."

"Did you straighten things out with Kedrick?"

"Yes."

"Do you want to talk about it?" She nodded, and he allowed her to pass through the door.

"I'm sorry that I haven't called or anything. I just needed some time and space to figure things out."

He stood in front of her. "I know. That's why I didn't bother you. I didn't want you to feel pressured."

She tilted her head and smiled. "You're always so considerate of my feelings. It's one of the things that I love about you."

"Well, I believe in treating a woman right and giving her space if that's what she needs." He paused for a moment. "Is that what you need, Vashti—space from me and this relationship?"

"I've been doing a lot of thinking, Lewis," she launched, pacing the living room floor. "And seeing Kedrick again threw my whole life out of balance, you know what I mean?"

"I think I do."

"I didn't want to mislead you or make any promises that I couldn't keep."

"No, I don't want you to do that either." He rubbed the creases in his forehead to ease the tension.

She went on. "I had so many unanswered questions in my mind, and these were questions that only Kedrick could answer."

"Things like what?" He looked up at her.

"I needed to know why he left me and if I still loved him. I had to answer that question honestly before we took our relationship any further. That's why I couldn't accept your proposal."

Lewis sank down into the couch and clasped his hands together. "Well, Vash, you and Kedrick were together for a long time. Heck, you were supposed to marry the guy. I guess it's only natural that you'd still have feelings for him and that he'd still have feelings for you."

"He wants to pick up where we left off and start a new life with me. He said that he wants to make all of my dreams come true, for real this time."

"And you deserve that, Vashti, you do," he agreed, nodding. "Don't I always tell you that you deserve to be treated like a queen? I'm glad that he finally wised up and realized what a jewel he had in you."

"That's real sweet of you to say, Lewis."

"I mean it, and I hope that you're happy together." He stood up to let Vashti out.

"What?" She turned around.

"I want you to be happy," he repeated, becoming

misty-eyed. "That's all I ever wanted, and I love you enough to want you to find happiness with whomever you can find it with. Granted, I was hoping that it'd be with me, but . . ." He shrugged his shoulders, dismissing the idea.

"Lewis, baby, I think you're confused. Come sit down." She led him by the hand back to the sofa. She looked him in the eyes. "Lewis, I love you. You're my best friend."

"I know that, Vashti. You love me as a friend, and we will always be friends. I don't want to lose that."

She put her hand to his mouth. "Lewis, just shut up and let me finish." She resumed. "You're my friend, my protector, my comforter, and my lover. Second to God, although I know it seems like I haven't been putting Him first lately, you're everything. Yes, I had questions about Kedrick that needed to be answered, and a part of me thought that I still loved him but after seeing him, I realized that he's not the one for me. You are."

"What are you saying, Vashti?"

"For as long as I can remember, just about every decision I've made has been a fleshly one, based strictly on my emotions or out of some fear of rejection. This time, I prayed and asked God what He wanted me to, and He kept leading me back to you. The devil tried everything to stop us, even throwing Kedrick in the mix. Obviously, God had a different plan." She took a deep breath and kneeled down beside the sofa.

"What are you doing?" he asked.

Vashti grabbed Lewis's hand. "I'm doing something that I should have done a long time ago. Lewis Anthony Brown, I love you with all my heart. I was a fool for not accepting your proposal before. I only hope that you can forgive me and will do me the honor of becoming my husband." She gulped. "Lewis, will you marry me?"

He laughed and helped her off the floor. "Get up from there with your crazy self!" He seated her on his lap. "Are you sure about this? Is this really what you want to do?"

She nodded. "I've never been so sure about anything in my life."

"All right, but you know I can't have my queen asking me to marry her. Let's do this right." She stood up, and he took her spot on the floor.

"Queen Vashti Marie Hunter—"

"Yes! Yes!" She squealed, jumping up and down like an impatient child.

"Let me ask you first!" He cleared his throat. "Now, Vashti Marie Hunter, will you marry me? Will you be my wife and let me love you for the rest of my life?"

She pounced on him and planted a big kiss on his lips. He curled his arms around her waist and balanced her on his knee.

"So is that a *yes*?"

"That's a *heavens yes*!" They embraced again. They were still kissing when Kirsten burst through the front door and slammed it shut. The noise startled them.

"Girl, are you crazy coming in like that?" barked Lewis.

"What's going on in here?" she asked.

Vashti beamed proudly. "Your dad and I are getting married! Isn't that great?"

Kirsten's face contorted into an icy glare. "Is this true? Are you seriously going to marry her?"

"Just as soon as she'll have me!" He playfully kissed Vashti on the cheek.

"Daddy, you don't know the truth about her. You're making a mistake!"

"Kirsten, watch your mouth!" he warned.

Vashti shook her head to quiet him. "Lewis, it's okay, let her speak her mind."

"Oh, you're giving me permission to speak my mind in my own house! How thoughtful of you," Kristen snapped sarcastically and flung her purse on the sofa.

"Kirsten, we're going to be family soon. We need to be honest with each other," replied Vashti.

"Oh, I can be *real* honest! *Honestly*, you are not my mother, and you never will be. *Honestly*, I don't care if he does marry you and the two of you have a thousand brats running around here, you will never be my family! You might be able to fool my dad, but I know that you're just some tramp he pulled off the streets, trying to prove that he's still young."

"Kirsten!" roared Lewis.

"I'm serious, daddy! If you marry her, I'm leaving. I'll go stay with mom, maybe even Damon."

Vashti stood up. Lewis went over and seized Kirsten's arm.

"Kirsten, you're being childish and rude. You need to apologize *now*!" he gritted through his teeth.

"And you need to make a choice—me or her!" She snatched away from him and stormed off, slamming her bedroom door shut behind her.

Lewis and Vashti looked at each, neither of them wanting to acknowledge the magnitude of Kirsten's reaction.

"Lewis, she's never going to accept me," Vashti concluded sadly.

He put his arm around her. "She's a kid, she'll come around."

"She thinks I'm taking you away from her and that I'm trying to replace her mother. I'm not trying to do either. I just want us to be one, big happy family." He invited Vashti into an embrace.

"Kirsten has to realize that she can't have her way and that this is *definitely* not the way to go about it." He released her. "Don't worry about her. I'll handle Kirsten; you start planning our wedding."

Vashti smiled up at him. "Really, Lewis?"

"Yes, it can be as big and as elaborate as you want it to be."

"Oh, baby!" She impulsively kissed him.

"Now, we do need to pick a wedding day. Do you want to be a July bride?"

"It's already May. Do you think that's too soon?"

"If it was up to me, I'd take you to the courthouse right now. But I know that you want a church wedding in front of all your friends and family, and I want to give you that."

Vashti thought of her wedding deadline. "Let's make it September." She gingerly touched his face. "Do you have any idea how much I love you?" They were so enthralled with each other that they didn't see Kirsten approaching.

" 'Cuse me," grumbled Kirsten, deliberately bumping against them as she made her way to the front door. She had changed into a midriff-revealing tank top and ripped jean skirt just inches shy of showing her behind.

"Where do you think you're going dressed like that?" grilled Lewis.

"Damon's on his way. He's taking me to look at prom dresses."

"He's not taking you anywhere dressed like that! You need to change."

Kirsten sulked and stomped into her room. Vashti rubbed Lewis's back. She was sympathetic; she wasn't that far removed from her rebellious teen years herself.

A few minutes later, Kirsten stepped out of her room wearing a tight pair of jeans and a tube top.

"That ain't much better," complained Lewis.

"Just let it go," whispered Vashti. "She's okay."

"I heard you," fired Kristen. "I don't need you taking up for me."

"Why don't you let Sabrina take you to look for dresses?" suggested Lewis.

"Or I could," volunteered Vashti. "I don't mind. I have pretty good taste."

She glared at Vashti and rolled her eyes. "I don't think so," she hissed. "Damon's taking me." A horn blared outside. Kirsten peeked out of the window. "That's him, I gotta go."

"You never did apologize to Vashti," Lewis reminded his daughter.

"Apologize for what? She ain't nobody!"

"Kirsten, this wedding is going to happen whether you like it or not. I love Vashti, and she's going to be my wife and a part of this family. You need to start accepting that."

She smacked her lips and shifted her weight from leg to the other. "Damon's waiting. I have to go."

"You ain't going no where until you get in there and cover up."

Kirsten exhaled and snatched up a knit shrug she had lying on the sofa. "If I don't leave now, I'm going to be late."

"We're going to talk about this, Kirsten."

"Fine, we'll talk about it when she ain't here. Can I leave?"

"I want you back here by 8:00."

She frowned. "8:00?"

"You know you *could* stay home," he warned.

She mumbled "fine" before throwing a sharp glance in Vashti's direction and stomping out with the door slamming behind her.

"I don't like that guy," said Lewis, looking out of the window at Kirsten hopping into her boyfriend's truck. "She wants me to like him, but I don't trust him. I know he's going to break my baby's heart, but she won't listen to nothing I tell her."

"Aw, she's just trying to test you, Lewis. All teens go through that." She hugged him from behind.

"Not Sabrina, she never acted out like this."

"Then consider yourself lucky because I know I gave my mother plenty of headaches! And Monique— I'm surprise that she doesn't have her mother's finger-prints permanently engraved into her skin as much as her mother had to slap that smart mouth. But we got over it, so will Kirsten." He turned and put his arm around Vashti and kissed her on the forehead.

"I think that having you here is going to be good for her. A lot of this stuff that she goes through and does is over my head. Now that Sabrina's gone and her mother's away, she needs a woman around to confide in."

"I would love to be there for her if she'll let me."

"Don't fret. Before you know it, she'll love you as much as I do."

"And don't *you* fret about her; she'll be fine."

"Now about this wedding . . ."

"Yes, Lewis, we need to start making plans. There's so much to do, especially if we're going to be married by September. Oh, I need to call mama and Monique! We've got to get out invitations; I need to get a dress and you a tux. I've got to get a caterer," rattled off Vashti.

"Slow down, mama." Lewis grabbed her hands and pulled her close to him. "The only thing you need to do right now is come over here and celebrate with your man."

"Hmm, celebrate with my man, you say," she smiled, locking herself in his arms.

"That's right. You know it's about five o'clock now. Kirsten won't be home until eight."

"Just what did you have in mind, Mr. Brown?" she teased. "A little wedding night preview," Vashti shrieked as he scooped her up and tossed her over his shoulder. "Come on, woman!" He gave her a whack on the behind. With Vashti laughing and screaming all the way, he carried her off to the bedroom for an evening of kissing and cuddling.

Chapter 48

"**C**ome on—let me see it!" egged Monique. Vashti extended her finger. Monique held up her hand to inspect the ring in a different light. "A solitaire— he spent some money on this, V! It looks like it's a couple of carats, too."

"Isn't it pretty?" gushed Vashti, admiring the ring again. "I wasn't expecting something so extravagant."

"You better get used to it. Lewis believes in spoiling his women."

A scowl washed over Vashti's face. "That's not always a good thing."

"You mean that daughter of his?"

"Kirsten," mocked Vashti. "You know I have really tried to be nice to her, but there are some people that you just can't be nice to. Thankfully, Sabrina's being supportive. I just wish that some of that would rub off on her little sister."

"Does Lewis know how she treats you?"

"Yes, but she's a teenager. You remember what

that's like; he can't do anything with her. Now that we're engaged, she's just going to get worse."

"Have you tried talking to her? Not in an I'm-sucking-up-to-you-to-get-close-to-your-father kind of way. I mean by being real, being yourself."

"I've tried, but she's so suspicious of me."

"Can you blame her? She's sixteen; she probably wants her parents back together, so that makes you the enemy."

"It seems like there's more to it than that. She's very hostile towards me."

"Why don't you have her over for a girls' day or something. Let her see how you live and that you're a normal person, not some wicked stepmother."

"That's what this dinner tonight is supposed to be all about. Thank God that Lewis will be there to neutralize Kirsten. Hopefully, I'll be able to find out what's really going on with her." She shook her head. "This has to work, Monique. Otherwise, it could spell the end for me and Lewis."

"Well, if it doesn't work, there's always boarding school!"

"You're crazy!" Vashti glanced over at her clock. "Look what time it is. I haven't even gone shopping yet."

"You might want to add valium to your shopping list," suggested Monique.

"She's not that bad, 'Nique."

"I meant for you! You're probably going to need it sooner than she will."

"Come in, I have dinner set up in the back," invited Vashti, welcoming Lewis and Kirsten back home from shopping for Kirsten's prom shoes. Lewis greeted

Vashti with a kiss. Kirsten rolled her eyes and sucked her teeth at witnessing the display.

"Kirsten, remember our agreement," warned Lewis.

"And thank you both for giving me free reign of the kitchen to prepare dinner," added Vashti.

Kirsten sniffed the air. "Eeww, what's that smell!" she complained, frowning and covering her nose.

"It's roasted chicken. Your dad told me that it's your favorite, so I thought it would be a good choice for dinner."

"I don't want it," replied Kirsten, shaking her head. "I can't eat anything that smells like that."

"It smells just fine, Kirsten," bolstered Lewis. "Honestly, baby, it smells great. When do we eat?" Lewis rubbed his hands together in anticipation.

"It'll be a few more minutes," answered Vashti, caught between Lewis's loving gaze and Kristen's icy stare. "Kirsten, I brought my cat if you want to play with her," she offered.

"A cat?" echoed Kirsten. "Do you even know how old I am?"

"I thought that all girls liked cats."

"Sure, Vashti. Do you have some Barbie Dolls and tea sets I can play with, too?" Kristen added sarcastically.

"Kirsten, that's enough! You are on very thin ice, young lady." Lewis's tone was grave and formidable. Kristen heeded the warning and slouched down on the couch as Lewis went over to comfort Vashti.

"She hates me!" whispered Vashti to Lewis once they had their backs to Kirsten.

"She doesn't hate you. She's just being difficult. Trust me, she's just as bad with me. Now that she thinks she's grown, she's impossible to deal with."

Vashti exhaled and decided to try again. "Kirsten, I could really use your help setting the table," she hinted.

"I don't feel like it," replied Kirsten, propping her feet up on the coffee table. Lewis snatched her up by the arm.

"Get over there and set the table," he ordered, giving her a slight shove. She pouted but obeyed.

It was quite possibly the most uncomfortable meal that Vashti had ever sat down to. No one spoke. The silence was sporadically broken by their forks clanking against the plates and the occasional one-word answer from Kirsten in response to their questions.

"So you have prom next weekend?" began Vashti, hoping to spark a conversation.

Kirsten shrugged nonchalantly. "So."

"Well, are you excited?"

"Not really."

"Not really?" replied Lewis. "It's all you've been talking about for weeks! I can't tell you how much I've shelled out in hair and dresses and a bunch of stuff she'll never wear again!"

"Ah, that brings back memories of my prom," recalled Vashti. "It was one of the most memorable nights of my life. I could stop by and help you get dressed if you want."

"No!" screeched Kirsten. "I don't want you stopping by! I don't want you to help me! And I don't want your friendship! Why can't you just leave me alone?"

"Why, Kirsten? What did I ever do to you, huh? I've tried to be nice. I've tried to be your friend. I don't want to take your father away from you, and I'm not a bad person," she argued.

"Do you think I'm stupid, Vashti? I know all about

you! I know way more than you think I know, and I'm not afraid to tell it," threatened Kirsten.

"Kirsten, get into the kitchen right now!" bellowed Lewis, rising and throwing down his napkin.

"No, I want to hear what she has to say. Let's put it all out there and deal with it once and for all," declared Vashti.

"Okay, we'll put it all out there," Kirsten began sweetly. "Do you know what I do during the summer, Vashti?"

"No," Vashti answered.

"She volunteers at the church," answered Lewis, trying to figure out where Kirsten was going with this. "She works in the pastor's office."

"I was working there last summer, too," continued Kirsten.

While Lewis may have been in the dark, the pieces began to fall into place for Vashti. The minute she realized who Kirsten was, something seemed to cauterize inside of Vashti. She already knew what Kirsten was going to say before she finished her speech.

Kirsten turned to Lewis. "Daddy, do you remember that woman that I told you about? The one that ran me over coming out of Pastor White's office? It was Vashti! She's the one who was in his office that day. She's the one who broke up his marriage and got him fired. It was her! I know it was because when she called, I was the one who made the appointment. I saw her with my own eyes."

Vashti couldn't speak anymore than she could stop the tears from rolling down her cheeks. She was paralyzed and stared down at the plate of chicken and at the end table cloth—at anything that would keep her from seeing the disillusionment in Lewis's eyes. It all came rushing back to her—the tryst in the pastor's office, her running out there, and for the first time, the face of the woman she bumped into. It was Kirsten.

Chapter 49

A deathly still lingered in the air following Kirsten's proclamation. Vashti knew that Lewis would never look at her the same way again. She had already tested his love and patience when she sought closure with Kedrick; she knew that seeking his forgiveness now would be asking too much.

"Are you finished, young lady," he rumbled in a tone that Vashti had never heard him use before. "Are you satisfied? Did it make you feel good to try to humiliate the woman I love?"

"How can you still love her? Look at her—she can't even deny it, can you, Vashti? She knows it's true."

"Now that's enough!" roared Lewis, slamming his fist down on the table. The plates and silver quivered, startling Vashti and Kirsten. "Now, I want you to get up and go into your bedroom and sit down and be quiet until I come to get you," he ordered, his teeth tightly clenched. Having never seen her father react this way before, Kirsten moved quickly and quietly from the dinner table.

It was just the two of them now, alone with the weighted silence and tension and the inevitable storm that was sure to follow. Vashti hung her head.

"I know that I should've told you," she sobbed heavily. "But I just couldn't." Lewis didn't say anything. In fact, he showed no emotion at all.

"I know what you must be thinking," she went on.

"You have no idea what I'm thinking," he answered curtly. Vashti looked up at him, hoping to see some semblance of the man who wanted to spend the rest of his life with her five minutes prior.

"I've lost you, haven't I?" She sank down in her chair, crying so hard that her whole body shook. She felt as though she had lost her ability to speak or even think. Lewis offered no sympathy and looked on as she cried.

"Are you finished?" he asked. She composed herself long enough to wonder aloud how he could be so cold and unfeeling toward her. "What do you expect me to do, Vashti?" he inquired, folding his hands together.

"I guess I expected more, Lewis," she fired. "I guess I expected the man that I love to give a crap about our relationship. How can you just sit there like nothing's happened?" She began to ponder whether or not she had fooled herself into thinking that Lewis was the kind and gentle soul that she desperately wanted to believe he was.

He leaned forward to talk to her. "Vashti, do you know what love is—what *real* love is?"

"Lewis, don't you dare question my love for you! Now I have made a lot bad choices, I'll be the first to admit that. But I love you, and I'm not going to sit here and let you tell me otherwise!" she protested.

"I never questioned your love for me, but, obviously, you doubt the love I have for you."

Vashti shook her head in disbelief. "What?"

"Vashti, what Kirsten did to you was cruel and unprovoked, but I will love her anyway, just like I always have, just like I always will. My feelings for you are no different." He smiled. "I like to call what I have for you no-matter-what love. Do you know what that means? That means that there is nothing you can do to ever make me stop loving you, including this."

"You still want to marry me?" she asked, astonished.

"I know that a lot of men would think I was crazy for saying this, but I don't care. Now, I don't condone what you did with Pastor White, but I'm not going to condemn you for it either. It was wrong, but I suspect you know that. And I know that you weren't yourself after everything that happened with Kedrick."

"So you forgive me?"

"It's not up to me to forgive. I don't have a heaven or hell to put you in. Besides, we weren't even together then, so how can I hold that against you? As long as you've asked God for forgiveness, that's good enough for me."

Vashti leapt from her chair and right into Lewis's arms. He crushed her to his chest and kissed her forehead.

"I thought it was over," she whimpered. "You are such an amazing man, Lewis. I'm so blessed."

"Listen, I'm yours and you're mine. That's just the way it is. And can't no ex-boyfriend or angry teenager or devil in hell do anything about it." He released her. "So, you might as well stop all that crying and save those tears for our wedding."

"Okay," she agreed and laughed, wiping her eyes with the back of her hand. "What about Kirsten?"

"I already told you that I will deal with her. Now, I can't promise that she's going to go to that prom after her little outburst today . . ."

"Lewis, don't take that away from her," pleaded Vashti. "She hates me enough as it is. Plus, she was only trying to look out for you."

He was touched. "I see I'm not the only one with a forgiving heart."

"Oh, I'm not so forgiving that we can't make her wash these dishes!"

"All right, then," yielded Lewis, chuckling. "But, seriously, I'll talk to her. Regardless of her reasons, she has no right to treat you that way. And don't worry, I'll make sure she keeps this to herself. I won't let her tell anybody at the church."

She was relieved. "We're going to be very happy together, aren't we?" Vashti beamed all over.

"Yeah, until you get all fat and start whining and complaining all the time," teased Lewis. "I'm just playing. You could be 500 pounds, and I would still love you. Now, 600—we might have to sit down and have a little talk!"

Chapter 50

"How does it look, Daddy?" asked Kirsten, modeling her newly-hemmed prom dress. Her smile quickly faded once she noticed that Vashti had arrived in the interim between her arriving home with the dress and her trying it on.

"You look pretty, Kirsten," Vashti complimented.

"You do, baby. You're going to be the most beautiful girl there tomorrow night."

"Thank you, Daddy."

"Vashti said that you looked pretty, too, Kirsten."

"I don't want her looking at me."

The frustration showed on Lewis's face again. "Kirsten, what did we talk about?"

"Daddy, I know that you want me to like her, but I can't. I don't think she's a good role model for me. She sleeps with married men. I don't think that's right."

The look of contempt in Kirsten's eyes spoke as loudly as her words. It was clear that the life and family with Lewis that Vashti envisioned was a fantasy. Crushed, Vashti stood up and excused herself from the living room and hurried into the kitchen. Lewis scolded Kirsten and ran after her.

"This isn't going to work, Lewis," she sobbed. "Your daughter has made it very clear that she doesn't want me to be a part of this family, and, frankly, I can't keep putting up with her abuse."

"Baby, don't worry about Kirsten—"

"But we have to!" Vashti cut in. "Kirsten is a part of your life; you are a packaged deal." She sniffed and wiped her nose. "You know, I thought it was just a phase; that if I was patient and understanding, things would get better."

"And they will!" insisted Lewis. "I'll make her apologize and punish her if I have to, but I'm not going to let Kirsten run my life for me or drive you away."

"Lewis, don't you see? Making her apologize isn't going to change anything. She wants nothing to do with me. I can't change that, and neither can you." She turned away, crying into her hands.

Lewis held her and stroked her back. "We can get through this, Vashti. We've gotten through so much already. It's just another test, that's all."

She pulled away from him. "Maybe these aren't tests, Lewis. Maybe it's a sign that we don't belong together."

Lewis squared off with Vashti. "Now, you might as well stop all that talk, woman! We've come too far to give up now. You're going to be my wife, and that's all there is to it!"

"And if you have to make a choice between the two of us, Lewis, then what, because that's what it's come down to." Lewis lowered his head. He couldn't answer her. Vashti touched his face and gazed lovingly at him. "It's an impossible choice, isn't it? And I love you too much to force you to make it." She dropped her hand to wipe her tears away.

"Vashti, don't do this—*please*!" pleaded Lewis, pulling her close to him.

"Don't you know that my heart is breaking, too? Walking away from you is the hardest thing I've ever done. I love you more than I even thought possible, but she's your daughter, Lewis. She needs you more than I do, and you need her."

"I need you, too." Tears began rolling down Lewis's face. Vashti was heartbroken all over again. They clung to each other, accepting their reality, but desperately wanting to hold on to the dream, if only for a little while longer. The moment was interrupted by Kirsten's voice screaming into the telephone. They momentarily forgot their problems and rushed into the living room to find out what was wrong with her.

"Damon, come on; you can't do this . . . What do you mean? Damon, I already have my dress and everything . . . Damon, you can't—hello? Hello?"

Kirsten stared at the phone as if she couldn't fathom what she'd just heard. She threw the phone against the wall and dashed down the hall to her room, slamming the door behind her.

"What was that about?" asked Vashti.

"I don't know, but I'm going to find out." Lewis followed her to the room. He knocked on the door, but she didn't answer. He could hear her muffled crying through the door. "Honey, can I come in?"

"Go away!" yelled Kirsten.

"Kirsten, did you and your boyfriend have a fight?"

"He's not my boyfriend!"

"Baby, just tell me what happened."

"I don't want to talk about it. Daddy, please, just go!"

Lewis sulked back into the living room, shaking his head. "She won't talk. I knew that punk was going to do something to hurt my baby!"

"Well, Lewis, we don't know what happened yet. Why don't I try to talk to her," proposed Vashti.

Lewis put his hand on her shoulder. "I know that you mean well, but she's already upset. If you try to force the issue, there's no telling what she might do."

"I won't pry. I'll just let her know that you're here for her—we both are. I want her to know that she can trust us."

"All right, just go easy on her, okay? I know that she acts all tough, but she really is a sensitive kid."

"I know, Lewis. I was a sixteen-year-old girl once, too."

Vashti gently knocked on Kirsten's door and let herself in. "Kirsten?"

"What do you want?" she barked. "Better yet, I don't even want to know. Just leave!" Kristen was lying on her bed with her back turned to Vashti.

"I know that we haven't gotten along; I just wanted you to know that I'm here for you in case you want to talk."

"Don't act like you care," she snidely remarked.

"Kirsten, I do care."

"All you care about is looking good in front of my dad. I know that you can't stand me. You're probably glad to see me crying."

"Why would you say something like that?"

"It's true! I know you wish that I was out of the picture, but I'm not going anywhere. I'm not scared of you either."

"I don't want you to be. I want us to be friends."

Kristen crackled menacingly. "Yeah, right!"

"Just tell me what happened. Your father is worried sick about you, and I told him that I'd come make sure that you were okay."

"I'm fine, all right? And tell him he got his wish—me and Damon are over."

Vashti edged over to the bed and sat down beside her. "Do you wanna tell me what happened?"

"Why—so you can gloat?"

"No, because I care about you and I want to help if I can."

"What do you think happened? He dumped me—satisfied?"

"Do you want to talk about it?"

"Not with you!"

"All right," said Vashti, rising. "I'll get your father." Kirsten abruptly turned over.

"I can't talk to him!" she cried.

"Then talk to me."

Kirsten seemed to be on the verge of a confession then clammed up again. "You're just going to say that I got what I deserved."

"Kirsten, I'm not the enemy. Contrary to what you think, it kills me to see you hurting like this."

Kirsten smacked her lips and turned back over. "I didn't want to go to the stupid prom anyway. I bet it's gonna be lame."

Vashti saw an inch and seized it. "I'm sure you're right. It'll probably be a bunch of people standing around gossiping about who's wearing what."

"I'll bet that LaShawn Turner picked out the trashiest dress she could find, too!" Kristen added.

"Who's LaShawn Turner?"

"Damon's date," she informed bitterly. "She's this stoochie he's taking because he knows she'll give it up."

"What's a stoochie?"

"A stank hoochie. She's been with about every guy in school."

"Was he pressuring you for sex?" asked Vashti. Kirsten didn't deny it. "I take it that you weren't ready to take that step with him."

She shook her head. "He wanted to get a room, but Dad would kill me if he found out that I went to a hotel after the prom."

"Lewis wouldn't have known unless you told him. Is that the only reason you didn't want to sleep with Damon?"

"No," she divulged. "I just wasn't ready to go all the way. I was scared."

"Did you tell Damon how you felt?"

"I told him, and he said that I was acting like a li'l girl. He said if I didn't, he was going to the prom with someone who would."

"A guy should never try to put demands on you like that. You did right by not giving in. You shouldn't do anything unless it feels right to you, regardless of what anyone else says."

"I thought that I could do it, but, then, it just didn't feel right. All I could hear was my dad telling me that my body is a temple and that I'm supposed to wait until I'm married."

"That's true, and it goes to show that he raised you right."

"I wish that Damon could have seen it that way."

"I know, but a lot of guys, and girls, don't view sex the way God meant for us to."

"I don't get it," sobbed Kirsten. "He said he loved me. I thought I was special."

"You are special! A guy like that doesn't deserve you."

Kirsten brusquely turned away. "What do you know? You haven't had your heart broken like this."

"Oh no?" Vashti chuckled. "I've been there, trust me."

"You couldn't possibly understand," bemoaned Kirsten and buried her face in a pillow.

"Kirsten, you got stood up for the prom. I got stood up on my wedding day!"

She looked up. "Really?"

"Yes, and it was humiliating. More than that, I loved him, and he dumped me without so much as a word or explanation."

Kirsten managed a weak smile. "That's messed up, Vashti."

"Tell me about it! I didn't get out of bed for, like, a week. When I did start dating again, it was just one loser after the other. I was ready to give up on love altogether. Then your father asked me out, and he showed me what it was like to be loved and treated like a queen."

"My dad really loves you," Kirsten admitted.

"I know, and I love him, too, very much. And one day you'll meet someone who loves you and respects your decisions."

"*One day* could be ten years from now! What am I supposed to do in the meantime?"

"You meet people, you date, and you enjoy being a kid."

Kristen hugged her pillow close to her chest. "It just hurts so bad, you know?"

Vashti nodded. "Yeah, I know. And it may hurt for a while, but one day you're going to wake up and it's not going to hurt anymore."

Kirsten sighed. "Why are you being so nice to me? I've been a total b—you know what—to you."

"Not a *total* one," joked Vashti. "Besides, I've been through what you're going through, and I'm a good listener. You don't have to go through this alone."

"It's hard sometimes. I can't talk to my dad about boys and stuff, and Sabrina's always busy."

"What about your mom?"

"She's always like, 'yeah, let's do lunch, Kristen,' but we never do. I can't really talk to her either."

"Well, you can talk to me. I'll always be here for you."

She lowered her head. "I can't talk to you either. You'll just go back and tell my dad everything that I say."

"Not if you tell me in confidence and not if it isn't anything that's going to hurt you. If you want to talk about boys or school, even sex, I'm here."

"Thanks, Vashti."

"And even though your father and I are breaking up—"

Kirsten was startled. "Breaking up?"

Vashti paused and took a deep breath. "Kirsten, I know how you feel about me, and I love your father too much to come between the two of you. I would never want you to be miserable in your own home, so I won't marry him without your blessing."

"Now, he's going to blame me because you guys aren't together."

"No, he won't. Your father loves you, Kirsten. Your happiness means everything to him."

"I want him to be happy, too," she added softly. "And I know that you make him happy."

Vashti put her arm around her. "Well, maybe we all can be happy if we tried. I mean, I know that things won't change over night, but I'm willing to try if you are. I really want to marry your dad and for us to be a family."

Kirsten thought it over a moment. "I think I can do that. I guess you're not as bad as I thought. I guess you're sort of all right."

"I guess you're pretty cool, too." The two shared an awkward hug. It was at least a start.

"What are you going to tell my dad about Damon?"

"Only that you realized what a jerk Damon was and that you're holding out for a man just like him."

"What about me telling Daddy about the pastor? Aren't you mad at me for that?"

Vashti shook her head. "The truth is that I should have told him myself, but it's a big relief to have that over and done with. Now, there are no secrets between us."

Kirsten smiled and nodded. "Vashti, I didn't mean all that stuff I said about you not being a good role model. I didn't tell anybody else about the pastor, and I won't. I'm glad that you're going to be a part of my family."

"Me, too. Now, let's go give your father the good news—together!"

Chapter 51

Vashti watched herself nervously in the mirror as her mother secured the lily onto the side of head.

"Is he here yet? Has anyone seen Lewis?" Vashti couldn't help being paranoid.

"Are you kidding? Lewis was here thirty minutes early!" Joyce told her. "He probably would've camped out on the steps if they'd let him."

Vashti turned and stared intently at her mother. "But have you *seen* him, mama? Did you lay eyes on him yourself?" Joyce held Vashti's shaking hands in hers.

"Yes, baby, I saw him with my own eyes. He's here and he loves you and he can't wait to marry you," she answered tenderly and kissed her on the forehead. "Now, have you laid your eyes on *her*?" She turned Vashti back around to face the mirror. Vashti gasped she saw the stunning image staring back at her. It dawned on her that she was actually getting married. This time, it would be for keeps.

"You look good, girl," reassured Monique, "even

better than last time." Vashti stuck her tongue out her.

There was a knock at the door followed by Kirsten's and Sabrina's heads poking through the slight opening.

"Ohh, you look so beautiful!" wailed Sabrina and walked in. Kirsten followed gawkily behind her.

"Thank you. How's your dad? Have you seen him?" Sabrina nodded. "We just left him."

"He's trying to act all cool," added Kirsten. "But I can tell he's nervous because he's talking a mile a minute and keeps repeating himself. He asked me how I was doing about ten times."

"He's excited though!" noted Sabrina, not wanting to alarm Vashti. "He asked us to give you this." She handed her a neatly-wrapped box.

"He is so sweet!" Vashti tore open the box. "Ohh, look, mama!" It was a sparkling diamond necklace. "You are my queen, now and forever. Love, Lewis," read Vashti from the inscription on the card.

"It's gorgeous! Turn around, baby, let me put it on you." Her mother clasped the necklace around her neck.

"I guess I have something new now," smiled Vashti.

"Well, we've already covered something old, borrowed, and blue. I'd say it was time we got you married," teased Monique.

Vashti looked warily around at the small crowd gathered in her dressing room. " 'Nique, can I talk to you for a minute?" She pulled Monique off into a corner.

"You're not having second thoughts, are you?" Monique asked her.

"Of course not! Marrying Lewis is the smartest thing I've done to this date. I just wanted to know what happened when you met with the lawyers yesterday."

Monique sighed. "It's official—well, it will be in thirty days. My marriage is over."

"I'm sorry, Monique. I know that you loved him and that you wanted your marriage to work out."

Monique nodded and spoke didactically. "You're right, but I think that the most important thing to remember here is that I've learned something, that I've grown, and more importantly . . . that I got a two million dollar settlement!" The two broke into smiles and rejoined everyone else.

As the sanctuary doors flung open and the organ signaled Vashti's arrival, she slipped her arm into her father's and started the trek up the aisle. She spotted Lewis, proud, handsome, and weeping, and picked up the pace just a little, racing to her future, her king, to her love. Shedding her single self, she happily embraced her destiny. A September afternoon never looked more promising.

Reader's Group Guide

1. Authors will often give their characters names with symbolic meaning. What do you think is the significance behind naming the lead character Vashti Hunter? Does she exemplify the characteristics of her namesake? What is the significance of her last name?

2. The Bible tells us that people should be "equally yoked." This principle can be applied to both friendships and romantic relationships. In your opinion, are Vashti and Lewis equally yoked? Are Vashti and Monique?

3. After realizing that Pastor White was not the man she believed him to be, Vashti lost faith in him, the church, and God. Did she make the mistake of putting more faith in the man than in the message, or was she right to feel betrayed? Was her reaction typical of Christians today?

4. Ultimately, Vashti breaks up with Brentz because she is not ready to take on the responsibility of being a mother to his children. Was this a selfish act? Why or why not?

5. Vashti goes from dating nineteen-year-old Tyrell to forty-seven-year-old Lewis. After a certain

point, does age still matter when choosing a mate? Why or why not?

6. Aside from Lewis, Travis is the man most committed to building a future with Vashti, with the condition that she be willing to share him with his job, his girlfriend, and the rest of the world. Would you be willing to "share" your mate for a chance at true love?

7. Out of desperation, Vashti goes online to meet a man and winds up dating Fletcher. Do you think that there is anything wrong with Christian men and women using the Internet to find a mate?

8. Vashti becomes involved with Ezra because she thinks that he has "potential" and hopes that she can change him. Is there anything wrong with dating a "diamond in the rough" in the hopes that he or she will evolve into the person you would like for him or her to be?

9. Lewis is portrayed as the "good guy" throughout most of the story, but what flaws did you see in him?

10. Vashti rejects Lewis's proposal to rekindle her romance with Kedrick, she doesn't tell him about the affair with the pastor, and she calls off their wedding because of her on-going feud with his daughter, Kirsten. By continuing to take her back, is Lewis exhibiting unconditional Christ-like love or is he a pushover? Explain.